The Spousal Shuffle

Text Copyright © 2018 Paula Brooks

All rights reserved. No portion of this book may be reproduced in any form without permission from the publisher, except as permitted by UK copyright law.

Cover Design by Rebecca Handyside

Chapter One

It was Matthew's idea to do a wife swap. Though it was more of a husband swap really. Or a boyfriend swap to be more accurate. Jo was pretty keen too.

Abby wasn't so sure. They were at Jo and Nick's and were still sitting round the dinner table though they'd finished eating a long time ago.

'It's perfect. The magazine would love it,' Matthew was saying. 'Plus you girls do nothing but complain about me and Nick, so why not? Let's swap.'

'I think it's a great idea. Nick would love living with me after a week or two of Abby,' Jo said, grinning at her friend.

'Yeah cheers, Jo.' Abby wriggled back, trying to get comfortable in the beautiful but completely impractical ladder-back oak chair.

'You're the one who complains the most. And you know how much I want this job. All our other story ideas have been crap. Don't you think it's a good one?' Matthew asked.

Abby shot a look at Nick. Big and broad and Action Man handsome. He looked back at her, eyes steady over the rim of his glass. 'I think it's a crap idea.' She turned back to Matthew. 'You'd make a real effort for Jo and she'd never believe me when I complained about you.'

'I wouldn't have to make an effort, I'm perfect already.'

Abby snorted.

'It would only work if you did the same as you always do—' Jo said.

'Nothing,' Abby cut in.

Jo ignored her. 'Otherwise what's the point? On that programme that was on TV they swapped completely, worked on each others budget and everything.'

Abby shook her head and emptied some of her drink into her mouth. 'I need a cigarette.' She stood up and headed for the door.

'I'll come with you.' Jo jumped up and followed.

They walked through the kitchen, the dirty dinner plates looking abandoned on the vast expanse of shiny work surface. Standing on the freshly vacuumed doormat, they donned coats and shoes and slipped out the back door. Abby lit up and inhaled deeply.

Jo shivered and jiggled about a bit. 'I think we should do it. Seriously, Abs. It could fix everything.'

'I don't see how.' She took another drag and wished Jo would go away.

'Well for starters it could get Matthew his dream job! And if that's not enough then do it for me. Nick's driving me crazy at the moment. If he lived with you for a bit he might start to appreciate me more.'

'He should appreciate you already, Jo. You need a new boyfriend. Screwing your best friend over isn't going to help. And what do I get out of it? Matthew still might not get the job and he'd never be happy with me if he got to live with you.'

'Don't be ridiculous. You work remember. He can't expect you to do as much as I do. Plus you've got Olly to look after.'

Abby sucked on her cigarette again. 'True.' She exhaled. 'I don't know. It's just too weird. Wouldn't it bother you – me living with your boyfriend?'

'No. It's not as if you'd sleep together. Oh come on, Abs. It'll be a laugh.'

Abby stared at her. A laugh? Maybe for Jo, Matthew was good fun. But for her? Living with Nick? No way. But what if it got Matthew the job he wanted? He'd wanted a job on a magazine for years; hated his job laying cable for Virgin Media. And it *could* help Jo. She'd been so unhappy lately. 'Has he really been that bad?'

'What, Nick?' Jo gave a hollow laugh. 'It's been awful. He's been moody and uptight and bossy and . . . ugh.' She pulled a face.

'Have you asked him why?'

Jo looked surprised. 'No. He never tells me anything.'

'Is it something to do with work? Or his ex-wife? Is he okay with Tilly?'

'Fine. He's always fine with her. And I think work's okay. He hasn't said any different.'

Abby took one last drag on her cigarette and threw it on the floor, stubbing it out with her foot. And then she remembered where she was and picked the butt up and put it in the bin. 'Nick hasn't actually said anything. Do you really think he'll agree?'

'No. Probably not,' Jo said miserably.

Abby sighed. 'Come on. Let's go and find out.'

Matthew and Nick had gone through to the living room and were slouched on the settee and an armchair respectively.

'Abby's agreed.' Jo sat on the settee, a huge smile stretching her face.

'To what?' Matthew sat up. Abby looked at Nick. He stared back, expression inscrutable. 'To doing a wife swap? Really?' Matthew sounded surprised but very excited. Overly excited.

Abby turned to look at him. 'You know sex isn't part of the deal, right?' she said.

'I know.' He scowled.

'So when shall we start?' Jo asked.

'Monday?'

Abby stared at Matthew. 'Don't you think we need more than two days to organise it?'

'What's to organise? I move in here. Nick moves into our place. Nothing else'll change.'

'It does on the programme. They swap finances and all sorts. And don't the women usually swap houses?' Jo asked and then she looked around the immaculate living room, her face dropping slightly.

Abby grinned, but was quick to argue. 'Well we're not doing that.' She wasn't living on an allowance like Jo did. 'And I'm not leaving Olly either.'

Jo looked disappointed. 'But how will we do it?'

'We can't move Olly, it wouldn't be fair. Matthew and Nick swap. We all carry on as usual.'

There was a silence, broken only by Snow Patrol singing quietly away in the background.

'That sounds okay,' Jo said eventually.

'Sounds okay to me.' Matthew reached for another can of beer.

They all looked at Nick. He was sitting back in his chair, long legs stretched out in front of him, glass in hand, eyes hooded.

'So, Nick? You game, mate?' Matthew asked.

Nick looked at Jo. And then he looked at Abby. 'Ok,' he finally said, gaze not wavering.

'Yes! This is going to be so much fun,' Jo said happily.

And still Nick stared.

And then he looked round the room. 'How long are we doing this for? I'm not giving up my weekends with Tilly.'

Matthew and Jo shrugged. 'A week? Two weeks?' Jo suggested.

'Two weeks. And Tilly stays with me and Abby Saturday nights.'

Everyone stared at everyone else.

And that was it. Settled. They were swapping partners.

Chapter Two

'**D**o you fancy Abby?'

Nick did a big sigh and rolled over to face his girlfriend. 'Look, Jo. It's you that wanted it so badly. I should be asking you the same thing about Matthew.'

Jo lay back and stared at the ceiling. 'You've just been so uptight lately. You can't blame me for asking.'

'I have not been uptight. I've been busy. There's a difference.' They lay in silence for a few minutes. 'Don't you wonder why Matthew's so keen?'

'No. Why?' Jo sat up, heart picking up a little.

Nick opened one eye to look at her.

'You're not worried are you? You know I wouldn't do anything,' she said. More because she was terrified he'd change his mind than to reassure him.

Nick leant up on one arm and looked at her. 'I know.'

Jo stared at him, thinking that he shouldn't be so confident. It wasn't as if their relationship was perfect. Far from it. He treated her like a child. Giving her an allowance and making her ask and explain if she needed extra. Expecting her to do as he said all the time.

Nick grinned and ran a finger along her face. 'You're looking at me as if you hate me.'

'Maybe I do.' Jo stretched and smiled back.

Nick dipped his finger along her chest and round a breast.

Jo moved towards him and thought that maybe sex would be a good idea. Get her into practice just in case she decided to sleep with Matthew. And it had been a long time. Probably wise to make sure everything was in working order.

Just in case.

Nick waited until Jo's breathing got even; until he knew she was sleeping and then he gave up all pretence of sleeping and rolled out of bed. Dressing quickly in jogging bottoms and t-shirt, he crept downstairs and out the back door. Jesus it was cold! He zipped up his coat and lit a cigarette.

He looked round the garden. And then up at the house. At the things that were draining the life out of him. He was just so damn tired all the time. He worked all the hours he could. Every penny went on the mortgage and bills. Jo didn't work.

When he met her she'd been working as a secretary for a local recruitment agency. She earned a pittance and hated every minute. Then just after she moved in with him she got laid off and hadn't worked since. That had been eighteen months ago. Every now and then she'd make a half-hearted attempt to find work but Nick knew it wasn't going to happen.

He couldn't complain. The house was always clean and tidy, meals on the table. And Jo wasn't frivolous. She managed okay on the allowance he gave her. But every month there was something else. The cars needed servicing or Tilly had to have new shoes. They'd had to replace all the windows at the end of last year and they badly needed the kitchen re-fitting.

And Jo wanted a baby. He sucked hard on his cigarette. Tonight was the first time they'd slept together for months, so how she thought that was going to happen he didn't know. He thought of living with Abby. It was a weird thought. He barely knew her. He'd been with Jo for over two years and he still didn't really know her best friend. They got together as a foursome fairly frequently and they were the only two smokers in the group but they were rarely alone. She seemed okay, a bit headstrong. And she and Matthew had a strange relationship. They were like two completely separate people who happened to live together.

He took another deep drag on his cigarette. Bloody sexy though. Not as pretty as Jo but sexier somehow. He wondered why she'd agreed to do it. Matthew was always game for anything; it *would* be a good story for his article plus he was probably hoping to get Jo into bed. Nick tried to be bothered by this. He liked Matthew but he was never going to be his best buddy. Matthew was too immature and too full of himself. And Nick was pretty sure he wouldn't turn Jo down. Would Jo do it though?

He hunched his shoulders. Against the cold and the thought, and then he chucked his cigarette in a nearby puddle and went back inside.

Chapter Three

Monday couldn't come quick enough for Matthew.
'Do you want Olly at the weekend?' Abby was lying on the bed watching him pack.

Matthew looked up, a startled look on his face. 'Won't it confuse him? It might be better just to stay away for the whole two weeks. Remember, I'm going to be working on my article while I'm there so I won't have a lot of free time.'

'Fine, whatever.'

Matthew gave her a long look. She sounded okay but she looked a little tense. Was she bothered about the swap? He'd worried that he'd seemed too keen but she hadn't said anything. 'Are you okay?'

Abby shrugged. 'I'm fine. A bit tired.'

'Are you nervous?' he asked curiously.

'A bit.' The surprise must have shown on his face because she rushed on, 'I don't really know Nick that well. And their relationship is very different to ours.' She gave him a strange look. 'Won't you miss Olly?'

'Of course I will,' Matthew lied. He loved Olly but in general he wasn't keen on kids. Though they did help attract women.

'So I guess I won't see you for the two weeks either,' Abby was saying and Matthew looked up guiltily.

'Is that a problem?' He went away a lot with work and sometimes he just went away but said it was with work. Abby never seemed to mind. Just carried on as usual. They were very independent of each other – it was one of the things he really liked about their relationship. That and the sex. That was pretty good too. Abby loved sex and rarely turned him down.

He wondered fleetingly if she and Nick would sleep together. He didn't think so. Nick wasn't the type. And then he wondered how long it would take to get Jo into bed. And then he felt himself grow hard and went to take a cold shower.

Abby phoned Jo the next morning. 'Just checking in. Are you ready for this evening?'

'Yep. Nick's got his stuff in the car.' She gave a nervous laugh. 'It feels strange doesn't it?'

'A bit. Don't worry, it'll be fine. And I've decided to give Nick an extra hard time. Make him really miss living with you.'

'Really?' Jo didn't sound as pleased as Abby had expected. 'Listen, Abs. Do you think it'd be best if we didn't talk for the two weeks? I was thinking maybe it'd make it easier.'

Abby stared at the phone. 'Why? Does it bother you thinking of Nick living here? We don't have to do this, Jo.'

'No! No. It's fine. I just thought it might be easier. We can concentrate better then.'

'Hm. Okay. What about our girl's night on Saturday?'

'Oh. I'd forgotten about that. You can still go. I'll give it a miss. Concentrate on making Matthew appreciate you.'

'Huh. He'll probably just go out. Okay. If that's what you want. Will you let Becky and Fiona know or shall I?'

'I'll text them later.'

'Okay. I have to go. I guess we'll talk in two weeks.'

'Fine. Good luck.'

'You too.' Jo hung up and Abby was left with a dead phone. Weird. Jo hadn't shown that much initiative for years. And she'd never managed a day without phoning or seeing Abby, let alone two weeks. She must be more nervous than she'd let on.

Abby went to put a wash on. And then she looked round the kitchen. It really could do with a clean. She checked her watch. She had two hours before Olly finished nursery. She could do some housework. Or she could go to the gym.

She decided on the gym. Changing into her workout gear, she went through to the garage, lighting a cigarette the minute she got through the door. She loaded her bag into Olly's seat on the back of her bike and wheeled the bike out of the garage. By the time she'd locked the door and got on the bike she'd finished her cigarette and ten minutes later she was at the gym.

It was busier than usual; Monday morning syndrome probably. She got straight on the treadmill and did thirty minutes at a run. Mind focused on her pace and the music from her MP3 player. She moved onto the bike and then the rowing machine and finished up with some weights.

She felt a lot better when she showered. So what if her best friend was acting weird and her boyfriend was moving out for two weeks? She trusted Jo. Uh-oh. That wasn't good. Didn't she trust Matthew? She lathered her hair and rinsed, thinking of Matthew and his frequent nights out. His business trips and his late nights at work. She was pretty sure he'd cheated on her. More than once probably. For the first time ever, she let herself think about that. It was a bit strange – thinking of him actually doing it with another woman – but not as upsetting as she'd have expected.

She pushed the thought from her mind and finished getting dressed and half an hour later she locked up her bike and walked up the nursery slope to collect Olly.

'Bloody cold isn't it.' Jamie's mum was already waiting, coat clutched round her, hat pulled down over her ears.

Abby grinned. 'I've just been to the gym and cycled. I'm alright at the moment. How was your weekend?'

They chatted for a few minutes and more mum's arrived and then the doors opened and they went inside.

'Mummy!' Olly belted across the room and threw himself in her arms. She held him tight for a minute, loving the feel of his warm bulk against her. 'We went to the park, Mummy, and I went on the slide. Jamie said rude words.'

'Did he?' Abby smiled at him and went over to collect his folder.

'Yes. He said brick and stupid.'

'That was naughty wasn't it?' Brick was prick.

'Yes. And then he kicked me so I put fire in my gun and shot him dead.' He made a gun with his fingers and aimed it across the room at his friend. 'Can we go to Fleet Toys and buy me a car?'

'Not today, honey. We need to go home and clean a bit. Nick's staying at our house tonight.'

'Why?' Olly frowned.

'Because daddy's staying at Jo's house.'

'Why?'

'It's a game. You and Tilly are swapping daddy's for a little while.'

'Why?'

Abby gave up, waved goodbye to his pre-school teachers and took him out to the bike.

She did the basic cleaning that afternoon. The toilet, the kitchen surfaces and the vacuuming. She finished the washing and made up the spare bed. And then she made tea. She and

Olly ate theirs and she put Nick's in the fridge for when he got in. What time did he get in anyway? She stepped towards the phone, all ready to phone Jo. And then she remembered. Jo didn't want to be contacted.

Feeling a little strange, she bathed Olly and put him to bed. And then she cleared up and washed their dinner stuff. And all the time she had one ear on the door. Seven o'clock. Normally she went Aerobiking with Fiona on Monday nights. She'd cancelled this evening because of Nick and it being the first night and everything. Just as well really – the class started at seven thirty.

She put on the TV and made coffee. And then she went out for a cigarette. And then she watched some more TV. At seven thirty there was a knock on the door and with heart pounding, she went to let him in.

'Hi. Sorry it's so late, things were a bit hectic today.' He looked exhausted. Tie undone and hanging loose round his collar, eyes rumpled, hair tousled.

Abby stood aside to let him in. 'That's okay.' He stepped into the hall and put his bag down. Abby shut the door and led him to the kitchen.

'Do you want your dinner now?' She switched the kettle on. 'Coffee?'

'No thanks.' He looked around.

'It's in the fridge.' Abby got his dinner out and put it in the microwave, wedging the door shut and setting the timer for three minutes. 'Matthew just comes in and heats it up when he's ready.'

'Oh right. Jo gets it all ready for me when I come in.'

'Right.' She made her coffee. 'Well I work, so four out of eight nights I'm asleep when Matthew comes in.'

She took his dinner out of the microwave and put it on the table.

He thanked her and sat down, his huge frame dwarfing the rickety kitchen chair. 'When are you working next?'

'Tomorrow.'

'What time do you start?'

'Ten. I have to leave at half nine and I get home just after seven.'

'You work all night?' He sounded surprised and Abby turned to look at him, so amazed that she was speechless for a minute.

'You didn't know?'

'No.' He shook his head.

'I've worked there for two years now. I can't believe you didn't know that. What did you think I did?'

'I never really thought about it.' He cut some meat and loaded his fork.

Abby took a sip of her coffee feeling really crap all of a sudden. All the time they'd known each other and he wasn't even curious about what she did.

'This is really good.' He pointed to his meal. And then he stopped to stare at her. 'Have I upset you?'

Abby stared back. 'A bit,' she admitted. 'I know we're not particularly close but I though we were kind of friends.'

He finished another mouthful. 'What do I do for a living, Abby?'

She thought for a minute and he grinned. And then she remembered. 'IT. Project Manager!'

He looked disappointed. 'So tell me what you do.'

'I work on a helpdesk for Arial Airlines.'

'Doing?'

'Not a lot. We're pretty quiet most nights. It's mainly helping the night staff with system problems.'

He ate some more. 'Do you like it?'

'Yeah. I do actually. I work with nice people and its easy work. The money's not bad either.'

'Really? Maybe you should get Jo a job there.'

Abby chuckled. 'Yeah right.'

Nick swallowed and looked up in surprise. 'Why's that funny?'

Abby sobered. 'You live with her, Nick. You must know how crap she is without sleep.'

'She'd get used to it.'

'No. She wouldn't. Either you need a lot of sleep or you don't. I've seen enough employees pass through to know that. Besides, she knows nothing about computers.'

They were quiet for a few minutes. Nick eating. Abby drinking her coffee.

11

'Do you want her to go back to work then?' Abby asked eventually. She knew Jo had half-heartedly looked around but she'd never mentioned Nick's views on her working.

'It would help. There's not much around at the moment though.'

Abby didn't comment. There was more than he realised. Abby knew. There'd been the threat of redundancies at work and she'd looked round for something else. There was plenty there. Unfortunately it was mostly full-time or in school hours. No good for her because Olly wasn't at school yet, but perfect for Jo.

'So? Do you have any plans I need to know about? Over the next two weeks I mean?' Nick asked, finishing his meal and putting his knife and fork down.

Abby wondered if he expected her to remove his plate. 'I normally go Aerobiking on Monday nights, but only if I'm not working. And I'm going out with Fiona and Becky on Saturday.'

'Oh yeah. Jo's going too isn't she?'

'Actually no. She's decided we shouldn't communicate for the two weeks.' Abby watched him closely while she spoke and his head jerked up at her words.

'Really? She said that?'

'Yep.'

'And what did you say?'

Abby shrugged. 'If that's the way she wants it.'

'But she's always phoning you. How will she last two weeks?'

Abby shrugged again.

He sighed and pushed his chair back. 'I need a cigarette.'

'I'll come with you.' They put coats and shoes on and stepped outside the back door.

'Are you out at all? Over the two weeks I mean?' Abby accepted a cigarette and let him light it for her.

'Jane drops Tilly off at nine on Saturday mornings. I take her swimming Sunday afternoons and drop her home at six. And I sometimes go out on Friday nights. I run in the morning when I can and if I go to the gym I go in my lunch hour.' He exhaled and eyed her through the smoke. 'Do you do stuff with Olly at the weekends?'

'I sometimes take him swimming or to soft play. I don't drive so we're limited by public transport. We got the train over to Basingstoke last weekend. I took him to the cinema.'

'You could come swimming with us on Sunday if you wanted. Or is Matthew taking him this weekend?'

'Nope. He thought it best if he stayed away completely for the two weeks. He never takes Olly anywhere anyway. He does his own thing at weekends.'

'Really?' Nick paused mid-puff. And then he continued, 'Well, the offer's there if you want it.'

'Thanks.' Abby finished her cigarette and they went inside. Nick's dinner plate was still on the table. 'I'm going to watch TV in bed for a while. Olly was up in the night last night and I'm knackered. Help yourself to coffee and stuff. The spare room is first on the right at the top of the stairs. The bathroom is next to it. I've left towels on the bed for you.' She went to the sink and poured a glass of water. 'The dishwasher's there.' She pointed behind her and then wondered if he'd ever used one before. From what she could gather Jo did all the houseworky stuff at home. 'You need to rinse the stuff before you put it in.'

Nick looked a little taken aback. He glanced at his plate and then back at Abby. 'Right. Thanks for dinner.'

'No problem. See you in the morning.' And she walked upstairs, heart beating just a tiny bit faster than usual.

Nick watched her walk upstairs and then he finished making his coffee and went through to the living room. It was weird doing everyday stuff in someone else's house. Although their houses were similar in many ways – both neo-Georgian and alike in size and layout – his was very different to Abby's. He looked around. One wall was red, another silver. There was a fireplace on the wallpapered wall – the wallpaper was cream and green. The last wall was covered in a rainbow of tiles. Big tiles, little tiles, shaped tiles. Some were mirrored; most were brightly patterned. It hurt his eyes just looking at them. He thought of his own tastefully decorated living room. Cream walls, cream carpet, oak furniture. Abby's furniture was a mixture of pine, beech and coloured stuff. It didn't look bad – just weird. As if she'd put everything she liked in one place without worrying about how it all looked together.

Nick wondered who'd done the decorating and then he sat down and drunk his coffee and watched a bit of TV. And then he got his laptop out and got to work.

It was almost one when he heard crying. He was still engrossed in the project he was working on and it took a few seconds to get his bearings. It wasn't Tilly crying. He was at Matthew and Abby's. It was Olly. The crying continued for a minute or two and Nick got up to investigate.

He wasn't sure if Olly knew he was staying and he didn't want to scare him, but on the other hand Abby had looked really tired and she was working tonight. She needed her sleep.

He followed the crying and was halfway across the landing when a door opened and Abby hurried out and into the room next door. She hadn't seen him and he stepped back, watching her quietly. She was wearing a t-shirt. A very short t-shirt and his eyes went straight to her legs.

'What's wrong, honey? Did you have a bad dream?' He heard her croon.

'Yes,' Olly sobbed back. 'Charlie bit me.'

'Nobody bit you, darling. It was just a dream.'

There was a moment's silence and then he watched her back out of the room. He cleared his throat, watching her spin round in surprise.

'Everything okay?' he asked in a low voice.

'Yes. He had a bad dream.' She looked back into the room. 'Who's Charlie?'

Nick shrugged.

'Haven't you gone to bed yet? What time is it?'

'Just gone one. I'm just finishing up some work.'

'Oh. I'm sorry Olly disturbed you.'

'That's okay.'

Abby moved towards her door. 'Goodnight then.'

'Yeah goodnight.' Nick managed to keep his eyes on hers but it didn't make any difference. He'd seen her legs now; they were imprinted on his brain forever.

'Nick?'

'Yeah?'

She stared at him. 'Nothing. Don't worry. Goodnight.'

'No. Tell me what you were going to say.'

She cleared her throat. 'Are you going to see Jo? Over the two weeks?'

'I don't think so. Why?'

'Just wondered.' She took a deep breath. 'I just didn't think about the sex part. The not getting it for two weeks I mean.'

Nick felt his mouth drop open in amazement and quickly pulled it shut. He'd had sex once in two months. Two weeks was nothing to him these days. Did Abby and Matthew do it that often?

'Sorry.' She shivered. 'I'm going to get my dressing gown on. I want a cigarette now I'm awake.' She slipped into her bedroom and Nick headed downstairs, suddenly wanting sex so much he was almost hard with it.

'Do you want one?' Abby poked her head round the living room door to ask.

Nick saw the cigarette packet just in time. 'Yeah okay. Let me just finish up here, I'll be out in a sec.' He quickly shut down his computer and put it away, switching off the lights and heading outside.

Abby was already puffing away, looking far less enticing in bulky dressing gown topped with her coat and a pair of trainers.

Nick lit up and leant back against the wall. 'Do you and Matthew do it a lot then?'

Abby gave a half smile. 'Yeah. Most nights when I'm not working and he's around. Why? Don't you?'

Nick concentrated on inhaling and exhaling.

'Sorry. I know a lot of people don't do it that often and you do work long hours. I just got the impression from Jo that you did it quite a lot.'

'Really? Well we don't.'

'But aren't you trying for a baby?'

Nick stared at her, half annoyed and half amused.

'Sorry, sorry. I know. I'm nosey. I'm just curious.'

And horny. Jesus. Was he meant to spend two weeks lying in the room across from hers knowing she was gagging for sex? How desperate was she? Shit no. Don't even go there. He gave a long hard pull on his cigarette. 'Jo wants a baby.'

'And you don't? Are you turning her down then?'

'Nope. If the offer was made I'd take it. And I gave up making the offer myself a long time ago.'

Abby looked so surprised that he had to wonder what Jo had told her. They smoked in silence for a couple of minutes and then headed back upstairs and to their separate rooms.

Nick lay awake for a long time. Trying to replace the image of Abby's legs with one of his girlfriend's. Only he couldn't picture Jo's legs to save his life. They were very thin. Not like Abby's. Hers were long and strong and shapely. And then he thought of Abby lying in bed, wanting sex. And then he thought of her pleasuring herself, her hand moving across her stomach, touching herself and he rolled over with a groan.

How the hell was he going to last two weeks?

Chapter Four

Jo was loving having Matthew to stay. He'd bounded through the door at six thirty, full of chat and laughter. He'd been overjoyed when she waited on him while he ate and then he'd got up and loaded the dishwasher.

She'd left him watching TV while she tidied up and then she'd joined him and they'd watched it together. He'd started yawning at eleven and they'd gone upstairs to bed.

'The spare room's through here.' She opened the door to show him and he dumped his bag on the bed. 'There are towels in the bathroom across the hall.'

He turned to smile at her and she felt her face flush.

'Um. So I'll be off. Just shout if you need anything. Goodnight.' 'Goodnight.' He grinned.

They locked eyes for long moments and she felt warmth flood through her.

'They'd never find out you know,' he said and her heart flipped up to her throat. He moved closer, voice caressing. 'We wouldn't have to tell them.' He was right next to her now, body skimming hers. He breathed against her ear, her neck and she felt goosebumps run the length of her body. 'It could be our secret.' He pressed a kiss to her neck and she shivered.

'We can't,' she gasped as his tongue flicked against her ear. 'What about your article? And Abby? I couldn't do that to Abby.'

He moved closer and she felt him against her, breath hot on her ear.

'Or Nick,' she added. He reached out a hand and brushed his thumb against her lips. She clamped down the urge to suck it into her mouth. His mouth moved to replace his thumb and she jumped back. 'We can't. I'm sorry. But we can't.' And she pushed past him, running into her room and slamming the door, leaning back against it with heart hammering.

And it was only the first night. How the hell was she going to resist him for another thirteen?

Matthew watched her go, a grin tugging at his lips. He'd never doubted that he'd get her into bed, just hadn't been sure he could do it in two weeks.

But now he was certain. He made a silent bet with himself that she'd be his before the weekend.

Chapter Five

Abby was woken by Olly climbing into bed beside her at six thirty the next morning. They lay and chatted and tickled and giggled until seven, Abby enjoying not having to keep him quiet so he didn't disturb Matthew.

Nick was standing by the kettle when they got downstairs. 'Good morning, Olly. How are you today?' He looked at Abby. 'Coffee?'

'Yes please.' Abby put some bread in the toaster and got the butter and jam and Marmite out. Olly trotted off towards the playroom.

'Did you sleep well?' Nick asked, eyes on the mugs as he poured water into them.

'Not really. Did you?'

'Nope.' He looked up at her and she quickly looked away. He was dressed for work, suit jacket draped over the back of a chair. His biceps strained against the thin fabric of his shirt and his trousers clung to his backside and Abby closed her eyes. Thank God she was working tonight – she couldn't stand another night being in the same house as him.

'Look, Nick. This is my gun.' Olly came back in, arms full of toys.

Abby put his toast on the table. 'Breakfast, Olly.'

Olly grabbed a slice of marmite and toast and turned back to Nick. 'Do you like my car? It's a racing car.' He took a bite of his toast and put it on the work surface, lining his cars along side.

Nick looked at Abby.

'What?' she stopped mid chew to ask.

'Shouldn't he sit at the table to eat?'

Abby almost dropped her toast. 'Why?'

'Because that's what he'll have to do at school. And at restaurants. Don't you ever sit at the table for your meals?'

'What do you think I'm doing now?'

'The three of you I mean.'

'No. Never.'

'So Olly never eats at the table?'

'Sometimes. When we eat at Matthew's parents'.' She put her toast down. 'No offence, Nick, but it's really none of your business. Olly's healthy and he eats well. What's important here?'

'Socialisation?'

Abby snorted.

Nick's jaw clenched slightly. 'Right. Time to go.' He glared at her for a beat then said goodbye to Olly and left.

Abby sighed. And then her eyes caught on his dinner plate. The table was such a mess she almost hadn't noticed. He hadn't put it in the dishwasher. And there were three mugs scattered around the kitchen too. And who the hell did he think he was telling her how to raise her son? Bloody cheek.

Well she wasn't clearing up after him. The plate would still be there when he came home tonight. And if she ran out of plates she'd simply stop cooking for him. And how come she felt so happy anyway? Well maybe not happy – she *was* pissed off about the Olly thing – but definitely kind of excited and alive. Still. It was better than horny. And if they were fighting they weren't wanting sex which was best all round. She sobered a little, guilt squashing the upbeat feelings. Nick was her best friend's boyfriend. And she'd lain awake fantasising about his hands on her body. How horrible was that? Still, at least she could put how crap he was in her notes for Matthew. She wondered briefly how he'd react if she put that she'd shagged Nick in there too? Would he even believe it? And if he slept with Jo? She bet that wouldn't end up in the article!

Chapter Six

Jo woke with a smile on her face. Matthew wanted to sleep with her. She knew she should feel bad for Abby, Matthew obviously wasn't the faithful type, but she couldn't do it. In a sick, evil sort of way, she was almost pleased. Abby had everything. She had a child, Matthew, a job she enjoyed. She was independent, happy. And she had big boobs. She'd never put up with the stuff Jo put up with.

Maybe she should just leave Nick. That's what Abby would do. Though she'd never have got together with him in the first place. Jo stretched and wondered how they were getting on. Nick and Abby. Probably, she didn't need to worry about leaving Nick. Chances were good that he and Abby would kill each other before the first week was through.

'Knock, knock.' The door opened and Matthew walked in. 'Coffee.' He put a mug down on the bedside table.

'Thanks. Do you always do that?'

'Nope. Never.' He winked. 'Don't tell Abby.'

Jo smiled happily.

'I have to go to work.' He looked her over. 'Feel free to stay like that all day.'

Jo watched him leave, the excitement almost choking her. She'd love to resist. To say that she couldn't do it to Abby. But let's face it, Matthew wasn't faithful. If it wasn't her, it'd be someone else. She would actually be doing her friend a favour. Keeping it in the family as it were.

She sat up and reached for the mug of coffee, mind on what she was going to wear when she met Matthew at the door that evening. She checked the clock. Eight thirty. Ten hours. Two to tidy and clean. One to shop. Seven to get ready.

Abby woke to her alarm and looked round, disorientated. The clock read nine twenty. Had she overslept? Christ, she was knackered. How long had she slept for? And then the fog cleared. It was evening. She had to go to work.

She'd had a really hectic day. She'd spent the morning sorting out the finances. Paying bills, balancing the accounts. Filing, filling in forms. She'd collected Olly at twelve fifteen and gone into Fleet to get some food. And then she'd come home and apart from feeding Olly, had been gardening non-stop. She'd filled fourteen bin bags with leaves. Three with grass cuttings and with Olly's help had weeded one of the flowerbeds.

Olly had been asleep by six thirty, Abby not much later. It felt like ten minutes ago. With a groan as her aching muscles protested being disturbed so soon, Abby rolled out of bed and into her jog suit. She did a quick bathroom stop; wee, deodorant and teeth, and then she checked on Olly and headed downstairs.

Kitchen first. She got her dinner from the fridge, putting it in a plastic bag with a can of Pepsi, apple, Twix and a bag of crisps. The kitchen was tidy and Nick's plate from yesterday was soaking in the sink. Abby swallowed a smile and went through to the living room.

Nick was tapping away at his computer again.

'Do you ever relax?'

He looked up. 'Oh hi. Yeah, sometimes. We've got a lot on at the moment. Did you sleep well?'

'Very. Just not for long enough.'

'Will you get to sleep tomorrow?'

'I get a couple of hours while Olly's at nursery.'

'That's it?' He looked horrified and Abby would have smiled if she wasn't still feeling annoyed at him for criticising her parenting skills. She'd been stewing over it on and off all day.

'It's okay. I manage. I have to run I'm afraid. I'll see you in the morning.' She hesitated. 'What if Olly wakes up before I get home?'

Nick smiled. 'We'll be fine. Go!'

Abby went. It was almost midnight before she had time to chat with her colleagues. The first night was always the worst. E-mails, problem updates, following up on work from the previous shift. They'd been given extra work tonight too.

Sixty-year-old Sally was the first to sit back. 'How was your week, hen?' she asked.

'Matthew moved out and Nick moved in,' Abby told her with a grin. Two heads immediately bobbed up on the other side of the partition.

'What?' supervisor Sid asked.

'Who the hell is Nick?' This from Judy.

Abby sat back. 'Jo and I have swapped men. You know that job Matthew applied for? The one with Men's Stuff magazine? He got through the first part and now he has to write an article. It can be about anything but has to be so many words long and about something original. We were all complaining about each other at the weekend and came up with the idea to swap partners for a couple of weeks.'

'Sex swapping?' Sid asked with bulging eyes.

'No! Just like on the programme. Apart from we're keeping the finances as they are. And the men have swapped houses instead of the women.'

Judy came round and perched on the edge of Sally's desk. 'Whose idea was it? And what's Nick like?'

'Sexy, but hell. And it was Matthew's idea.'

'Why's he hell?' Sally asked.

'It's been two days. We've spent half an hour together and he's already tried to tell me how to bring up Olly. He's used to being waited on so it took him until tonight to start clearing up after himself.'

'So you're not going to sleep with him?'

'Sid! For God's sake.'

'And it's for two weeks you say?'

It took almost half an hour to answer all their questions.

'You canna win this one, hen,' Sally said when Abby had finished. She tipped her chair back and put her legs up on the desk.

'Nice leggings,' Abby said.

Sally admired her yellow lycra leggings. 'Thanks, hen. Marks and Spencers. Twenty eight pounds.' She crossed skinny black arms over her chest and glared at Abby. 'Let me finish. You canna win. Jo has no wee-uns. No job. She's the perfect housewife. Matthew's never going to want to come home.'

Abby shrugged. 'If he loves me, he'll want to come back whatever.'

Silence.

'Bet he sleeps with her.'

'Sid!'

Sid grinned and smoothed his already over-smoothed oily hair. Judy nudged him and he almost fell off the desk. 'Hey!

I'm an old man.' He straightened and walked back round to his computer.

Judy grinned, the jewel on her front tooth sparkling under the strip lights. 'Pervert!' She turned back to Abby with serious eyes. 'Cigarette?'

Abby followed her down the stairs and they lit up.

'Is this your way of getting rid of Matthew?' Judy asked, sitting down on the top step.

'It wasn't my idea.' Abby sat down next to her and zipped her coat up. 'Christ, it's March. Shouldn't it be getting warmer?'

'Don't change the subject. You already think Matthew's been sleeping around. Why are you giving him this opportunity?'

Abby shrugged. 'He really wants the job. It's better pay and he'd be around more. And I did it for Jo. Nick treats her like a maid and completely takes her for granted.'

'Isn't she the one who doesn't work?'

'Yes.' Abby squashed the disloyal thought that her friend actually *was* a maid. She did sod all and Nick supported her *and* paid her an allowance. More than he'd actually pay a live in maid probably.

'Well I think you're crazy. I don't know why you didn't just give them a pack of condoms and the Kama Sutra.

Chapter Seven

Matthew didn't come home until ten thirty that night. He let himself in with the key Jo had given him the night before and followed the sound of the TV to the living room.

Jo was dressed in a silky lilac dressing gown and she was lying on the settee. Matthew eyed her pale slim limbs accentuated by the flimsy fabric and moved closer. He cleared his throat. No reaction. And then he realised that she was sleeping.

Damn! He perched on the coffee table and looked her over. Enjoying the opportunity to do so unobserved. Shoulder length blonde hair framed a tiny round face. She was really petite, maybe five foot, five foot one, and she had an almost boyish figure. She was as different from Abby as you could get, yet Matthew found them both sexy. Though thinking about it, there weren't many attractive women Matthew didn't find sexy.

And then he realised that Jo meant him to find her looking like this. Maybe not asleep. But probably freshly washed and dressed in silk. Her legs were clean shaven too. He felt himself harden and grinned a wide, satisfied smile. She was his for the taking. If he woke her with a kiss, slid a hand up soft creamy thigh . . . He gave himself a mental shake. Not yet. It was too easy. He wanted to play for a bit longer.

He got to his feet and left the room.

Bedtime.

Abby got home at ten past seven and unlocked the door quietly. Usually if Olly was awake, he'd come running down the stairs. Matthew would still be in bed – nothing got him to move before seven thirty. Today, the house was awake. The curtains were open, coffee and toast smells lingered and voices came from the kitchen.

'Good morning.' She walked into the kitchen and glanced at Nick. He and Olly were sat at the table eating toast. She bent to kiss her son.

'I'm eating at the table, Mum,' he said. 'I'm big boy.'

'You are.' Abby had been fuming at Nick all night but it was so nice to come home to find Olly up and dressed and eating, that she found it hard to hold on to her anger.

'Was he okay? What time did he wake you?'

'He woke at two. Another bad dream about Charlie. He was fine. And he was up at six thirty.'

'Nick was up 'fore me, Mummy. I got dressed all by myself.'

'Really?' Abby poured herself a coffee and put bread in the toaster. And then she turned back to the table. 'Who's Charlie?'

'Charlie in the mini. He bit me, Mum. Tomorrow I'm going to take my gun to bed and shoot him dead.' He made gun noises.

'Olly. Toast,' Nick said and Olly carried on eating.

Abby buttered her toast and thought that maybe she was asleep. This was all a dream. Nick and her son weren't really sitting bonding over toast. Olly hadn't dressed himself and he wasn't sitting at the table doing as he was told. Unless they were aliens. Maybe they'd been invaded and their bodies taken over.

'Did you have a good night?' Nick asked and she thought that if he was an alien he was a polite one.

'Quiet. I got almost two hours' sleep.'

'So that's what? Four hours in all?' He shook his head. 'Why don't you go up to bed now? I can take Olly to nursery.'

Abby gaped at him. Matthew had *never* taken Olly to nursery. Not once. She wasn't even sure he knew where it was. 'Thanks, but don't worry. He doesn't start until nine fifteen.' Definitely aliens.

'That's okay. I can work from here until it's time to leave. Seriously, Abby, I don't mind.'

'But . . . you don't even know where it is.'

'So? Tell me.'

'The Point. Behind the Harlington Centre.'

'By the park. Nine fifteen. Got it. Say goodnight.'

'Can I eat my toast first?' Abby grinned.

Nick smiled back and Abby thought how nice this was. When he wasn't telling her how to raise her son or leaving dirty plates and mugs all over the place, he was nice. Very nice.

For an alien.

Chapter Eight

Jo woke at four thirty. She was cold, her neck was stiff and the TV was blaring music at her. She rolled to her feet, groaning when her muscles protested, switched the TV off and went upstairs. Matthew's door was ajar and she could hear him breathing. It was just below a snore and it told her he was home.

She wondered what time he'd come in. Nick would have phoned to say he'd be late. And he'd have carried her up to bed. At the very least, he'd have covered her up and switched the TV off. And where had Matthew been? Last she'd noticed it was nine forty-five, so she knew he'd come in after that. Was he working late? Drinking? Was he alone? Or with a woman?

She'd been so excited all day. The house was gleaming. The kitchen was fully stocked. She'd shaved, trimmed, exfoliated, plucked. She'd spent almost two hours deciding what to wear. Obviously she'd made the wrong choice. He'd certainly managed to resist her. Unless he hadn't actually seen her. Maybe he'd come in and gone straight to bed.

It took almost an hour to get back to sleep and when she woke it was five past ten. The house was in silence and the day stretched endlessly ahead. Jo itched to ring Abby. She picked up the phone and thought of phoning Becky or Fiona but she was scared they'd see through her. What if they knew she planned to sleep with Matthew? Putting the phone back she went downstairs. No sign that Matthew had been there. She checked the dishwasher. Plate and mug. He'd had toast and coffee.

Oh well, there was nothing else for it. She'd have to go shopping.

Abby woke to her alarm at twelve and stretched happily. She felt great. Four and a half hours sleep. More than she ever got in one stretch when she was working. She quickly pulled on last night's clothes and stopping only to brush her teeth, jumped on her bike and headed for nursery school.

She fed Olly and then took a shower, dressing in jeans and t-shirt. She got downstairs just as her mobile started ringing.

'Abby? It's Nick. How are you?'

'Fine. I feel great actually. Thanks for this morning. Where did you get my number?'

'You wrote it down for me when you gave me the door key?'

'Duh, oh yeah, sorry, I'm really not with it today.'

'That's okay. Listen, I was thinking that when I'm in the office I could pick Olly up for you too. That'd give you longer to sleep.'

'You can't do that! I thought you went to the gym at lunchtime.'

'Not every day. It'd be no trouble.' His voice faded for a second. 'Sorry about that. Oh, yeah. The other thing I was ringing about. How do you get to work?'

'I cycle.' Abby watched Olly play fighting with his Power Rangers and wondered why he always made the red one win.

'To Farnborough? At night?'

'Yeah. I've been doing it for two years.' Abby switched the phone to the other ear and sat down. 'Why? What's wrong?'

'Nothing. I'll call you back.' The line went dead and Abby put the phone down. Weird.

Two minutes later it rung again. 'Why haven't you got a car? Or why aren't you on Matthew's insurance?'

'Because I can't drive. Nick, I'm fine cycling. I like it.'

'Even in the rain?'

'Well, no. But I can't afford to learn to drive and I don't have the time.'

'I'll teach you.'

'What?'

'When we're back to normal. When I'm back home and you can leave Olly with Matthew. I'll teach you to drive.'

'You can't do that.' Abby looked at the ceiling. 'Look, no offence, Nick, but two days ago you didn't even know what I did for a living. Now suddenly you're worrying about how much sleep I get and how I get to work and you're going to teach me to drive. It's very nice and all that but in two weeks you'll be gone and I'll be back to being Jo's best mate. Don't make rash promises.'

'I *will* teach you to drive. End of conversation.' And the connection was broken.

Abby put the phone down again. And then she smiled. He really could be lovely.

She set her alarm for nine fifteen that night. She wanted an extra fifteen minutes so she could thank Nick properly.

He was outside having a cigarette when she went downstairs.

'Couldn't sleep?' He lit her cigarette for her and she concentrated on the first drag, pulling it deep into her lungs before blowing out and turning to Nick.

'I slept wonderfully thanks. I just wanted time to say thank you. For taking Olly to nursery and being so nice and stuff.'

Nick stared at her through a haze of smoke. 'You work, Abby. I'm surprised Matthew isn't more supportive. And I'm surprised you put up with it. From what Jo says I thought you fought him on everything.'

'I pick my battles. I've given up on nagging him to do more for Olly. And I get enough sleep.' She shrugged. 'It's fine. We're fine.'

'It's not fine. Five hours isn't enough sleep and you shouldn't be cycling at night. I've got you a lift for tonight. My nephew, Will. He's training for some Gladiator like thing and has been on at me to give him some instruction. I've promised him some pointers if he'll chauffeur you to work.'

Abby dragged her jaw from the ground and puffed at her cigarette. 'That's very nice of you but how will I get home?'

'Olly and I'll collect you.'

'But you'll have to wake Olly up. Sometimes he's not awake that early.'

'It won't hurt him.'

Abby sighed. 'You'll be gone in less than two weeks. What's the point?'

'The point is that you're my responsibility while I'm here.'

'Oh.' Abby sucked in some smoke and tried to steady her pounding heart. His responsibility. God that sounded good. It made her feel looked after, a feeling she hadn't had for a long time. If ever. 'It's really not necessary. I can take care of myself.'

He put out his cigarette, expression stony.

'Fine. Thank you. And why are you giving him pointers? You're not a Gladiator?' She looked at the thick arms. 'Are you?'

'No. But I used to be a personal trainer, and body building was my speciality.' He checked his watch. 'You'd better move it. Will'll be here in two minutes.'

Abby stamped on her cigarette and went inside to get her bag.

Nick saw her to the door and into Will's red escort. 'Will'll phone me with directions. I'll see you at six forty-five.'

Abby shut the car door and wound down the window. 'Okay. Thanks. Goodnight.'

He smiled. 'Drive carefully, Will.'

Will saluted. 'Yes, Uncle.'

'Cheeky fucker.'

Will pulled away from the curb and Abby watched Nick fade to nothing in the wing mirror.

'Thanks for this,' Will said. 'I've been after Uncle Nick to train me for ages.' He was a skinny thing, how he expected to bulk up to Gladiator level was beyond Abby. He had Nick's dark hair and square jaw but that's where the similarity ended. Will had dimples in both cheeks and his chin, impossibly long eyelashes and a permanent smile. Abby wondered if Nick had ever looked so young and carefree. She couldn't imagine it, but who knew?

'No problem. Nick insisted. Normally I cycle.'

Will shot her a look. Almost as if checking she was serious. 'That's not sensible. Women shouldn't cycle alone at night.'

Abby bit back a sharp retort. The boy was doing her a favour. And if his dad was anything like Nick it wasn't surprising he thought like they did. And it *was* nice to get a lift.

'So? Who's related to Nick? Your mum or dad?'

'My dad.'

Abby leant her head back against the headrest and closed her eyes. 'Thought so.'

Sid and Judy were already at their desks when she got in.

'Was that Nick who dropped you off?' Judy asked the minute she opened the door. They'd obviously been watching the security cameras.

'Nope. His nephew.' Abby sat down and turned her PC on.

'Where's your bike?' Sid came round the partition, closely followed by Judy.

'At home.' Abby entered her network password and tried to ignore them.

The door banged open. 'Evening.' Sally walked over, bright as ever in a lime green tracksuit. 'Where's your bike, hen?'

Abby gave up. 'Nick wasn't happy with me cycling in. Thought it was dangerous. He has his nephew chauffeuring me in for the next two weeks and he's picking me up in the morning. And when he goes back to Jo, he's teaching me to drive.' She shrugged and logged onto her e-mail.

The silence stretched for all of thirty seconds and then:
'Good on him.' Judy.
'About time someone started looking out for you, hen.' Sally.
'Definitely wants sex.' Sid.
'He does not want sex!' Abby glared up at him. 'And I can look after myself. Matthew knows that.'

Sally snorted. 'Matthew knows nothing beyond the end of his dick, excuse my French.'

'Sally!' Abby said without heat. Sally was best buddies with Matthew's mum and had got Abby the job here. She'd known Matthew since he was a baby and she wasn't impressed. She clearly thought Abby was far too good for him.

Abby sighed and started opening e-mails. The other three got bored and wondered back to their desks. Sally was right. Matthew wasn't the most considerate of boyfriends. But they were happy together. Abby got her freedom and regular, uncomplicated sex. Matthew got to live with his son and was free to come and go as he pleased. The relationship suited both of them.

For now.

Chapter Nine

Matthew rushed home from work that night. He didn't expect to be greeted in silk again, but you never knew.

Jo was in the kitchen, emptying the dishwasher. She was wearing the dressing gown again and her hair was damp.

'Oh, hi,' she said, face flushing and he knew it wasn't intentional this time. She'd genuinely just got out of the bath or shower. She was naked under the dressing gown. Matthew felt his entire body go hard and gave her a very slow smile.

'Hi, yourself. Good day?'

'Yes, thanks. You?'

He nodded, still smiling.

'Are you ready for your dinner?'

He moved closer, eyes never leaving hers. He shook his head. 'Not yet.' Jo tried to lower her eyes and he hooked a finger under her chin, holding her face still. He lowered his mouth and watched hers drop open. Her eyes fluttered shut and he swallowed a grin. And then his mouth touched hers and she stumbled against him, hands automatically coming up against his chest.

Matthew deepened the kiss and felt her hands slide round his waist. He stroked hands down her back and across her buttocks and then he slid his hands up her thighs, pulling the dressing gown up with them. The tie fell open and he looked down at tiny creamy breasts, nipples large and hard as walnuts. He lowered his mouth, totally aroused, completely relaxed about the entire situation. But at the same time he was aware of a faint twinge of what felt very like disappointment.

It had been almost too easy.

Chapter Ten

Nick and Olly were waiting outside the door when Abby walked out at six fifty-two.

'Hi.' She climbed in the passenger seat and smiled back at Olly.

'I'm in Tilly's seat,' he said.

'You look knackered,' Nick said.

'I am. I got no sleep at all last night.' She leant her head back and closed her eyes.

'Why don't you go straight to bed when we get home?'

'Are you sure?'

'Yes!'

'Okay.' Abby gave a weak smile.

Next thing she knew Nick was trying to get her awake enough to get inside.

'Sorry,' she muttered, taking his hand and easing sleepily out of the car. Olly was already inside, the door open. Nick put an arm around her waist and led her into the hall.

'Go to bed,' he said, voice soft.

Abby gave a sleepy smile and turned to her son. 'Have a nice time at nursery, baby.' She kissed his cheek.

'I will, I love you, Mum.'

'I love you too, honey.'

'I'll collect him, Abby. Do you need to write a note or something? I'll wake you when I have to go back to work.'

'Okay.' Abby sleepwalked into the kitchen and scribbled a note giving permission for Nick to collect Olly. 'Thanks for this.'

'No problem. We'll have fun won't we, Ol?'

'Yes. Can we go to the park?'

Abby smiled and left them to it.

Nick knocked on the bedroom door at one thirty. There was a pause, then a rustling of bed clothes and Abby called out, 'Come in.'

He opened the door and put a mug of coffee down on the bedside table. 'I have to leave in twenty minutes. We've been to the park and had lunch. Olly's in the playroom.'

'Thanks. Has he been okay?' Abby asked, voice husky from sleep. Nick let himself look at her for the first time and was shot through with desire. She was sitting up in bed, the bedclothes clasped round her chest. Her skin was light ebony against the cream of the duvet, her almost black hair framing slashing cheekbones, bright green eyes and the most kissable lips Nick had ever seen.

Nick swallowed and looked away. 'He's been fine. I'll see you downstairs.' And he left before he was tempted to check if she was wearing any underwear.

He looked in on Olly and slipped outside for a smoke. Abby joined him a few minutes later. She'd pulled on running shorts and a sweatshirt. Nick raised an eyebrow.

'I'm dropping Olly at Fiona's so I can go for a run. I don't get to go to the gym when I'm working and I'm not cycling.' She shrugged. 'I have to do something.'

Nick checked out her legs. Long and strong and shapely. Her thighs were smooth and toned, waist small in comparison. She was as different to Jo as you could get and Nick found himself increasingly attracted to her.

'How far do you run?'

'I try to run different distances through the week. Usually three miles, then six, then eight. I'm aiming for six today.'

'Mum! Mum!' Olly yelled, running through the kitchen. 'My car's broken.' He held up a big police car. One of the wheels was hanging at a weird angle.

'Never mind,' Abby said. 'We'll put it in the kitchen and Daddy'll fix it when he comes home.'

'When is Daddy coming home? Is he on holiday?'

'Yes. He'll be back soon.'

Olly stared at her for a beat, short blonde hair sticking up, so cute in his dungarees and shirt.

'Don't love Daddy,' he said. He looked at the car and then he looked back at Abby. And then he threw the car at her and ran back through to the playroom.

Abby rubbed her arm where the car had hit and dragged hard on her cigarette. Nick stubbed his own cigarette and went inside. He found Olly watching TV.

'That wasn't very nice was it, Olly?' Nick said, sitting down next to him.

'Don't like Mummy,' he said mutinously.

'You shouldn't say that. It upsets Mummy. You hurt Mummy's arm. Would you like it if I threw a car at you?'

'Throwing's naughty.'

'Yes, it is. Don't you think you should say sorry?'

'Don't want to.'

'Fine.' Nick stood up. 'Only good boys get to go to the park. If you can't be good and say sorry, I won't take you to the park again.'

Olly stared at him, surprise etched on his little freckled face, and Nick realised that he wasn't used to this. He wasn't used to being taken to task for misbehaving. Granted Abby was busy. But what the hell was Matthew doing? Nick gave a mental shrug. It was nothing to do with him.

He went through to the kitchen to put the lunch stuff away and found Abby making a sandwich.

'Your mum phoned a little while ago. She wanted to remind you about next Thursday. And she wanted to know why the window cleaner was answering the phone.' He grinned and Abby chuckled.

'What did you tell her?'

'I told her you were in bed.'

'That's it? That's all you told her?' Abby gave a bark of laughter. 'Thanks a lot!'

'So what's happening next Thursday?'

Abby stopped laughing. 'It's Keith's sixtieth. My mum's husband. They're having a dinner party. I'd completely forgotten about it.'

'Not fun?'

Abby scowled. 'I can't stand Keith. Or his daughters. Or dinner parties.'

Nick stopped just short of smiling. She sounded like a petulant child. 'Was Matthew meant to be going with you?'

'Yeah,' Abby said on a sigh. 'Becky's babysitting.' She looked up. 'I don't suppose you want to come? It'll be boring as hell, but the food'll be good.'

She looked almost pleading and Nick nodded. 'Sure,' he said and wondered what he was letting himself in for. Abby was an odd woman. God knows what her family were like.

Nick put the last mug in the dishwasher and gathered his laptop and case. 'I have to go. I'll see you tonight.'

'Okay, have a good day.'

'You too.'

'Are you going, Nick?' Olly said from the doorway.

35

'Yes. I'll see you in the morning,' Nick said.

'Okay.' He turned to Abby. 'I'm sorry, Mummy. I'm sorry I threw my police car at you.'

Abby swung round and stared at her son in stunned disbelief.

'Is it fixed now?' Olly went on and Abby laughed. She looked at Nick and shook her head.

'What are you doing to my son?' she asked.

Nick just grinned.

Abby came down at nine that night. Nick was in the living room watching TV.

'Blimey! Not working?'

Nick looked up with a grin. 'Just finished. Couldn't you sleep?'

'Nope. Got enough this morning I guess.' She smiled. 'I feel great. Are you sure you want to move back with Jo?'

Nick went still, grin disappearing.

Abby felt her heart stop and then it picked up speed. 'I was joking,' she said.

Nick just stared, face expressionless.

'I need a cigarette,' Abby said and left the room.

She'd only just lit up when Nick followed her out.

'Be horrible. Criticise my parenting skills,' she said.

Nick gave a small smile. 'Okay. You don't discipline your son enough. He has no routine and he gets away with murder.' He sucked on his cigarette. 'Happy?'

'No,' Abby said miserably. She sighed. 'I could really get used to having you around. You're spoiling me.'

Nick gave her a long look. 'I'm supporting you. It's different from spoiling and no more than Matthew should do. You work a thirty-two hour week. That's practically full-time. You shouldn't have to do everything at home too.'

'I'm used to it.' She sighed again. 'Sorry, ignore me. I'm probably hormonal or something.'

Nick chuckled. 'You're a woman, Abs. You're meant to be coy and secretive. And you should never admit to hormones.'

Abby smiled. 'Sorry. I make a crap woman.'

Nick looked at the curve of her breast against her jacket. And then he looked at her mouth. Abby watched him and unconsciously licked her lower lip.

Nick groaned. 'Jesus.' He pulled hard on his cigarette and stubbed it out with his heel. 'You make a hell of a woman.'

'Nick?' Abby stepped closer.

'Don't,' he said.

'But . . .'

'No.' Nick put out a hand and placed a finger against her lips.

They stood there in silence. A dog barked in the distance and still they stood. Abby let her eyes close and moved her head so her lips brushed Nick's finger. Heat spread away from her mouth, through her body, washing over her limbs and turning her legs to ribbon.

He snatched his hand away and lit another cigarette. Abby tried to do the same only she couldn't get hers to light. Her hands were shaking too much. Nick cursed under his breath and gave her his. And then he took hers and lit it himself.

'Do you cheat on Matthew?' he asked, voice rough.

'No! Never.'

'Because you love him? Because you get enough sex from him?'

'Because I don't cheat.'

'Right.'

'You don't believe me?'

He gave a hollow laugh. 'All women cheat.'

'That is such bollocks. Is this because of your ex-wife? Jo's never cheated on you.'

He stared at her but she couldn't read his expression in the dark. 'Yet. Do you really think she won't sleep with Matthew?'

'Of course she won't.' Abby went still. 'Will she?' She shook her head. 'Jo wouldn't do that.'

'But Matthew would?'

'Matthew doesn't turn anyone down.'

'You know Matthew cheats on you?' Nick's voice was harsh now. 'And you put up with it?'

Abby shrugged. 'I don't know for definite, but I'm pretty sure.'

'Do you even care?'

'No. Not really.' Abby stared at him, defiant.

Nick snorted in disgust. 'I can't believe you have so little self-respect.'

'Me? What about you? You're standing here saying how Matthew and Jo are shagging. Where's yours? You're letting it happen.'

'If it happens, I'll kick her out.'

Abby smiled without humour. '*If* you find out.'

'Oh, I'll find out.'

The doorbell shattered the silence between them and Abby looked away first. 'That's probably Will. And I'm telling him not to pick me up again.'

'The hell you are!'

'I am. And you can stop doing stuff for Olly. It'll screw him up when you go. And stop taking him to nursery school. We're fine on our own.'

'There's fine and there's getting by. You're getting by. Stop being such a fucking doormat and make Matthew pull his weight.'

'Stay out of it, Nick,' Abby said and went through to Will before she gave in and cried.

'Hi, Will,' she said. 'Thanks for coming out but I don't need a ride tonight.'

'Oh. Are you sure?'

'Yes.' She forced a smile and watched him walk away. And then she turned to fetch her bag and walked into Nick's chest.

'You sent him away?' He put out a hand to help her balance and then crossed his arms over his chest.

'Yes. I don't want you doing me any more favours.' Abby moved round him and put her rucksack on. And then she went through the kitchen to the garage to get her bike.

'You know, if you were my girlfriend you wouldn't be doing this.' Nick had followed her out.

Abby snorted and opened the garage door. 'If you were my boyfriend you'd be dead.'

She got on her bike and started pedalling. She didn't look back and she didn't say goodbye. Sod him. He could take his concern and his consideration and his sexy body and stay the hell away from her.

She didn't need him. She cycled faster and faster, and pretty soon the urge to cry went away and by the time she got to work she had her emotions back under control. She didn't need anyone.

Chapter Eleven

'I'm going to leave Nick.'

Matthew froze.

He felt Jo shift closer and her hand slid round his waist. He closed his eyes.

'I mean it. I'm leaving him. I'm sick of being treated like a child. I want fun and laughter and a good time.' She wrapped her hand round him. 'And mind-blowing sex.'

She snuggled against his shoulder and kissed his neck. Oh God. She didn't expect a response did she?

'Matthew?'

Oh bloody hell. He rolled so she was underneath him. And then he kissed her mouth. Best way he knew to shut-up a woman. She relaxed beneath him and he kissed his way to her neck.

'Matthew?'

Jesus! 'I'm here for you. You know that. But I can't leave Abby. We have a son, remember?'

Jo went quiet and Matthew moved quickly, taking her nipple into his mouth and sucking it so hard she jerked. And then her fingers were in his hair and he moved lower, and lower and pretty soon she wasn't complaining and Matthew thanked God for Olly. And then he thought about how passionate Jo was and how he was pretty sure she'd faked her orgasm and how much he liked a challenge. Especially if it involved sex. Jo may have been too easy to seduce and was way too clingy; but Matthew wanted to succeed where he suspected Nick had failed. He heard Jo groan when his tongue flicked against her clitoris and her hips pressed up against his mouth. He eased a finger inside her and moved back slightly.

'Do you fake it with Nick too?' he asked and immediately felt Jo's muscles tighten.

'I don't know what you're talking about,' she muttered.

Matthew licked her again, his finger pressing against her insides. Another moan and everything grew more moist. He continued to lick, over and over, circling, pressing harder then so gently she strained upwards. He licked her until she was moaning incoherently and then he pulled away and moved up the bed. 'Do you ever orgasm?'

Jo's hand paused halfway down his stomach. 'Yes.'

'With Nick I mean.'
Another pause and then a sigh. 'No.'
'With any man?'
Jo shook her head.
'On your own?'
'Yes.' Jo worried her lower lip between her teeth. 'Don't worry about it. I still really enjoy it. You don't have to orgasm to have fun.'
'No. But it helps.' He tweaked her nipple between his thumb and forefinger, rolling it until it tightened. 'If you can make yourself come, then I can make you come. What do you think about? Do you use a vibrator?'
Jo's eyes jerked to his, and then slid to the ceiling, her face flushing. 'Sometimes.'
'And what do you think about?'
Jo still wouldn't meet his eyes.
'Other women, threesomes?'
She shook her head.
'Anal, S&M?'
More shaking.
Matthew slid three fingers inside her and she jolted against him, jaw going slack.
'Come on, Jo. Help me out here. Tell me what you want.' He slid his thumb against her clitoris and moved the other hand to cup her buttocks. She squirmed against him and he went through every fantasy he could think of, watching her closely.
And then he rolled her gently onto her stomach and moved her hands above her head, trapping them there with one hand wrapped around her wrists. With the other he kneaded her buttocks. Her breath came faster. Still holding her wrists, he leant across her and hooked open his gym bag which was next to the bed. His hands moved against cold metal and he pulled out his handcuffs.
'What are you doing?' Jo twisted beneath him, voice panicked.
'Trust me.' Matthew kissed her neck and snapped a cuff round her right wrist.
'Hey!' Jo tried to pull away but she was too slow. Matthew hooked the cuffs through the bars of the headboard and clipped them on the other wrist. He considered a gag but then

decided he wanted to be able to hear her. Jo buried her head in the pillow and whimpered as his hand slid south again.

He teased her for a while, stroking her thighs and buttocks, never touching her quite where she wanted.

'So you want to be smacked, huh?' he whispered and raising his

hand, gave her a sharp slap on her right buttock. The fingers still inside her were suddenly coated with fresh evidence of her arousal. He slapped her again, and then again, alternating between cheeks. Her internal muscles clenched his fingers and he let a finger slide over her clitoris. One more smack, lower this time.

Jo whimpered. 'Please,' she muttered and that was all it took.

Matthew all but lost control. He quickly ripped a condom open and slid it on and then grasping a buttock in each hand, lifted her and spread her legs with his. He moved close against her and slid easily inside, his hands squeezing and stoking her cherry-kissed bottom. He moved slowly, thinking of cleaning the windows, work on Monday, anything to try and stop himself coming. Jo moaned loudly and he moved faster. He couldn't hold back any longer and thrusting harder he gripped her tightly, his fingers leaving red marks and he felt her tighten around him and suddenly she screamed and he could feel her muscles spasm around him, milking him hard and fast. And then he was exploding inside her, crying her name as he collapsed on top of her.

Jo was still throbbing around him when he regained his senses. He reached for the handcuff key and released her wrists, letting her cuddle against him. Her hand stroked his chest and he crossed his arms behind his head. He'd done it.

He'd beaten Nick.

Chapter Twelve

Abby got home at five past seven on Saturday morning to what was fast becoming a familiar sight.

'Morning, Mummy,' Olly said from the kitchen table.

'Morning, sweetheart.' She kissed his forehead and switched the kettle on.

'There's coffee in the machine,' Nick said.

'I want instant,' Abby told him, spooning Nescafe into her mug.

Nick shrugged.

Abby glared at him. 'Don't patronise me.'

Nick stared back, expression inscrutable.

'And stop sucking up to my son.'

'Nick's not sucking me, Mummy,' Olly said and Nick's jaw tightened.

'Have you finished your breakfast?' he asked.

Olly nodded.

'Go and play then. We'll do your teeth when I've finished my coffee.'

Olly jumped down and ran from the room.

Nick stood up, chair scraping along the floor. 'I know you're tired but don't take it out on me. Would you prefer I left Olly in his pyjamas and told him he couldn't eat his breakfast until you came home? Or should I just stay in bed? Is that what Matthew does?' He loaded the dishwasher and shut the door. And then he was looming over her and she flushed. Of course that was what Matthew did.

'Go to bed,' Nick said.

'No.'

'You can't go around in this mood all day. It's not fair on Olly.'

'Let me decide what's fair on Olly—'

'Jesus, Abby. Let go would you. I'm not taking over your son.' He paused and took a deep breath. 'Tilly'll be here in two hours. Olly will want to play with her for a while. Go to bed. At least for a couple of hours. You won't last the evening otherwise.'

He was right. And even Matthew would have taken over for a while so Abby could get some sleep. She just didn't want to take anything from Nick. He was getting to her. Making her want to rely on him. She had actually started to enjoy being taken care of.

'Alright then,' she said. 'Thanks.'

She went through to say goodnight to Olly and then shuffled up to bed. She woke at two thirty to the sound of squealing children in the garden and took a quick shower before heading downstairs. Nick was working in the dining room where he could watch Tilly and Olly through the patio door.

'Don't you take weekends off?'

'I've got some stuff to catch up on.' He finished typing something and looked up. 'Feeling better?'

'Yes.' Abby blew out a sigh. 'I'm sorry I was a cow earlier.'

'Don't worry about it.'

Abby sat down across from him and drummed her fingers on the table, eyes staring unseeingly through the patio door.

'Abby?'

'What?' She jerked round.

'What's wrong?'

'Nothing.' She went back to drumming.

Nick sighed and shut his computer down. He closed the lid with a whoosh of air and sat back, arms folded across his chest.

The phone rang.

Abby carried on drumming.

'Shall I get that?'

Abby drummed a little faster. Nick picked up the phone and pressed the pick-up button.

'It's your mum. She phoned earlier.'

Abby took the phone. 'Hi, Mum.'

'Hello, darling. Who is that man that keeps answering your phone? And what have you done with Matthew?'

'He's an alien. He took over Matthew's body.'

'Very good, dear. I'm ringing about Thursday. You will be there won't you?'

'Yes. I'll be there.'

'And Matthew? You know how the girls love him. Speaking of which, when are you getting married? Sharon's desperate to be bridesmaid.'

'I'm not getting married. And I won't be bringing Matthew.'

'But you have a child! And why aren't you bringing Matthew? You can't come alone. I've done the seating plan and everything. You have to bring someone.'

'Fine. I'll bring the alien.

'Good, good. Very good, darling. See you on Thursday then. Seven thirty for eight?'

Abby jabbed the end button and chucked the phone across the room. It landed in the ironing basket.

'Alien?' Nick said from across the table.

Abby looked up. 'You're the alien. My mother never listens to me.'

'I kind of figured that one out. Are you okay?'

'Yes, no. I don't know.' She ran a hand through her hair and fixed Nick with a glare. 'Do you miss Jo?'

Nick looked at her carefully. 'No. Not at all.'

'Do you love her?'

Another long look. 'Probably not.'

'So why are you with her?'

'Are you asking as her friend?'

'No. I don't know who I'm asking as but the answer bothers me more than it should.' She shot him another angry look. 'I don't even like you that much. You're bossy and you work too much and you're too strict with Olly.'

Nick grinned.

'It's not funny!'

He grinned some more. 'I was with Jo because it was easy.'

'Was?'

'I plan to ask her to move out when I go home.'

'Well that backfired didn't it?'

'What?'

Abby stood up. 'I need a cigarette.'

Nick followed her outside and they sat at the picnic table. Tilly and Olly were in the playhouse, probably playing mums and dads, or Power Rangers or something.

'Jo wanted to swap so that you'd appreciate her more. She thought after two weeks of having to pull your weight here you'd love going back to her waiting on you.'

Nick snorted. 'I pay her bloody well to wait on me. And it's not worth it. I could get a live in maid a lot cheaper.'

'And you might get regular sex then too.' Abby exhaled and squinted at him through the smoke. 'She's my best friend. We really shouldn't discuss her like this.'

'But you agree with me?'

Abby sat back and looked at him. 'I think she should work. She shouldn't be living off you and it's not doing her any favours spending all day shopping and keeping house. She needs a child. Or a job or something. Basically she's spoilt. She's used to being the centre of attention at home. She was the same at school. I'm not criticising her,' Abby added quickly. 'I love her like a sister, but she *is* spoilt.' Abby glared at Nick. 'And you probably haven't helped. You spoil her just as badly as her parents and brother.'

'I know.' Nick watched Tilly and Olly through the playhouse window, cigarette forgotten, smoke curling around his arm.

'So what are you going to do?'

Nick looked at her, gaze direct and unwavering. 'I told you. I'm going to ask her to move out.'

Abby looked away. That would mean he was available. Her heart jumped around in her rib cage and she got warm all over.

'Abby?' Nick said, voice soft.

Abby shook her head and kept her eyes averted.

'Look at me.'

Abby shook her head some more and he leant across the bench, hand grasping her chin, forcing her to look at him. 'What's wrong?'

'She's my best friend, Nick.'

'I know.'

'Even if she slept with Matthew, I still couldn't do it to her. Do you know how much it'll screw her up when you kick her out?'

'Maybe she and Matthew will hook up.'

'No way.' Abby smiled sadly. 'He'd sleep with her but he wouldn't live with her. She's too needy for him. He couldn't cope with it.'

'Shame.'

Abby cut her eyes in his direction. 'Besides, Matthew is with me.'

'Why d'you think I'm so keen for them to get together?'

'Nick, don't,' she said on a whisper.

'Why? What are you so scared of?' he demanded.

'Matthew is Olly's dad and Jo is my best friend.'

'But you'd like to?'

Abby looked at him. All big and handsome and strong and dependable. She sighed. 'You know I would.'

He smiled.

'But I can't and I won't.'

He carried on smiling.

'I mean it, Nick.'

'I know you do.' But still he smiled.

Stupid, arrogant alien.

Chapter Thirteen

Nick took Tilly to the cinema after lunch and Abby and Olly went to the park and did some shopping in Fleet. Olly was in bed by six-thirty and when Nick and Tilly got home at seven, Abby had just finished putting her make-up on.

Nick was in the kitchen making hot chocolate when she went downstairs.

'Why are you wearing a bra? Where's your t-shirt?' Tilly asked. She had a packet of mini-marshmallows in front of her and was picking out the pink ones.

Nick looked up, did a quick body scan and turned back to his mugs.

'This *is* my t-shirt, honey.' Abby got a bottle of beer from the fridge and tried to find the bottle opener.

'It's in the living room,' Nick said.

Abby went through to get it and when she came back Nick was at the table with Tilly. 'Are you getting a lift?' he asked.

Abby nodded. 'Becky's picking me up at seven thirty.'

'How are you getting home?'

Abby shrugged. 'I'll probably walk. Or get a taxi.'

'How do you normally get home?'

'Walk. I never have enough money left for a taxi.'

Nick nodded at the windowsill. 'Take a tenner. I'd rather you didn't walk.'

'I'm not taking your money.'

'Abby—'

'No!'

They glared at each other.

'I'll take a taxi. I'll make sure I have money left.'

'If you run out, get a taxi anyway. Call me and I'll come out and pay.'

'Fine,' Abby said, thinking *no way*.

Nick sighed and shot a quick glance at Tilly before turning back. 'Cigarette?'

'No.'

'Coward.' He grinned and Abby picked up her cigarettes and lighter.

They went outside and Nick pulled the door shut. 'Are you going to Moo's?'

'Not planning to.'

He lit their cigarettes and watched her suck on hers. 'Your nipples are hard.'

Abby worked very hard at not reacting to this. 'It's cold. And you shouldn't be looking at my nipples.'

'It's hard not to in that top.'

'Are you complaining?'

'Not at all. I like it.'

They puffed in silence for a few minutes.

'How drunk are you likely to be?' Nick asked conversationally. 'Is it worth me trying to get you into bed?'

Abby coughed and smoke flooded her airways.

Nick banged her on the back.

'Nick!'

'Just thought I'd ask.'

His eyes were on her nipples again and Abby had to smile. 'Never hurts to ask.'

When Abby answered the door at seven thirty both Becky and Fiona were on the doorstep.

'Hi, gorgeous.' Becky kissed her cheek and squeezed past her. 'Just need to use the loo.' She took a step forward and froze. 'Nick?'

Nick waved from the kitchen. 'Becky. Fiona.'

'What are you doing here? Where's Jo? I thought she wasn't coming out tonight.' Fiona walked in and went through to the kitchen. 'Hi, Tilly. How are you?'

'Okay. I've got a wobbly tooth.' Tilly demonstrated and Fiona pretended to be impressed. 'Jo and Abby have swapped Daddy and Matthew. Daddy's living here for two weeks. It's so they can all ap-app-ap . . .'

'Appreciate,' Nick said helpfully.

'Appreciate each other. Daddy doesn't help enough and Abby's a slob.'

'Thanks, Tilly.' Abby ruffled her hair.

'That's what Daddy said.'

Abby turned her frown on Nick and he grinned. 'Just telling it how it is.'

'I am not a slob. At least I can load a dishwasher.'

'What about emptying it? And wiping surfaces. And housework?'

'I work.'

'So do I.'

Abby glared at him but he was smiling and it was hard to pretend to be mad.

'Okay, so I'm a slob. At least I know how to have a good time.'

'I wouldn't know.' Nick's smile got wider and he winked. 'Yet.'

Becky and Fiona were staring, mouths hanging open. Speechless.

'Don't you need the toilet, Becky?' Abby asked.

Becky nodded in a dazed kind of way and disappeared into the hall.

'How are Mark and Rachel?' Nick asked Fiona. 'And Edward?'

'All fine. Rachel has a boyfriend.' She paused. 'Have you really swapped partners?'

'Didn't Jo tell you? Matthew got through to the next stage of the magazine job and has to send in an article. Swapping partners was the best story idea we came up with.'

'Really? No. She just sent a text saying she couldn't make it tonight. Why is that? Have you spoken to her?'

'Nope. She didn't want any contact for the two weeks. With either of us,' Abby said. She felt Nick move in behind her, his body just short of touching hers.

Fiona looked from him to Abby. 'Jo didn't want any contact? Are you sure? She's actually gone a week without speaking to you?'

Abby nodded.

'But she can't get dressed in the morning without consulting you. Sorry, Nick.' Fiona gave Nick an apologetic look.

Abby looked up at him and he inclined his head slightly, smiling. His eyes caught on Abby's and the smile got wider. 'Your nipples are hard again.'

'That's because you're breathing all over me.'

'Jesus. Is sex included in the swap?' Becky asked walking back in the room.

'Not yet.'

'No!' Abby glared at Nick and he grinned, unrepentant.

'Christ. Let's get out of here.' Abby moved away from Nick.

'Have a good night, girls,' Nick said.

'Bye bye.' Tilly waved.

Fiona and Becky said goodbye.

Abby looked down at her chest. 'See. It's you. They're normal now.'

Nick rocked back on his heels and winked.

'What the hell is going on?' Becky asked when they were in the car. 'You're like bloody newlyweds.'

'I've never seen him like that. And I can't believe you haven't told us about all this. When did you start?' Fiona said from the backseat.

'Monday.'

'Monday! It's Saturday. Shit, Abby. I don't believe this. Whose idea was it? And you haven't heard from Jo? Not even once?' Becky's tone held pure disbelief.

'I'm ringing her.' Fiona pulled out her mobile and dialled. 'Jo? Why aren't you coming out . . . Why? He knew you were going out. He'd have had to stay in if he was at home . . . Oh. Okay. Alright, see you later.'

'Well? What'd she say?' Becky swivelled in her seat and almost mounted the pavement. 'Oops.' She indicated and turned into the car park.

For once they managed to find a parking space without circling fifteen times. Becky jumped out and got a parking ticket and then they walked into the pub. All in silence. And then they ordered drinks and found a table. Still in silence.

'She's sleeping with him,' Fiona said flatly when they were settled.

Becky and Fiona both stared at Abby. She stared back, took a long gulp of her drink and then sighed. 'She probably is. She was really keen for the swap. And I haven't heard from her. And you know what a tart Matthew is.'

Fiona and Becky exchanged looks.

'It's okay. I actually expected it.'

'And you don't mind that your best friend is sleeping with your boyfriend. The father of your child?' Fiona asked.

Abby shrugged. 'I haven't really thought about it to be honest. And we don't know for definite that they have.'

'What would you do?'

Another shrug. 'Kick him out and never speak to Jo again.'

'And beat the crap out of them both I hope,' Becky said.

Abby grinned. Becky wasn't keen on Jo. She thought she was weak, spoiled and insipid. Becky had very little tolerance.

'I can't believe Jo would actually risk losing your friendship,' Fiona said.

Becky snorted. 'Jo probably hasn't thought far enough ahead to realise it'd upset Abby.'

'I think you underestimate her. She knows more than you think,' Abby took another long swig.

'I agree,' Fiona said.

'That makes it even worse!' Becky exclaimed.

'Yep.' Abby leant back in her chair and swung her beer bottle between thumb and forefinger.

'Hello, ladies. Hi, Abs. I know I'm not meant to speak to you but you look too gorgeous to resist.' Abby's head jerked round in surprise, Matthew smiled and dropped a kiss on her nose. 'How are you? How's Ol?'

'He's fine,' Abby told him, turning back to her beer.

Matthew pulled up a chair and sat astride, arms hanging loosely over the back. Abby looked at the silver ring he wore on his middle finger and tried to work out how she felt. Nervous? No. Pleased to see him? Not really. *Anything*? Nope. Nothing at all. Oh dear.

'How's Jo?' Fiona asked.

'She's fine.'

'Have you slept with her?' Becky asked.

Matthew's smile faltered slightly. 'You what?'

'Jo. Have you slept with her?'

Matthew gave a nervous laugh and Fiona frowned at her friend. 'How's the swap going? Are you enjoying living with Jo? Getting lots of exciting material for your article?'

'Of course he bloody is,' Becky said.

'Actually I'm looking forward to moving back home,' Matthew said with another look at Abby's top.

'Boring in bed is she?' Becky snapped.

'Can I talk to you outside for a minute?' Abby said to Matthew.

Matthew finished glaring at Becky and stood up. Abby led him outside and they sat on a bench. She immediately lit a cigarette.

'Are you okay?' Matthew asked.

Abby shook her head. 'Actually, no. I want you to move out.'

'What?' Matthew straightened and looked at her with pure disbelief. 'Why? Don't tell me you believe Becky.'

'I know you shag around, Matthew,' Abby said flatly. 'I've known for ages but sleeping with my best mate is low. Even for you.'

'I. Have. Not. Slept. With. Jo.'

They locked eyes.

Matthew looked away first.

'I don't care. I don't care if you have or you haven't. I just want you to leave.'

'It's Nick isn't it?' Matthew stared at her with wide eyes. 'Are you sleeping with him?'

'No. I'm not. I wouldn't do that. To you or to Jo. But living with him has made me realise what I want. I want to be looked after.'

'*You*? But you hate all that! You're independent. It's the biggest thing we have going for us.'

'I know. It was. Maybe I've changed.' Abby shrugged and sucked hungrily on her cigarette. 'Nick takes care of me. He makes sure I get enough sleep and he's offered to teach me to drive so I don't have to cycle at night.'

'I didn't know that was what you wanted. I can do all that.'

'No you can't.' Abby shook her head sadly. 'And I didn't realise that was what I wanted either. And I'm not saying I want it with Nick. But I don't want us anymore. I'd rather just be alone.'

'But what about Olly?'

'Olly'll be fine. You'll see loads of him. I still have to work.'

'And the house?'

'We'll have to sell it, of course.'

'But you love the house.'

'I know.' Abby shrugged. 'But I can love something smaller just as much. It's the only way. I can't afford it alone. We can barely afford it together.'

'True.' Matthew nodded and sat back. 'Are you sure about this? Have you thought it through?'

'No. Not at all. I just knew when I saw you tonight.'

They sat in silence for a beat and then Matthew gave a sad laugh. 'Maybe I should have stayed away tonight.'

'It wouldn't have made any difference. And steer clear of Jo, Matthew. She's too high maintenance for you.'

Matthew nodded.

'How come you're out tonight anyway? Why isn't Jo out?'

'She said she didn't want to go out. Then Jason rang and I decided I fancied a beer.'

'And Jo didn't mind?'

'No. Well maybe a little.' He looked grim and Abby smiled to herself. A few of Jo's tantrums and Matthew might learn to keep his dick in his boxers.

'Right. Well I'd best get back to the girls. Why don't you start looking for somewhere to stay while you're still with Jo?'

'I'll probably move back in with Mum and Dad for a bit. Then when we sell the house I'll look for something else.'

'Are you going to stay with Jo for the rest of the two weeks?'

Matthew went still. 'You don't think I should? What about the article?'

Abby thought about it. 'No. I think we should stick with the original plan. You need it for the magazine. And who knows? Maybe it'll do Nick and Jo more good than it's done us.' Unlikely considering Nick was already planning on ending his relationship but it felt like the right thing to say.

'Maybe.'

Abby stood up and they looked at each other for a few long moments.

'I'll call you when the fortnight's up. You can come and get your stuff and we can work things out.'

'Okay.' Matthew stood up and put his hands in his pockets. He looked at the bench for a beat. 'Are you sure you don't want to think things through a bit more?'

'I'm sure.'

'Well if you change your mind—'

'I won't.'

'But—'

'You can't be what I want, Matthew. It wouldn't be you. And would you really want to be? Think about it. You like us because we're so independent. We're like roommates that have good sex. I want more than that. I want a relationship.'

Matthew looked up slowly and nodded. 'You're right.' He gave a little grin. 'I'll miss the sex though.'

'Yeah me too.'

They shared a smile and then Abby leant forwards and kissed his cheek. 'I'll call you. Take care.'

'You too.'

Abby stubbed out her cigarette in the ashtray and went back inside.

Chapter Fourteen

Matthew went back to Jo's house after his conversation with Abby. He didn't feel like beer. Or pulling a strange woman. He wanted adoration. And he wanted sex.

Jo was watching TV and pretended not to hear him when he walked in. He sat down next to her and pulled her onto his lap.

She went stiff. 'You're home early.'

He nuzzled her neck. 'I missed you.'

'Really?'

'I saw Abby.'

She lost her smile. 'And? Did she guess? You didn't tell her did you?'

Matthew kissed his way to her ear. 'No. I didn't tell her.' He wrapped an arm around her waist and unbuttoned her jeans.

'Did she say anything about Nick? Have they killed each other yet?'

Matthew gave a dry laugh. 'Not quite.'

'What's funny?'

Matthew sighed and wished he hadn't mentioned Abby. And then he stroked his hands into the front of her jeans and moved his fingers around a bit.

Her head fell back and her mouth opened slightly.

'She's kicked me out.' He said and angled himself so he could get a finger inside her. She jerked against him.

'You're kidding! Why?' she said on a gasp.

'Seems she's realised she prefers living without me.' He pulled her jeans down and watched her kick them off. Her underwear followed and she turned so she was straddling him.

'But, why? Why would she suddenly do that?'

Matthew shrugged and scissored her clitoris between his fingers. Her eyes closed and she gasped slightly. He moved them back and forth a few times then rubbed them together.

Matthew watched her cheeks flush. She groaned and moved harder against him. He felt himself get hard and confidence washed through him. Why the hell was Abby throwing it away? He thought of sex with Abby and let his eyes go shut. She was phenomenal. He couldn't remember a time she'd ever said no. He thought of his married friends. Jeff whose wife only slept with him once a month. And poor old Pete. He hadn't had sex in months. They couldn't understand why Matthew was always picking up strange women. He didn't know why he did it, really. Because he could, maybe?

Jo moaned and he opened his eyes. Sod Abby anyway. He didn't need her. Women loved him. And she'd be back. She loved sex too much to go without for long. He thought of Nick and the way she'd looked when she talked about him. Nick was a good-looking bloke. Fit body too. He was pretty sure Abby wasn't sleeping with him though. She wasn't the type to have sex with just anyone.

He looked at Jo again. He was using both hands and she was writhing in his lap. She certainly wasn't complaining. Maybe Nick wasn't so hot in bed. Or maybe he had a small cock. Matthew had heard that was quite common with bigger men. He couldn't be that great a lover if he hadn't given his girlfriend an orgasm in two years. Though, to be fair, if Matthew hadn't had a previous girlfriend who could only get off on domination, he probably wouldn't have guessed that was what Jo wanted.

He gave a mental shrug and twisted until Jo was face down across the settee. He reached into his jean pocket for a condom and stripped from the waist down. He quickly rolled the condom on and entered her from behind. He smoothed a hand across her buttocks and watched her tense. He smiled to himself. He'd managed to bring her to orgasm a few times without actually smacking her. Just the thought that it could happen seemed to do it. And once she'd actually come without him laying a finger on her. He'd simply pinned her over the back of the settee and told her what he was going to do to her. She'd had an orgasm from a combination of anticipation – her butt was in the air, ready and waiting, his words, and the memory of the night before – he'd downloaded a good old fashioned spanking film off the net and carried out a lot of the scenes while Jo watched it.

He decided not to give her what she wanted this time. Instead he moved gently in and out. He stroked her body until she was pushing back against him, clearly frustrated beyond words. He carried on with the teasing thrusts and the barely there caresses, every now and again moving his hand around to brush against her clitoris.

He thought of Abby and Nick and pictured them doing the same thing and he was suddenly shot through with anger. Grasping Jo's hips so hard she gasped, he rammed against her. She instantly screamed out her orgasm, every muscle clenching around him. Matthew felt no satisfaction. He could make Abby cry with the same abandonment and she'd left him anyway. Jo collapsed onto the settee and he pulled her hips back up, still hard inside her.

'I'm not done,' he growled, wanting, *needing* to share his pain. Abby wasn't here, he couldn't punish her and he wouldn't have dared even if she was. He smacked Jo's buttocks. As hard as he could. She cried out and his handprint appeared, first white and then bright red against her pale flesh. He hit her again, lower this time, even through his rage he remembered his ex telling him to hit low – apparently it wasn't a "nice" pain if you did it too high. He smacked her again and again, over and over, until his arm ached and Jo's bottom glowed. His anger disappeared along with his strength and he pulled out.

'Turn over,' he said and Jo quickly obeyed. Her eyes met his, bright with unshed tears and he took her face between his hands. He kissed her gently, sorry for taking his anger out on her, sad because he felt so little for her and guilty because he knew Nick would leave her and he wouldn't be around to offer any comfort. He slid inside her, lifting her legs until he was in so deep she gasped. And then he gently held her burning buttocks while he thrust into her. He kissed her neck, nipping just short of hurting her. He moved faster and she twisted in his arms, writhing, sobbing, trying to move away from his relentless pounding and then she went still, every muscle in her body rigid. Matthew slowed down a little, he scissored her legs and moved a little higher and she started to shake. Matthew felt her muscles contracting around him, squeezing him so tight he exploded without warning. His orgasm went on for ages and when he finally collapsed on top of her, he realised that Jo was still in the midst of her own orgasm, she was still rigid, still shaking and he pressed harder against her and she broke beneath him. She cried out and her body went loose, her eyes closed, mouth slightly parted.

He thought of Abby while he watched her come down to earth. He thought of never watching Abby orgasm again and felt tears prick his eyes. He'd get her back. He had to.

Chapter Fifteen

Abby proceeded to get completely and utterly plastered. She was approaching thirty years old. She had a son. A huge mortgage. And now she was a single parent. She thought of what her mother was going to say and bought another round of drinks. Fiona and Becky were keeping up. Just. They were worryingly happy that she'd dumped Matthew. Strange. Abby thought they liked him. Maybe it was because they thought he was cheating on her.

They said goodbye at the Oatsheaf traffic lights at just past midnight and Becky and Fiona headed home. Abby, who lived in the opposite direction, promised to hail a taxi, and waved them away.

She started walking. She wondered what Matthew was doing? He was probably drunk too. Not that she was drunk but she *had* put away quite a few. They'd played some drinking games and she was pretty sure she'd lost quite a few times. She had no money left anyway. And she probably owed Fiona some too. She lit a cigarette and thought that maybe Nick had said something about a taxi. She could sleep with him now. Actually she couldn't. He had Jo. And even if he kicked her out like he'd said, Abby wouldn't sleep with him. She couldn't do that to Jo.

It didn't take long to walk home – see, she couldn't be that drunk, and it was only twenty past twelve when she unlocked the door. First time too. Hah – and Fiona said she was rat-arsed. Or was it rat-faced. It was rat-something. Bloody stupid expression. What'd it mean anyway?

'Abby?' Nick appeared at the living room door and she realised she was still standing in the hall.

He was wearing jeans and a white t-shirt. The t-shirt was tight and the jeans sat low on his hips. He was barefoot.

Abby stared at him for a minute. 'You have a hairy big toe.'

Nick looked down. 'All my toes are hairy.'

'I can't see all of them. Your jeans are too long.'

Nick smiled and pulled them up slightly.

Abby checked out his feet. 'You're right. But the big ones are the hairiest.'

Nick let go of his jeans and straightened. 'Did you have a good night?'

Abby slumped against the wall. She'd dumped Matthew. She was pretty sure he'd slept with Jo. 'I need a cigarette,' she said and headed back outside.

Nick followed a few seconds later. He put the front door on the latch and pulled it shut. And then he joined her on the doorstep. 'What happened?'

Abby exhaled a stream of smoke. 'I broke up with Matthew.'

Nick froze, cigarette just short of entering his mouth. 'You what?'

'I broke up with Matthew. I bumped into him and suddenly realised he wasn't what I wanted.'

Nick took a very long, hard drag on his cigarette and stared into the street. 'Jesus. You don't hang around do you? Were you planning it?'

'Nope.' Abby shook her head and flicked ash in the flowerbed. 'It hadn't even crossed my mind, and then he was there, in front of me and I just suddenly knew.'

'What'd you tell him?'

'That you'd spoilt me. And that I'd realised that was what I wanted.' She shrugged and inhaled some smoke. 'Me and Matthew are just good buddies. It's only worked this long because neither of us have wanted anything more.'

Nick stared at her. 'So what are you saying?'

Abby stared back, gaze unwavering. 'That I want someone like you.'

'You want me?' He looked totally bewildered. Not scared or pressured or hunted. Just surprised. Very surprised.

Abby shrugged. 'I don't know that I want *you*. You're a bit bossy. But I like the way you look after me.'

Nick grinned. 'Bossy?'

'Very.' Abby put out her cigarette and leant her head back against the door. It flew open and she fell backwards. 'Whoa!' She put out a hand to steady herself and then closed her eyes. Her head was on the carpet and her back was on the ridge between hall and doorstep. It was kind of uncomfortable but it was nice to be lying down.

She heard Nick chuckle and he stood up. 'Time to go inside.'

Abby gave a sleepy smile. 'I'm fine here.'

Nick held out his hands. 'Come on. I need to shut the door. Then you can sleep in the hall if you want to.'

'Okay.' She shuffled backwards and flopped back down. Nick closed the door and hauled her to her feet. 'Bed.'

'Hmmm.'

He shook his head and pulled her arm round his neck. And then he led her up the stairs and into her room. He dumped her on the bed, removed her shoes and reached for the duvet.

Abby sat up and whipped her top off. And then she lay back and pushed off her trousers. Nick paused, duvet in hand and looked down at her.

'Black top. Black trousers. Bright pink thong.'

'Uh-huh.'

'It's see through.'

'Uh-huh.'

'And your nipples are hard again.'

'It's you.' Abby closed her eyes and wriggled against the soft cotton sheets. 'You make my nipples hard.' She sighed. 'God, I love my bed. I love going to bed and being able to stay in bed all night.' She opened her eyes and looked at Nick. 'Do you love my bed?'

Nick was still looking at her thong. And her nipples.

'I can't sleep with you.' Abby told him. 'I'd like to. I really would. But you live with my best friend.'

'So why'd you just strip for me.'

Abby looked at him in surprise. 'I'm getting ready for bed. I didn't strip for you.'

Nick looked down at her, eyes dark. And then he leant down and kissed her. His mouth pressed softly against hers, his tongue parting her lips. And then he deepened the kiss and Abby twisted her fingers in his t-shirt. She felt a spark start somewhere deep within her stomach. It got brighter and hotter and spread through her entire body. In her mind she pushed him away. In reality, she pulled him closer and when his tongue twisted against hers, she curled her hands in his hair and responded without thought.

And then he pulled away.

And walked from the room.

Abby flopped back and sighed. It was good that he'd stopped. She definitely wasn't going to sleep with him.

She rolled over and buried her head in the pillow. And wondered what would have happened if she'd removed the thong as well.

Chapter Sixteen

Abby's first thought on waking was that she was halfway through her time with Nick. And then she moved slightly and hell exploded in her head. And then she remembered that she'd dumped Matthew.

'Oh shit,' she moaned and rolled over, burying her head in the pillow.

She could hear Olly laughing and she was pretty sure that Nick was with him. She struggled to listen, to make sure. Olly didn't need to be with someone else to laugh. Olly would laugh at grass growing.

Clutching her head with both hands she forced herself out of bed and pulled her dressing gown on. She followed her son's voice, the pounding in her head growing with every movement.

He was in the spare room with Nick. Nick was sat up in bed, chest bare, hair tousled. He was reading Olly a book and Olly was tucked up next to him.

'Mummy sick?' Olly asked. 'Nick's reading me funny book.'

'Okay, darling.'

'Go back to bed, Abs. Me and Olly are fine. And Tilly'll be up soon.'

Abby nodded. 'Thanks,' she said weakly and went to the bathroom to use the toilet and throw up.

She woke again at eleven and felt much better. She showered, dressed in jeans and sweatshirt and headed downstairs.

'Hello, Abby. Are you feeling better?' Tilly was in the kitchen, drawing at the table.

'Yes, thank you. What are you drawing?'

'We have to draw our favourite animal for school.'

'And what's yours?'

'A rabbit. He's called Nemo and he's got long ears. Look.' She held up her drawing and Abby admired it.

'Very good.'

Nick walked in from the garden, Olly riding piggy back. He looked at Abby. 'How are you feeling?'

'Better. Thanks for watching Olly for me.'

'No problem. Matthew called. So did Jo.'

'Jo called?' Abby met his look. 'Did you talk to her?'

He nodded and switched on the kettle. 'She tried to be subtle but she was trying to find out if I knew about you dumping Matthew.'

'What did you tell her?'

'Nothing.' He grinned. 'She wants you to call her. So does Matthew.'

Abby poured herself a cup of coffee and grabbed her coat, phone and cigarettes. Nick followed her outside and they sat on the bench. Tilly and Olly sat with them for all of four seconds before heading for the playhouse.

'Any regrets this morning?' Nick asked when he'd lit both their cigarettes.

Abby met his look for a second. 'Oh. You mean Matthew?'

Nick smiled. 'You thought I meant kissing me?'

'I didn't kiss you. You kissed me.'

'You kissed me back.'

'Well it would have been rude not to.'

Nick grinned and sipped at his coffee.

Abby sighed. 'How am I going to tell Olly?' She buried her head in her hands and almost poked her eye out with her cigarette.

'Abby.' Nick reached out and put a hand to the back of her head, stroking her hair back until her head came up. 'Olly will be fine. I've never met a more secure child.' Abby gave him a hesitant smile and he tucked her hair behind her ear. 'Just tell him he'll have two beds and two lots of toys and he'll be happy.'

'I don't know—'

'As long as you're honest with him.'

'I guess him and Matthew aren't particularly close. And I'll still have to work so he'll stay with Matthew half the time anyway.'

'Exactly.'

Abby straightened up and pulled on her cigarette.

Nick took his hand away and wrapped it round his coffee mug. 'When will you tell him?'

'When the two weeks are up. When Matthew comes back.' She shrugged.

'We're finishing the two weeks then?' Nick had gone still and Abby stared at him with pounding heart.

'You don't want to?'

He gave her a long look and then he smiled a little half smile. 'I do want to. Very much.'

'Even though we can't sleep together?'

The half smile again. 'I can wait.'

Abby snorted. 'Forever?'

'Sweetheart, it won't be forever.' He gave her a look so intense that her heart stopped and she went dizzy.

'Jo?'

'She's history.'

'Nick, I can't sleep with you just because you've kicked Jo out. It won't stop her loving you, or wanting you, or thinking of you as hers.'

'Not to start with. But she'll get used to it and then she'll meet someone else and then you can sleep with me.'

'I may have met someone else by then too.'

She was joking but Nick's eyes darkened and the line of his mouth straightened.

And then her phone rang. She turned it over and saw Jo's photo on the screen.

'Hi, Jo,' she said. Nick's scowl got darker and he stubbed his cigarette out viciously. And then he lit another one.

Abby raised an eyebrow.

'Hi, Abs. God, I've missed you. How are you? How's Nick?'

'Sulking,' Abby said and then she realised that she hadn't missed Jo at all. Oops.

Nick was scowling and Jo was quiet. Then, 'Nick doesn't sulk.'

'Yes he does.'

'No. He doesn't. He yells and has tantrums. He never sulks.'

Abby looked at Nick. Definitely sulking. 'If you say so.'

'I've been with him for two years, Abby. You've had him for a week. I know. He does not sulk.'

'Fine. So how are you? I thought we weren't talking for the two weeks.'

'What on earth made you end your relationship with Matthew?'

Abby thought for a minute. Not sure what to say or how to say it. 'I saw him and I knew it wasn't right.' *And he slept with my best friend*, she thought but didn't say. That was up to Nick to find out, she wasn't forcing it.

'But . . . surely that's not the only reason. Are you sure? Maybe you'll change your mind when the swap's over. Are you sure you weren't drunk?'

Abby rolled her eyes. 'No. I wasn't drunk. I haven't missed him at all. I like living without him. Doesn't that tell you something?'

'So there's no other reason?'

'What other reason would there be, Jo?' Abby asked, aware of the edge in her voice.

'I don't know,' Jo replied, her voice fading as if she'd turned away from the phone. 'Matthew's back. I have to go,' she said and hung up.

Abby ended the call and slammed the phone down in disgust. She looked at Nick. He wasn't scowling and he wasn't smiling. He looked . . . intrigued.

'I love that you're so damn honest,' he said.

Abby returned his smile but her heart wasn't in it.

Yelling started up from the playhouse and Tilly came running out. 'Olly just broke my Barbie's head. He pulled it off and ate it and now it's all wet and ruined.' She burst into tears and handed Nick the beheaded Barbie. He made soothing noises and they went inside to fix the doll.

Abby lit a cigarette and thought how likely it was that Jo and Matthew had slept together. With a sinking heart she realised that she was almost certain they had. The thought made her feel sick. More because Jo would do it than because of any real feelings of jealousy. Yes, she wanted to sleep with Nick but she hadn't succumbed and her feelings weren't based on a flattered whim like she suspected Jo's were. She knew without a doubt that she was close to falling head over heels in love with Nick. Just as unequivocal was the knowledge that Jo felt little for Matthew.

She watched Nick and Tilly come back out, hand in hand. It was easy for him. Jo and Matthew's probable deception wouldn't be the double whammy it was for her.

Nick sat down and lit another cigarette. Tilly went and sat on the swing, eyes big and sad in her pretty pale face.

'Where's Olly?' Nick asked.

Abby shrugged. 'Still in the playhouse.'

Nick froze. 'You haven't told him off?'

'No. Why would I?' Abby flicked the ash from her cigarette, mind still on Jo and Matthew.

'Because he just ripped Tilly's doll apart.' Nick looked at her in amazement. 'You don't think that's wrong?'

'He's a boy.' Abby said, thinking how much else there was to stress about. 'And he's three. Three-year-old boys do stuff like that.'

Nick flicked his ash into the ashtray and glared at her. 'No. They don't. Fuck, Abby. You can't let him get away with stuff like that. He needs discipline.'

Abby felt her throat close over and she glared at him. 'I will deal with my son in my own way.'

Nick stared at her for a couple of beats and then he stood up and stalked over to the playhouse. He called Olly out and stood talking to him for a minute or two. His voice was quiet and calm and Abby couldn't hear what he was saying. Olly said something and then he walked over to Tilly and apologised.

Nick came back over to the bench and stubbed his cigarette out.

'You shouldn't have done that,' Abby said. 'You had no right.'

Nick glared down at her. 'I had every right.' His eyes pinned her to the seat for a short while and then he straightened up and called Tilly and Olly in for lunch.

Abby stayed outside and chain-smoked and Tilly brought her out a sandwich. 'Me and Daddy are going now. Thank you for having me and I'll see you next weekend.'

Abby returned her kiss. 'It's been a pleasure, Tilly. Have a good swim.' She watched the little five-year-old trot inside and wondered at her perfect manners.

Olly came out a few minutes later and then the front door banged and Abby buried her head in her arms. Wishing the day was over and she could go to bed. Her head still hurt and she felt sick. Sick from too much alcohol, the thought of all the hassle involved in splitting up with Matthew and with wanting Nick so damn much she was crazy with it.

Chapter Seventeen

Jo found the fun had gone out of the swap. Apart from when they were having sex, which admittedly was most of the time, Matthew was moody and uncooperative.

She found herself missing Nick. She missed the routine, the predictability. Matthew was too capricious. One minute joking, the next snapping at everything she said. But then there was the sex. Jo only had to think about the things he did and she'd feel her insides open out. Surely it was worth hanging onto him just for that. She thought of going back to Nick and never experiencing that again and felt something close to panic.

But she knew Matthew wouldn't stay. And she'd rather have Nick and her memories than nothing at all. At least she could relax with Nick. She couldn't sustain life with Matthew. She didn't have the energy.

She caved Monday night and rang Nick.

'She's not here, she's Aerobiking,' he said when he heard her voice.

'I phoned to talk to you actually.'

'Oh.' He sounded surprised. 'What's up?'

'I just wanted to see how you were.'

There was a short pause. Then, 'You wanted to see if I was going to accuse you of sleeping with Matthew.'

Jo closed her eyes. Jesus, why did he do that? He and Abby were so alike in that way. Brutally honest. Too much so. If they ever clashed, Jo wouldn't want to be around 'Why would you do that?' she asked, all innocence.

Nick sighed. 'Never mind. It's irrelevant anyway. I want you to move out before I come home.'

'But—' she started to say but he overrode her.

'You can go to your parents. It hasn't been right between us for a long time, Jo. You know it hasn't. This is way over due. And don't try to move in here.'

Jo gave a sob. 'Why not? Did Abby say that?'

'No. I'm saying it. Why don't you try and stand on your own two feet for a change?'

Jo gasped. And then she swiped at her eyes and stood straighter. 'Maybe I'll move in with Matthew.'

Nick gave a mirthless laugh. 'Where? At his parent's? He can't afford to support himself never mind you as well. You're on your own, Jo.' And he hung up.

Jo put the phone down and stared unseeingly out of the window. And then she cried. Real tears this time. Tears of pity, and fear, and apprehension. She hated being alone.

Nick went out when Abby got back from Aerobiking. He got home at just gone ten and she was in bed. She listened to him close the front door and then a door opened and the TV came on. A few minutes later the sound of Windows starting on his PC resounded faintly up the stairs and Abby gave up all pretence of trying to sleep.

She pulled her jogging gear on and crept downstairs and out the front door. She started off slowly, went a mile or so and then got into her stride. She stuck to the main roads and ran her four-mile route. She could have gone further but didn't want to run the same route twice and the alternative, to go down the side roads, was not a wise move at eleven at night.

She crept in the front door and went straight up to shower. Fifteen minutes later she donned her dressing gown and went down for a cigarette.

Nick followed her out almost immediately. 'Your face is red. Where did you go?'

'For a run.'

'At eleven at night?'

'At ten fifteen. I couldn't sleep.'

'Do you do that a lot?' Nick lit a cigarette and concentrated on the first drag.

Abby shrugged. 'Sometimes.'

'Stupid.'

Abby ignored him.

'You know it's dangerous, right?'

'It's my life.'

'True. I'm just thinking of Olly.'

'So do I. Every minute of the day,' Abby said coldly.

Nick put his hands in the air. 'Jo phoned.'

'Oh?'

'I told her I wanted her out before I got home.'

Abby dropped her cigarette.

She picked it up and pulled in some smoke. 'How'd she take it?'

'She cried.'

Abby nodded. 'Of course. I'm surprised she hasn't phoned me.'

'Me too.'

'I suppose she'll want to move in here.'

'Would you mind?'

Abby thought about it and then she nodded. 'Yes. I'd hate to live with Jo.'

'That's good because I told her she wasn't to ask you.'

Abby looked at him in surprise and then she watched a cat jump onto the playhouse before disappearing into the night shadows. 'And you think that'll stop her?'

It was Nick's turn to look surprised.

Abby smiled. 'You're right. It probably will.'

'It better. She probably screwed your boyfriend. She's lucky you're even speaking to her.'

'I know. I'm such a nice, forgiving person.'

Nick gave a wide smile.

Abby narrowed her eyes. 'You arguing with me?'

'Nope. You are. A nice, forgiving person.'

Abby nodded. 'Thank you. I am.'

'But only because we don't know for definite and because you don't give a shit anyway.'

'Hey!'

'It's true.' Nick put out his cigarette and shoved his hands in his pockets. He rocked back on his heels and grinned.

Abby smiled back. 'I know.' She put out her cigarette and they went inside.

They paused at the bottom of the stairs. 'Well, goodnight,' Abby said.

Nick smiled. 'Goodnight.' And then he reached out and grabbed her dressing gown, pulled her gently forwards and placed a featherlike kiss on her lips.

Abby's lips parted involuntary and Nick deepened the kiss. His tongue wound its way round hers and his knee pressed between her thighs.

Abby groaned and felt herself go limp. He pulled her closer so all her weight was in his arms and around his leg.

He kissed her neck, his lips scorching a path from her ear to the curve of her shoulder and back again. He nipped her earlobe and fire exploded in her belly. His hands were at her belt and then her dressing gown was open and he was pushing it from her shoulders. His hands and then his eyes roamed her body.

'Christ, you are gorgeous,' he said and yanked her harder against him. Abby didn't even try and talk herself out of kissing him. He was too yummy. All hard and soft and yielding and dominating at the same time and although sex with Matthew had been amazing it had never been like this. This wasn't good sex, or good kissing, though the kissing was extraordinarily good, it was lust, self-denial and pure and simple chemistry.

Though there was nothing pure about it. Abby unsnapped his jeans with one hard yank and then she was pulling him free and wrapping her mouth round him. Nick went down on one knee and grabbed her hair. Abby put one hand on his buttocks, one cupped his balls and then she circled her tongue, flicking and sliding and sucking him, whole and hard, over and over and in the end he pushed her away. She rolled on to her back and smiled up at him and he looked down at her, eyes like the night sky, deep and dark and velvety black. And then he pinned her to the floor. His hands grasped her hips and he licked into her, over and over, without stopping and without mercy as she writhed and sobbed beneath his mouth. She felt herself fighting orgasm. Not yet, not yet. She wanted to come with him inside her.

'Nick—' she tried to say, tried to tell him what she wanted.

'Not yet,' he said, eyes meeting hers, fierce with the depths of his passion and suddenly images started to flash through her mind – like a disjointed movie. Jo laughing, Jo introducing Nick when they first met, so happy and excited and in love. Then she saw Nick criticising Olly's eating habits. Olly throwing his car at her and Nick's shock at her lack of reaction. Nick chastising Olly for breaking Tilly's doll. And then the future. She saw a grown up Olly and a middle aged Nick. They were standing side by side and they were both wagging their right forefingers at her – identical expressions on their faces.

She placed her hands on Nick's head, pushing him away. Wriggling away and pulling her dressing gown back on while she stood, she tightened the cord round her waist. 'I can't,' she said, voice uneven, just above a whisper.

Nick was already on his feet, raking a hand through already dishevelled hair. 'Because of Jo? Abby I—'

'No. Not because of Jo,' Abby said and then she sighed. 'Well not just because of Jo. Because of Olly and me and you. We're too different Nick. It could never be more than sex and I can't risk hurting Jo for that. If we had a future, then maybe it would be different. At least Jo could understand that.'

The frustration slowly left Nick's expression, leaving something soft, almost tender. 'But we do have a future. You know it's more than sex, Abby.'

'How can it be? We can't agree on anything. You drive me mad where Olly's concerned. You think I'm a crap parent—'

'No I don't. I just think you're too lenient. It's nothing we can't work out.'

Abby shook her head sadly. 'It's too much, Nick. You make me crazy. Maybe without Jo it'd be worth trying but I just can't risk it. There's too much at stake.'

Nick held her look, expression unfathomable. And then he shrugged. 'Maybe you're right.' His eyes raked over her, eyes stony. 'It's probably not worth it.' And he turned and walked into the living room, closing the door firmly behind him.

Chapter Eighteen

When Jo told Matthew that Nick had asked her to move out, his first instinct was to run. Very fast.

'What are you going to do?'

Jo lifted her chin a fraction. 'Find somewhere else to live. Get a job and rent a room somewhere.'

'Good plan. So have you started looking? For a job I mean?'

Jo looked startled for a moment. 'Yes. Of course,' she said in a voice that told him she'd done no such thing.

Matthew went to have a shower and when he came back Jo was still sitting in bed.

'Don't you think it's weird that they've kicked us out at the same time?' Jo asked.

Matthew pulled on his boxer shorts and picked out some socks. 'Not really. Neither of us had particularly good relationships.' He shrugged. 'I'm not at all surprised to be honest.'

'You don't think they're sleeping together?'

Matthew paused with one sock on. And then he shook his head. 'I don't think so. Nick's not Abby's type.'

'Maybe it's fate.' Jo paused and Matthew centred all his attention on dressing. 'Maybe we should go with it. Find a place together.'

Matthew felt panic squeezing at his throat. 'Let's make separate arrangements to start with and see how it goes.'

'Why? We're really good together.' Jo crawled out of bed and moved behind him, sliding her arms around his neck.

'It's too soon.' Matthew squeezed her arm and got up to put his trousers on.

Jo pouted. 'Fine.'

Matthew sighed, too irritated to placate her. Why did women always do this? It was the reason he'd been so happy with Abby. She never put any pressure on him.

Jo watched him dress and then she seemed to make an effort to pull herself together. 'You're right it's too soon. I'll move in with my parents, you move in with yours and you can court me properly.' She grinned and Matthew fought back claustrophobia. 'Then after a decent amount of time we can find a place together.' Jo wound her arms round his waist and leant up to kiss him. Matthew forced a smile. Jo beamed back and he wondered what the hell he'd got himself into.

Nick was already awake when Olly got up so he took him downstairs and made him breakfast. He listened to him chatting and realised that he'd miss him when he went home. Olly was a good kid. A bit wayward, not surprising considering Abby's lack of discipline and Matthew's lack of attention. Stubborn too but that was to be expected considering who his mother was. But he was smart, and kind and funny. Cute too.

'Morning,' Abby said brightly and Nick forced himself not to snap.

He watched her kiss Olly. She was wearing leggings and a lycra cropped vest and her hair was tied up in a messy ponytail. She may as well have been naked. Nick closed his eyes but he could still see her. Her naked body was burnt into his brain. The lush curves, everything round and firm and warm.

He forced his eyes open. Abby was at the counter making coffee. She buttered her toast and sat down opposite him.

'Please can I get down?' Olly asked.

'Yes. Good boy for asking,' Nick said and Olly beamed and ran from the room.

Nick finished his coffee and finally met Abby's look.

'Good morning,' she said.

Nick scowled. 'What's so good about it?'

Abby looked surprised for a beat. And then her jaw tightened. 'Fine. If you can't even be civil then fuck off.' And she walked out, leaving her coffee and toast untouched.

Nick sighed and buried his head in his hands. What the hell was wrong with him? It was tiredness, he told himself. He shouldn't be taking it out on Abby. He'd known she didn't feel right sleeping with him. He even understood. So why was he being such a bastard? He should respect her for denying herself.

And he did. He just didn't like it. He wanted to be in her bed for the remaining week. But it was her decision and so what if she hated him? Six more days and they probably wouldn't see each other again.

Chapter Nineteen

Abby ignored Nick for as long as possible. He didn't get home until she'd gone to bed on Tuesday night. On Wednesday morning she woke when he came in from his run and she made sure she didn't go downstairs until he was leaving. But then she realised she had her mother's dinner party the following evening and a sulking Nick would be better than no Nick at all.

She went to bed at seven and set her alarm for nine. Nick was in the living room watching TV when she went downstairs. She stood in the doorway, waiting to see what kind of reception she would get.

'Hi,' he said quietly, expression guarded.

'Hi.'

'What's up?'

'Are you still coming with me tomorrow?'

'If you still want me to, of course I am,' he said, still without expression. And then he turned back to the TV.

'Thanks,' Abby said and turned to leave the room.

'You won't get any sleep before work tomorrow then?'

'No. I was going to book it off but then I decided it would give us a perfect excuse to leave early.'

'So, when will you sleep?'

'In the morning. I'll be fine.'

'On two hours?'

'Two and a half hours.'

'I'll work from home tomorrow afternoon,' Nick said and turned the volume up on the TV.

'Hey!'

'What?'

'Don't dismiss me like that. You won't work from home. I'll be fine on three hours sleep.'

'Two and a half hours,' Nick said and grinned.

Abby stared at him in amazement and disgust. 'You're a fucking psycho, you know that?'

Nick's smile got wider and she gave up. He was completely nuts. One minute stroppy and nasty. The next, laughing and taking the piss. Well, sod him. She got her coat and shoes on and went through to the garage.

No bike.

She stared round in bemusement. It had been here, she was sure of it. Yes, it had. She'd seen it when she got the dinner out of the freezer.

Nick. He'd moved her bike. Why would he do that? To stop her cycling. She went through to the living room, an icy calm settling over her.

'Will's picking you up at twenty to,' Nick said without looking up.

Abby walked outside without responding. Forcing herself to be calm – no slamming doors or kicking cars – she walked down the road to Elsie's house. Elsie was a friend of her mothers and she had teenage daughters. Abby used to babysit for them so felt quite comfortable knocking on the door at nine thirty at night.

'Hi, Elsie. Sorry to call round so late. My bike's been stolen and I was wondering if I could borrow Alison's. I have to get to work.'

'Of course you can, dear,' Elsie said and started on about the crime in the area. 'It's all the new pubs you know, dear.' Elsie had lived in Fleet for her whole life – almost fifty years – and her favourite topic was the good old days. When there were no big housing developments and only one pub on the high street. When there was no nightclub and no indoor shopping centre. When Fleet's entertainment had comprised of the pond, the canal, a swimming-pool-less sports centre and a pitch and putt park. Oh and tennis courts. Mustn't forget the tennis courts.

Abby managed to escape before Elsie got on to the Carnival and how much better it used to be. She made it to work with one minute to spare and cursed Nick for thinking he could re-arrange her life. She'd cycled to work quite happily for two years. She cycled everywhere. Pre-school, the gym, the pub, to see friends. And suddenly she was supposed to stop just because he felt responsible for her. For two weeks. And then what? He was hardly going to teach her to drive now. They probably wouldn't even see each other now he wasn't living with Jo.

'Still cycling?' Sid asked when she walked in.

'What happened, hen? Has Nick gone now?' Sally asked.

'No. I like to cycle. Nick has split up with Jo and I've dumped Matthew and no, we are not getting together. Nick's a stroppy, controlling, chauvinist pig and I hate him. I hate all men and I'm going to be single for the rest of my life.' Abby jabbed the power button on her computer terminal and tapped her fingers impatiently while she waited for it to boot up.

Judy and Sid came round the partition.

'Why did Nick dump Jo?' Judy asked.

'Because she was screwing Matthew?' Sid guessed.

'And that's why you kicked Matthew out,' Sally said, eyes wide with sympathy, 'Oh, hen, I'm sorry. Are you okay?'

'I'm fine. I kicked Matthew out because it was time. I don't want a room mate anymore. Nick dumped Jo 'cos he's a shit and I don't want to talk about it.'

'So you didn't sleep with him,' Sid said.

'Of course she didn't,' Sally snapped.

Judy shook her head and went back round to her desk.

They ploughed through the first night e-mails and then Judy dragged Abby away for a cigarette.

'What's wrong? I know you slept with Nick.' Abby opened her mouth to argue and Judy ploughed on, 'Come on, Abby. I've known you for two years and I know you wouldn't be this pissed off if you hadn't had sex with the bloke.'

Abby sighed. 'I didn't sleep with him. It was close, but I stopped him.' And then she told her the whole story.

'You're mad. You should have taken the sex for the rest of the fortnight. What harm would it have done? He's split up with Jo and anyway, she didn't need to find out. And so what if he took your bike? Take the sodding lift. Have a rest for once. You're so damn independent. You're going to end up alone forever if you don't start taking help from people.'

'He had no right to take my bike. If I want to cycle I will.'

'It's for one more week, Abby. Would it really have hurt to get a lift with his nephew? Humour the bloke. You could have been getting sex and having a laugh. Instead you're madder than I've ever seen you.'

'It's the principle.'

'The principle won't get you laid.'

Abby half expected to find Nick waiting outside the next morning. He wasn't. And he wasn't at the table with Olly either.

She crept upstairs and into Olly's room. He was asleep, hands stuck down the front of his trousers. Shaping up to be just like his father. There was no sound coming from Nick's room and she wondered if she should wake him. Not that he'd oversleep. Not perfect Nick. She shot a dirty look in his direction and went downstairs for breakfast.

She'd just finished and was thinking that maybe she should wake them up when Nick appeared in the doorway, Olly hanging off his arm.

'Morning,' Nick said. Not overly friendly but not nasty either.
'Morning.'

Nick flicked the kettle on and put bread in the toaster.

Abby put her stuff in the dishwasher and was surprised to realise that she was nervous. Very nervous.

'Did you want me to teach you to drive?' Nick asked conversationally.

Abby looked at him in surprise. 'If you still want to, of course I do.'

Nick finished making coffee and wondered outside. Abby settled Olly with his breakfast and followed.

Nick handed her a cigarette and watched her light it. 'I *will* teach you to drive. Starting on Tuesday. If we go at six you can bring Olly.'

'Really. Thanks.'

'But . . .'

Abby swallowed a groan. There had to be a "but" and she knew exactly what it was going to be.

'You have to promise you won't cycle to work at night anymore.' Yep, there it was.

'Fine.' Abby did a sigh and sucked hard on her cigarette.

'And you look knackered. I'll pick Olly up and bring him home. I can work from home this afternoon and you can sleep as long as you want to.'

'Otherwise, let me guess, you won't come tonight,' Abby said in sarcastic tones.

'That's right.' Nick looked annoyed. 'Hey, it's not my fault I have to bribe you to do anything. I have to do this with Tilly, I never expected to do it with a grown woman.'

Abby checked through the window to make sure Olly was okay. 'If you weren't such a bloody chauvinist you still wouldn't have to. I *am* a grown woman. I've cycled everywhere for over twenty years and I know how much sleep I can get by on.'

'I am not a chauvinist—'

'Right. So you'd try and stop Will cycling to work?'

Nick exhaled with a big sigh and stared at her in irritation. 'Fine. So I wouldn't mind a man cycling through Farnborough at night but that's because women statistically get hurt more—'

'I bet they don't. You're always reading in the paper about random men getting beaten up.'

'That's beaten up. It's rarely fatal. Women get raped and sexually assaulted and murdered.'

'Yeah, but—'

'Will you stop arguing with every fucking thing I say?' Nick ground his cigarette out, patience clearly pushed to the limit. 'I don't want you to cycle. End of conversation.'

Abby opened her mouth to argue and he cut her off, 'I don't give a fuck about anyone else cycling. They can all walk around naked for all I care. It's you I care about. I don't want you to get hurt. Is that so bad?'

Abby pulled the last bit of nicotine from her cigarette, heart twisting at his words. She held his look, feeling the flush climb her neck. She dragged her eyes away and stubbed out her cigarette, breathing a big sigh and trying to keep her voice even. 'You know, it's all irrelevant anyway. Even if you teach me to drive I'm not going to be able to afford a car.'

'You can borrow Matthew's. He'll be looking after Olly when you're at work.'

Abby scowled because he was right and went inside, heart still pounding.

'Can we go to the park today, Mummy?' Olly asked.

Abby smiled, glad of the distraction and kissed his cheek. She wiped some butter from his nose and lifted him down from the table. 'Maybe.'

'I'm picking you up today, Olly. I'll take you to the park for a little while before we come home.' Nick put his mug in the dishwasher and straightened up. 'Let's go and get you dressed.'

'Are you taking me as well? Are you going to bed, Mummy.'

'Yes, darling. Give me a kiss.'

Olly kissed her and gave her a tight hug. 'I love you, Mum.' He pulled back and looked into her eyes. 'When I come home and you wake up, then can we go to the toy shop and buy me a spaceship?'

'Not today, honey.'

'What about for my birthday? Can we get me one then?'

Nick laughed and took him from Abby. 'They don't sell spaceships in the toy shop, buddy. You have to go to the spaceship shop.'

'Where is the spaceship shop? Do they sell Power Rangers as well?'

Their voices disappeared up the stairs. Abby wiped down the table and put Olly's plate in the dishwasher. And then she went up to bed.

It was almost four when she woke and she had to check her watch and both clocks before she believed it. She'd slept for seven and a half hours.

Nick and Olly were in the living room. Nick was working on his computer and Olly was watching Peppa Pig.

'Hi, guys.' Abby ruffled Olly's hair and flopped down on the sofa. 'Have you had a good afternoon?'

'We went to the park and I was a pirate and then we had lunch and came home. Nick let me play on the 'puter and I played Cbeebies. I'm hungry. Is it dinner time now?'

'Soon.' Abby smiled. Olly climbed onto her knee and carried on watching TV. She gave him a hug and he wriggled away. 'Mu-um. I don't want a cuddle. I'm watching tel'vision.' He turned round and looked at her, expression earnest. 'I'll cuddle you after Peppa Pig. 'kay?'

'Okay. Thank you, darling.'

'You're welcome, Mummy.'

Abby stifled a smile and looked at Nick. He was grinning at Olly.

'What time are we going tonight?' he asked when Olly had turned his attention back to the TV.

'Seven thirty for eight. And we can leave at nine thirty.'

'I told Will I'll be driving you to work tonight. That gives us an extra ten minutes.'

'My mother doesn't need to know that. I'd rather spend the extra time at work.'

Nick smiled and turned back to his computer.

Abby put Olly to bed at seven. Nick was outside having a cigarette when she went downstairs. It was pouring with rain; drops pinging off the plastic awning, sloshing through the gutters and glittering on the patio under the cloud shrouded sunlight. She shut the back door and joined him where he leant against the house, huddled under the small piece of shelter the awning provided. Abby lit her cigarette and inhaled gratefully before she spoke.

'Thanks for today.'

'It's fine.' Nick gave a small smile. 'Funny how you slept so long when you didn't need it.'

'Yeah, yeah. Don't rub it in.' Abby grinned and flicked her ash into the ashtray. 'I'm going to miss you when you go.'

Nick turned serious. 'You need to get more sleep, Abby. Maybe you shouldn't work nights. Isn't there something else you could do?'

'Not without putting Olly into daycare and I refuse to do that. He's better off with me, even if I am tired.'

'What about childminding.'

'No way!' Abby stared at him, aghast. 'Fiona tried that and she had a nightmare. Her kids got picked on, she had problems with parents and payment. And she was so stressed all the time.' She gave a shudder and pulled on her cigarette.

'Fine. But there must be something else. What about working from home?'

'No.' Abby shook her head. 'I looked, there's nothing. I could work evenings or weekends but that would mean relying on Matthew to babysit and the pay's nowhere near as good.' She shrugged. 'I have no choice really. Anyway, I like my job. And Olly'll be at school next year. I'll get more sleep then.'

'That's almost eighteen months away.'

'It'll fly by.' Abby waved a hand and sighed, stubbing her cigarette out against the wall. 'We'd better go.'

Abby's mother and Keith were standing at the front door, light spilling out onto the rapidly darkening driveway. Abby's mother had her daughter's face but where Abby was tall and broad, her mother was five foot nothing and incredibly slim. The rain had eased off but it was still spitting and Nick and

Abby pulled their hoods over their heads as they ran from the car.

'Abby, darling.' Her mother kissed her and turned to Nick. 'And you must be Nick. Very pleased to meet you.' She looked him over and sent Abby an approving smile.

Abby rolled her eyes and Nick hid a smile. He watched Abby greet Keith. He was small too. Five foot six maybe. He had brown hair, a brown beard, brown moustache and there was absolutely nothing interesting about him. He was Mr Average. Mr Brown. 'Happy Birthday, Keith.' Abby handed him his present and let him kiss her cheek. She was tense as hell. Beautiful in black trousers and cream top, but more uptight than he'd ever seen her.

Keith welcomed Nick while Abby hung their coats on a handily placed coat stand and then they all went through to the living room. Two young women, Abby's step-sisters presumably, were already at the table. Abby introduced them and their respective boyfriends. The last couple at the table were Keith's brother Karl and his wife Chloe. Karl looked like Keith but more. There was more brown hair and more nondescript body. Chloe looked similar but without the facial hair.

Nick pulled out Abby's chair and they took their places. There were little silver chairs with typed names attached. Abby immediately started stacking them.

Nick put a hand on her knee and squeezed slightly. 'Relax,' he said under his breath.

Abby took a couple of deep breaths. Her mother and Keith came back in the room and Nick removed his hand.

A maid started handing out starters.

'So, are you the new boyfriend?' Michelle asked Nick. Her boyfriend, Alan, sighed and dug into his meal.

Abby met Alan's eyes. 'Get out while you can,' she said and he hid a smile.

Michelle hadn't heard her step-sister. Her piercing blue eyes were still fixed on Nick.

Nick glanced at Abby. 'We're friends. Good friends.' He and Abby exchanged a smile and he turned back to Michelle.

'So where's Matthew?' Michelle asked.

'He and Abby have split up,' Nick said when it was clear Abby wasn't going to answer.

'Who dumped who?' Sharon asked.
'Abby dumped Matthew.'
'Why?'
'Sharon, dear, now's hardly the place,' Abby's mother said gently.

Sharon ignored her and continued to stare at Nick.
'It's none of your business,' Abby said.

Sharon and Michelle looked annoyed but everyone was staring at them so they shut up.

Abby's mother and Keith started chatting to Karl and Chloe, and Abby and her step-sisters ate in silence for a while.

'He was probably cheating on her,' Michelle said to Sharon after a few minutes, 'You know what he's like.'

Sharon nodded. 'True.'

'Meaning?' Abby asked, putting her fork down.

Nick willed her to ignore them. They were winding her up on purpose – he knew the signs, he had sisters of his own.

'Meaning Matthew made passes at both me and Sharon,' Michelle said.

Abby went still. Nick reached out a hand and squeezed her knee again. She turned to look at him and he stared calmly back. She visibly relaxed and ignoring her sisters, picked up her fork and continued to eat.

Nick squeezed her knee again before resuming eating.

Michelle and Sharon scowled and exchanged looks. Nick watched them with interest. They weren't unattractive but they were so unpleasant it made them seem that way. They both had blonde hair – probably not natural - and blue eyes. They were slim, average height and they were okay looking. Very alike. And also very jealous of Abby. That much was obvious.

'So have you met Olly?' Michelle asked Nick. Nick finished his mouthful and wondered why she started every sentence with "so".

'Yes, of course. He's a lovely little boy.'

'And do you know Matthew? He and Abby have been together for years,' Sharon said.

'Yeah. She's probably on the rebound,' Michelle said. No "so" that time.

Nick gave a grim smile. 'Matthew is scum. And Abby is not on the rebound.'

'Have you just come out of a relationship too?' Michelle asked.

'Mind your own business, Michelle,' Abby said coldly.

'Ah. So he has. And you're worried he's on the rebound?'

Abby stared at her for a beat and then she turned to Alan. 'How's Lizzie, Alan?'

Michelle's face turned red and Nick guessed that Lizzie was an ex.

'F-fine,' poor Alan muttered and Michelle turned to glare at him.

'Still see her do you?' Abby asked and Nick didn't bother to hide his grin.

'S-sometimes.'

Michelle turned her murderous glare back to Abby. 'She's his next door neighbour. Of course he sees her.'

Abby raised her eyebrows and Michelle's colour deepened another notch.

'Abigail,' Abby's mother snapped from the other end of the table, 'Stop winding your sister up.'

Michelle gave a satisfied smile and Abby's hand tightened round her wine glass.

Nick put a hand round her shoulders and rubbed just below her ear with the back of his thumb. Her skin went rough with goosebumps and her knuckles lost their whiteness.

'Bit cosy for friends aren't you?' Michelle said. Abby looked down the table at her mother but she was deep in conversation with Chloe again.

Nick carried on stroking Abby's neck and locked eyes with Michelle. 'I'm trying to persuade her to be more than friends,' he said and Michelle looked startled.

He felt Abby's hand on his knee and turned to find her smiling at him. After that, Michelle and Sharon's barbed comments seemed to float over her head. Abby spent the rest of the meal chatting to him, and Michelle and Sharon started bickering between themselves.

They went through to the living room when they'd finished eating and Keith poured them all champagne.

'Twenty minutes,' Abby muttered when her mother stood to toast her husband. 'And then we can go.'

Nick squeezed her waist and they drank to Keith.

Nick went off to find the toilet a few minutes later. It was a feat – the house was huge. Horribly ostentatious too. Keith, or his wife, liked to show off their money. He returned almost ten minutes later to find Abby squaring off to Michelle. Before he could get across the room he saw Keith say something to Abby and she went beet-red.

'She just told me that she slept with Matthew and that it wouldn't be long before she had Nick in bed too,' Abby was saying. Nick didn't break stride and he was by her side before Michelle finished her protest.

'I did not say that! She's making it up.'

Keith looked from his daughter to Abby. 'This is my birthday party. It's not one of your drunken orgies.' He looked at Abby and she took a stricken step back. 'And I would appreciate it if you could curb your nastiness for one evening.'

'My nastiness?' Abby said and then she sighed. 'I don't know why I even let it upset me anymore. Michelle has done nothing but bait me since I got here. If she were anyone else she'd be on the floor by now.'

Keith opened and closed his mouth a few times. Michelle crossed her arms over her chest and smirked. Sharon struck a similar pose.

Abby snorted in disgust. 'I have to go to work.' She stopped to kiss her mother, grabbed their coats and headed outside. Nick said a quick thank you and followed her.

They drove in silence for a few minutes, the only sound the swishing of the window wipers as they fought to keep the windscreen clear of rain.

'I'm sorry you had to witness that,' Abby said miserably.

'It's not your fault. Did she really say that?'

Abby nodded. 'And it's probably true. She probably did shag Matthew.'

'Well she wouldn't get me,' Nick said.

Abby smiled. 'I know. Thanks.' She banged her head back on the headrest and sighed. 'I don't know why I let them wind me up. They've always been like that. Keith married mum when I was twelve and he tried to make me go to private school like his horrible daughters. He thought I was loud and common. He's loaded and me and mum never had any money. Dad lives in Canada and he's got a whole other family to support now. Michelle and Sharon were jealous that I stood up to Keith and got more freedom. They were always getting me into trouble. I couldn't wait to move out.'

'What happened to their mum?'

'Dead. When they were tiny.'

'Did your mum take their side too?'

'Not really. I don't think she likes them very much to be honest. But she's scared to go against Keith so she'd always let him go ape-shit at me and then she'd sneak up later and give me a cuddle.' Abby shrugged. 'It doesn't matter now. I rarely see them.'

Nick was quiet for a minute. 'And you think Matthew slept with Michelle? Even knowing how they treat you?'

Abby shrugged. 'I don't know. I can't believe he'd do that, but if Michelle really tried to entice him . . .' She shrugged again.

Nick gripped the steering wheel and tried not to show how angry he was. He'd never been particularly keen on Matthew but lately he was finding he almost hated him. How could he do that to Abby? It was worse than sleeping with her best mate. At least Jo wouldn't throw it in her face.

He looked over at Abby. She looked pale and unhappy, eyes wide and wet with unshed tears. 'Can't you phone in sick?'

Abby shook her head. 'No. I'm okay.' She forced a smile and Nick felt his heart contract. She might be stubborn and overly independent but she was so brave and determined and adorably headstrong that he couldn't help but respect her. He could quite easily love her too, he realised. And then he thought of a lifetime of fighting and making love with Abby and pressed his foot harder on the accelerator. He wouldn't make it past age fifty.

Chapter Twenty

Abby went into the building with Nick's kiss still burning on her lips. He'd driven her the rest of the way to work in silence and when she'd turned to say goodbye he'd yanked her into his arms and kissed her with such passion she'd almost had an on-the-spot-orgasm.

'What was that for?' she asked when he was finished.

He scowled. 'Fucked if I know.'

Abby got out of the car and walked inside on rubbery legs, barely registering the rain plastering her hair to her face. Her lips were tingling and she could feel his stubble on her chin. She got upstairs to loud applause.

'Saw it on the camera, hen.' Sally smiled.

'Sure you don't want to take your lunch hour now?' Sid said with a wink.

Judy watched her walk to her desk. 'You took my advice then?'

'No! We are still not together. He kissed me goodbye, that's all.'

'Hm. Lasted a long time for a "goodbye" kiss,' Sid said.

Abby pinched her nose. 'I don't want to talk about it.'

'Oh, come on . . .'

Sally's phone started to ring and Abby quickly picked up her headset, punching the button to intercept the call.

Sid sighed in a resigned way and turned back to his computer.

Jo missed Nick. She missed his strength and his reliability. Matthew was never around. Some nights he'd come in at six and others it could be anywhere up to midnight. They went out together on Friday night and had a wonderful night. They both got drunk and spent most of the night having sex. She didn't mention a future between them again. But she still hadn't contacted her parents about staying with them. Surely, when the time came, Matthew would agree that living together was the best thing to do. They had such a good time together - when he was around.

She woke up on Saturday morning and stretched happily. Muscles she didn't even know she had were aching. She'd been forced to sleep on her front after he'd carried out a particularly enthusiastic school girl scenario. She'd been a little disgusted with herself at how much she'd enjoyed it. Matthew had assured her that it was normal – apparently he'd had an ex who liked it even rougher, but she still felt a little . . . dirty somehow. And weird. Like she was some kind of sexual deviant. But then she thought of all the spanking books she'd read, the websites she'd looked at and the movies she'd seen. A hell of a lot of women must like it if there was so much of it around.

She rolled on her side to look at Matthew. The bed was empty. She listened for noise downstairs. Nothing. Sighing, she rolled out of bed and went downstairs. Everything was as they'd left it last night. And then she spotted the note. It was next to the kettle, held down by the sugar jar.

Dear Jo
I've moved out. I know it's early, but it's best this way. We had a fun last night together and I'll always remember you for that. I know you hoped for more, but it's just not me. I'm not cut out for relationships and commitment and stuff and I know you'll find someone wonderful who is.
Take care and thanks for a good time.
Love Matthew xx

Jo read the note three times. And then she blinked back tears and folded it into four. That was that then. She really was on her own. And as Nick wanted her gone before he got back on Monday, she'd have to start packing today. With a heavy heart and tears dripping off her chin, she picked up her phone and called her parents.

Chapter Twenty-One

Nick took Tilly and Olly out on Saturday while Abby slept. She woke at seven after six hours sleep and lay for a few minutes, just savouring the silence. She dressed in her work gear and went to check on Olly. He was fast asleep with his gun in his hand. Abby prised it away and tucked him in.

Nick was in the kitchen. 'Hey, good timing. I just made bolognese, you want some?'

'Yes, please.' Abby got cutlery and glasses while Nick spooned spaghetti onto plates and then they sat down to eat. The kitchen looked like a bomb had hit it. Nick still hadn't totally got the hang of being a new man but he was getting there. It'd be clean eventually. She hoped.

'Did you sleep well?' Nick asked.

Abby nodded. 'Yep. Didn't wake once.'

Nick wound spaghetti round his fork. 'Jo phoned earlier.'

Abby paused, fork in the air. 'And?'

'Matthew's moved out. She was crying, begging me to let her stay.' He sighed and drank some beer. 'It was horrible.'

'What did you say? Why has Matthew gone early?'

'At a guess, I'd say he ran away. I told her it wasn't right between us and she'd realise that once she got used to the idea. And then she told me she was going and I'd never see or hear from her again and she hung up.'

Abby ate some more bolognese. 'Do you think I should go and see her?'

Nick looked at her for a beat. 'It's up to you.'

Abby thought about it while she ate. 'No. She was the one who didn't want to speak for two weeks. She can phone me if she wants to talk.'

Nick nodded.

They ate in silence for a while.

'Was Olly okay today? Abby asked when she'd cleared her plate.

'Yes. I took them to Tilly's school and they rode their bikes round the playground. I reckon Olly's almost ready to lose the stabilisers.'

'Really? When did you do Tilly's?'

'I haven't yet. She's not as steady as Olly and she cries every time I suggest taking them off.'

Abby got another can of coke from the fridge and wished that Nick was sticking around so he could teach Olly to ride his bike.

'Will Matthew help him?' Nick got up and rinsed his plate.

Abby shrugged. 'I don't know. If Olly nags him enough, maybe.'

'Your mum phoned earlier.' Nick picked up his cigarettes and they went outside.

'Did she want me to call back?'

'Yeah. She asked if you were still upset. I told her she should ask you and she asked if I was going to marry you.'

Abby grinned. 'That's my mother. What'd you tell her?'

'I told her it was a little soon to be thinking of marriage but I'd let her know if things developed.' He chuckled. 'She sounded happy. I think she likes me.'

'She loves you. Didn't you see the way she smiled every time you touched me?'

Nick concentrated on his cigarette for a minute. 'Two nights to go. Have you spoken to Matthew at all?'

'Nope.' Abby frowned. 'You don't think we should finish early too do you?'

Nick looked at her, expression unreadable. 'No. I don't. Why? Do you?'

Abby shook her head. She inhaled, exhaling a stream of blue smoke and staring at him through the haze. 'I don't want to finish it at all,' she said eventually. Her heart was pounding and she felt sick, but she *didn't* want him to go. Where was the harm in a bit of honesty? He didn't have to see her again if he didn't want to. She really had very little to lose.

Nick put out his cigarette and moved to sit on the table part of the bench. 'Come here,' he said and held out a hand.

Abby felt like her rib cage had collapsed into her stomach. She moved to take Nick's hand and he pulled her closer until she was stood between his legs, her face inches from his.

'This doesn't have to be it, you know,' he said.

Abby watched his eyes caressing her face, lingering on her lips. She unconsciously licked her lower lip and wondered if he could hear her heart beating. She looked at his mouth and leant closer.

'Abby?' he prompted.

'I can't,' she whispered, eyes still on that gorgeous lower lip. It reminded her of Brad Pitt's and she couldn't look at a picture of him without wanting to suck and nibble at it. But Nick wasn't a picture. He was real. And she'd chewed on his lip before.

'Because of Jo?' Nick asked and Abby nodded. Nick stiffened slightly and Abby panicked. He was going to get all stroppy and he'd go inside and take his lip away. She leant forward, wrapping her arms round his neck and sucking his lip into her mouth. She ran her tongue across it and felt him slowly relax against her. His hands skimmed her back and rested on her buttocks, pulling her harder against him.

Abby smiled against his mouth and he gripped her tighter. 'I feel that smile,' he said, pulling his lip away and nipping her ear. 'What's so funny?'

'I love your mouth,' Abby told him and kissed him again.

Nick kissed her back. His mouth was soft and cool, his tongue hot and hard. His chest was crushing against her breasts and she could feel him hard against her thigh. She let out an involuntary groan and pulled back slightly. 'We can't, Nick. We have to stop.'

He stared at her for a moment and then his eyes narrowed and he jumped down from the bench, moving so he was stood over her. 'What is wrong with you? First you tell me you don't want the fortnight to end. Then you tell me you can't sleep with me because you don't want to hurt Jo. Then you kiss me. Don't you think you should make up your fucking mind what it is you do want?'

'You know what I want,' Abby said, trying to keep her voice even, working hard to stand still even though his expression and proximity made her want to retreat. 'You know I want to sleep with you. And you know Jo's not the only reason I won't.'

'It's bollocks, Abby. All of it. If Jo is such a good friend she'll want you to be happy. And what was that crap about Olly? You don't like me criticising you? The only reason I do criticise is because I want more than a quick fuck. I wouldn't bother if I thought things would stay casual. What difference would it make to me if Olly was a spoilt brat?'

'My son is not a spoilt brat,' Abby snapped.

'He bloody well can be and you know it. And that's not the point. The point is that you're a prick tease.'

'That's not fair,' Abby cried out.

'And you think it's fair to keep kissing me then pushing me away?'

'I don't think any of this is fair. If it was fair we'd be in bed right now,' Abby was fighting back tears now, desperate to make him understand. 'I'm not playing with you, Nick. I want you just as much, more probably, than you want me. I can't help kissing you and I can't help wanting you. But Jo is my best friend. Why can't you understand that?'

'I'm trying to understand. But *why* is Jo so important? You say you believe in fate and all that bollocks. What if fate is me and you? What if we're meant to be together and have two or three kids together? Jo doesn't love me. She'll forget about me as soon as she meets someone else. Why is she more important than you? And me? And Olly? Don't you think Olly would love us to be together? I know Tilly would.'

'Don't bring Olly into this,' Abby said, arms wrapped round herself, tears starting to fall, the lump in her throat making it hard to speak. 'I can't do this anymore, Nick.' She swallowed, swiping at her eyes with the back of her hand. 'I think we should end it now. Quit while we're ahead.'

'You call this ahead?' Nick said, voice quieter now. All the fight seemed to have left him and suddenly she was in his arms and he was holding her tight, one arm across her back, the other cradling her head against his chest.

She was powerless to do anything but slump against him, tears literally pouring from her eyes while she cried for what seemed like hours.

'I don't want to finish early. Apart from anything else, Jo is still at my house. If you want me to stay away from you, then fine. Olly is looking forward to playing with Tilly tomorrow and you'll get more sleep if I stay.'

Abby nodded and surreptitiously wiped her nose on her sleeve before pulling away. 'Okay. You're right. Best to stick with the plan. And you don't have to stay away from me.'

Nick lit a cigarette and passed it to her, before lighting one for himself. 'I don't think the most loyal of man could ever understand female friendship. Not completely.'

Abby gave a watery smile. 'I know. Everything you say is true, Jo shouldn't come first. But that's the way it is with friendship. And I could never justify hurting her.'

'Even if she has slept with Matthew? Even if she's not worried about hurting you?' Nick's tone was gentle and Abby was amused that he was still speaking his mind despite her tears.

'Even then.' She inhaled deeply. 'And if me and you are meant to be together, then it'll happen eventually. But I want to do it right. Jo will meet someone else and you'll learn that my parenting techniques are far superior to yours and we'll live happily ever after.' Abby grinned as his expression relaxed and he perched on the edge of the bench.

'Superior parenting techniques huh?'

Abby nodded. 'You could learn a lot, you know.'

'I imagine I could.' He looked thoughtful for a bit. 'Which bit is the hardest bit to learn? The completely ignoring everything they do wrong? Or the not saying anything when they're naughty?'

'Very funny. I thought we'd called a truce.'

'You brought it up.'

'So I did. You know you're not meant to say the word naughty. Gives them something to aim for apparently. *And*, Mr SmartyPants, for your information, thinking up excuses for bad behaviour is the hardest part.'

Nick stubbed out his cigarette, shaking his head in defeat. 'I'm sorry. Can we change the subject – I'm never going to be as relaxed as you about this stuff. Let's agree to disagree for now, okay?'

Abby followed him inside. 'For now.'

Chapter Twenty-Two

The rest of the weekend passed uneventfully. Nick took Tilly and Olly out again on Sunday while Abby slept. Then he took Tilly to the cinema early evening before taking her home. He got in at ten o'clock and Abby was already in bed. She told herself she was tired, but deep down she knew she was hiding. She just didn't trust herself round him anymore. It was easier just to avoid him than to rely on her failing self control.

Nick got up with Olly on Monday morning and woke her with a cup of coffee at eight thirty. 'Olly's ready for nursery. I have a meeting at nine otherwise I'd take him for you.'

Abby forced herself awake and sat up. 'Okay, thanks.' And then she really looked at him and realised this was the last time he'd wake her up. The last time he'd bring her coffee. And she forgot all about her morning breath and her friendship with Jo and jumping out of bed, flew into his arms.

He wrapped his arms tight around her and she buried her head in his neck.

'I wish you didn't have to go,' she said, blinking back tears.

'I know.' She felt him bury his face in her hair.

'Mummy!' Olly flew into the room and hugged her leg. 'Are you okay? Why are you crying?'

'I'm ok baby,' she said, ruffling his hair. He climbed onto the bed and started poking at her phone.

Nick pulled back and looked at her, eyes soft and warm, face sad. And then he reached out with both hands and wiped the tears away, his hands lingering on her face.

'Please don't cry,' he said gently as tears continued to run down her cheeks and onto his hands. 'It doesn't have to be over.'

'Yes it does,' Abby sobbed. And then she straightened up and gulped some air. 'I'm sorry. You'd better go. You'll be late for your meeting.'

Nick looked at his watch and then he looked back in frustration. 'I can't leave you like this.'

'I'm fine. I'm just overreacting because I'm tired,' Abby said and looked at him, eyes taking in every detail. The creases bracketing his mouth, the dimple in his chin. He stared back and time stood still.

And then Olly started bouncing on the bed and the moment passed.

Nick took her face in his hands and kissed her gently on the mouth. 'I'll pick you up at six tomorrow. Driving lesson,' he added at her blank look.

'Okay.' Abby stepped back.

Nick said goodbye to Olly and with one last look at Abby, he walked out.

Abby took Olly to nursery and then she went home and went back to bed. Her mobile woke her two hours later.

'Did you work last night? Shit, sorry, Abs, I didn't mean to wake you.' It was Jo.

'Don't worry. I didn't work, I just had trouble sleeping last night.' *Because I want your ex-boyfriend so badly it's killing me.*

'What are you doing? Today I mean. Can we meet? I've really missed you.'

Abby invited her round for lunch then got up and showered. She collected Olly and got home just as Jo arrived.

'Hi,' Jo said and watched her unlock the door.

They went inside to the kitchen and Abby switched on the kettle. 'How are you?'

Jo sat down at the table and her eyes got moist. 'You heard that me and Nick split up?'

Abby nodded. 'Are you okay?'

Jo shook her head and burst into tears. 'No. I'm living back with Mum and Dad and it's awful. They keep suggesting I get a job and I miss Nick so much.' She buried her head in her hands and Abby put an arm round her shoulders, perching on the chair next to her.

Jo cried in her arms for a while, Abby wondering what was upsetting her the most. Being apart from Nick or not living in his lovely big house anymore. She had a feeling Nick didn't count much at all and then felt guilty for not being sympathetic enough.

Jo eventually pulled away, wiping her eyes – no snotty nose, Abby noted – and heaved a sigh. 'I wish we hadn't done the swap. Look how much trouble it caused.'

Abby shrugged. 'It was enlightening.'

'How did you and Nick get on? Was he a complete slob?' Jo asked.

'No.' Abby shook her head and got up to make coffee. 'It took a few days for him to get in the habit of putting his stuff in the dishwasher but apart from that he was fine. He's tidy. And okay, so he doesn't clean or do washing or anything but he emptied the dishwasher a couple of times and he took a turn cooking at weekends. And he was really helpful with Olly.'

Jo's face had turned stony. 'You had a good time then?'

Abby put a mug of coffee in front of her friend and fought to be understanding. 'The swap was Matthew's idea, Jo. You talked me into it remember? Me and Nick just made the best of it.'

Jo stared at her. And then she sighed. 'I know. I'm sorry. I kept thinking that maybe he fancied you and that was why he was dumping me but I should have known. You're not his type.' She did another sigh. 'He loves kids. Did Tilly stay? Did the four of you go out?'

'No. Tilly did stay but I'd been working. Nick took Olly out though.' Abby concentrated on her coffee and tried not to feel hurt that Jo thought Nick wouldn't want her.

'Mummy? Can I have lunch?' Olly poked his head round the door and grinned at them both.

'Oh God. Sorry, Ol.' Abby jumped up and started gathering bread and butter and marmite.

Jo watched her while she sipped at her coffee.

'So how was Matthew?' Abby asked.

'Fine. He didn't expect me to serve his dinner and he loaded the dishwasher. He didn't do much else though.'

'No. He wouldn't. He expected me to keep the house spotless but he never did anything to help. Did he appreciate living in such a clean house?'

Jo shrugged. 'He never said.'

'I'm surprised. He used to moan about what a slob I was.'

Jo looked around. 'It's not that bad. A bit dusty.'

Abby bit her lip. 'I just finished working a four night shift. Cleaning hasn't been a priority.'

'But you have all day.' Jo looked surprised.

'I have to sleep.' Abby yelled for Olly to come get his lunch.

'Sorry. I don't mean to criticise,' Jo said. 'We're just different. I couldn't bear to live in a dirty house.'

Abby counted to ten. 'I'm just going to have a cigarette and then I'll make us a sandwich,' she said and slipped outside. She inhaled deeply. Then she inhaled again. A few deep breaths later and she felt calmer. Had Jo always been this tactless? She got eight hours sleep a night – minimum. She had no kids. She didn't work. All she did was shop and keep house. For two people.

Abby smoked two cigarettes and then went back inside. Olly was sat at the table and he'd finished his sandwich. 'I've minished, Mummy. Can I get down now please?'

'Of course you can, sweetheart.' Abby watched him run through to the playroom. And then she turned to Jo. 'What would you like in your sandwich?'

Matthew came round at six that evening.

'You're looking good,' he said and kissed her cheek.

'Thanks. You are too.'

'Daddy!' Olly ran out of the playroom and threw himself at Matthew. Matthew laughed and spun him around.

'God, I missed you, Ol.' He hugged him tight and Abby looked on in surprise. Matthew wasn't a bad dad but he wasn't particularly good either. Maybe separation would be good for him and Olly after all.

Abby left Matthew to put Olly to bed and went outside to wait for Fiona to pick her up for Aerobiking.

'Is Matthew back?' Fiona asked, watching the house while Abby fastened her seatbelt.

'Only to babysit.'

'Has Nick gone? Where's Jo?'

'Yeah. Nick went this morning. Jo's back with her parents. She came round for lunch.'

'She phoned me earlier but I didn't get a chance to call her back yet. Is she okay?'

'Not really. She was crying about Nick. She didn't say anything about sleeping with Matthew though.' Abby paused and looked out the window. 'She annoyed me a bit actually.'

Fiona glanced at her in surprise. 'She probably slept with your boyfriend. You should be more than annoyed.'

Abby waved her hand. 'I'm not annoyed about that. She was just so insensitive. More or less called me a slob and then she told me I wasn't Nick's type.'

'If only she knew.'

Abby stared straight ahead. She hadn't told Fiona anything. It felt too disloyal to Jo.

'I do know,' Fiona said softly. 'Don't worry I won't say anything.'

Abby immediately felt tears fill her eyes.

Fiona put her hand over hers. 'Are you okay?'

'Not really.' Abby heaved a sigh and swiped at her eyes. 'I really like him, Fi. But I've told him I can't do anything because of Jo and then today I suddenly realised that I don't actually like Jo very much. Do you think it's because of Nick? She never bothered me before.'

Fiona smiled. 'She's spoilt and she's selfish. You just never saw it because you never got a break from her before. You should go for it with Nick. What did he say?'

'He knew right from the start how I felt. He's not happy about it but I think he accepts it. He's still going to teach me to drive. He's coming over tomorrow night.'

'Are you going to be able to resist?' Fiona grinned.

'I think I'll manage. We'll be in his car and Olly'll be with us.'

'You can't take Olly! You won't be able to concentrate. I'll come and watch him for you.'

'Really? You don't mind?'

Fiona waved a hand. 'Nah. It'll be a good excuse to get out. Edward can deal with the kids for a change.'

Abby got home to find Matthew carrying boxes and bags from the house to his car. She waved goodbye to Fiona and helped him with the rest.

'There's some stuff we need to sort out. I can't remember if it's mine or yours or joint. Have you done anything about the house yet?' He asked.

Abby picked up a box and followed him to the car. 'No. I'll call some estate agents tomorrow. What stuff are you talking about?'

'The DVD player. The CD's. Some kitchen stuff. Your mum rang by the way. I said you'd ring her back. Why doesn't she just call your mobile?'

'I've never given her the number,' Abby told him with a smile.

It was almost midnight before they'd divided up all their belongings and decided what to do about Olly and money. Until the house was sold they agreed to keep the money as it was. It was hard to decide on visitation because of Abby's working hours. In the end they decided to play it by ear. If Abby's shifts fell during the week then Matthew could take Olly out over the weekend but if she was working weekends, she'd need to sleep so he'd see plenty of him anyway. And he'd have to stay the night whenever Abby was working whatever happened.

Abby went to bed feeling slightly happier. The split had been easy and amicable. She was lucky. And she had her driving lesson tomorrow. And maybe at the weekend she'd get her mum to babysit and she'd go out and get drunk and perhaps even find a new man.

Chapter Twenty-Three

When Nick phoned at ten o'clock the next morning Abby assumed he was cancelling.

'How are you?' he asked.

'Fine. What's wrong?'

Nick chuckled. 'I'm not cancelling. I just phoned for some stuff I need to know for insurance.'

'Oh.' Abby gave him the information and hung up, a goofy smile on her face. He was still going to teach her to drive.

He pulled up just after Abby opened the door to Fiona and they watched him walk up the path.

'He *is* bloody sexy,' Fiona said on a cough.

'Tell me about it.' Abby's eyes caught on Nick's and she lost her breath for a few long moments. She clenched her fists and willed herself not to run into his arms. From the expression on his face it didn't look as if he would push her away.

'Hi Abs, Fiona.' Nick kissed Fiona on the cheek. 'How are you?'

'Fine. I'm babysitting for Olly. Figured you'd be able to yell at Abby better without her kid in the backseat.'

'Why am I going to yell at Abby?' Nick looked surprised. He kissed Abby's cheek and straightened, eyes never leaving hers.

'Because you have no patience and Abby can't drive.'

'I have shit loads of patience,' Nick said. He grinned at Fiona and looked back at Abby. 'Are you ready to go?'

She nodded and turned to Fiona. 'Olly's in bed – he was up at five. I said you'd go and say hi.'

'Okay. We'll be fine. Have fun.' Fiona waved and went inside, shutting the door.

Nick and Abby were left on the doorstep. 'I hope she doesn't go anywhere, I haven't got a key. Or my phone.'

'Don't worry, I've got mine. Fiona can get the number from Jo if she needs it. Come on, let's go.'

They walked to the car and Abby slid behind the wheel. 'Are you sure about this?' she asked, looking around nervously. 'I'd hate to trash your car.'

Nick grinned and fastened his seat belt. 'Adjust your mirrors. Can you reach the pedals? Right. The pedal in the middle is the brake. It's the most important one.' He went through the gears and the pedals and showed her what buttons did what. 'Are you ready?'

Abby nodded. She was starting to feel quite excited. She turned the key and listened to the engine catch.

'Right. Foot on the clutch. Take the hand brake off. Check your mirrors. First gear. Ready. Check your mirrors again. That's it. Accelerate. Release the clutch.'

Abby followed his instructions and the car started to move. And then it jerked to a halt and all the lights on the dashboard lit up.

'Don't worry. You stalled. Let's try again. More acceleration this time.'

It took four goes but eventually they started to move. Nick took her round the block a few times, sticking close to home, avoiding the main roads. After half an hour she'd stalled another six times and almost crashed into a parked car. But she could pull away, change up to fourth and brake. And sometimes she could indicate too.

'Good.' Nick leant back in his seat. 'Let's try Kings Road now.'

'You're kidding! It's rush hour!'

'You'll be fine, Abs. Just take it easy. Okay? Handbrake off. Remember to check your mirrors. ABBY!'

Abby slammed on her brakes and watched a mini fly past. 'Sorry.' She started the whole sequence again, remembering her mirrors this time. She got to the end of Pondtail Road and indicated left and there was a gap in the traffic and suddenly she was driving along Kings Road.

'I did it! I did it!' she said, bouncing in her seat a little.

'Good girl. Watch the road. Okay, we won't brave traffic lights today, indicate left here. That's it. Mirrors! Good. Well done.'

Five minutes later they were parked outside Abby's house. Okay, so one wheel was on the curb and one was on the road, but the car was stationary, dent-free and it was *almost* parallel with the curb. Pretty good for lesson number one, Abby reckoned.

'Thanks for that, Nick. It was so much fun.' Abby beamed at Nick and he smiled back before getting out of the car. Abby removed the key and followed him up the drive. She accepted a cigarette and let him light it for her.

'How long do you think it'll take? Before I can take my test, I mean?' Abby asked.

Nick leant against the porch wall and smiled. 'Give it a couple of weeks, see how you get on. You did well. And make sure you tell Fiona how patient I was.'

'You yelled twice,' Abby reminded him.

'Out of fear! Not impatience. There's a difference.' He grinned and sucked on his cigarette. And then his expression softened and he moved closer. 'How are you?'

'I'm okay.' Abby fought to keep focused. Friend. Friend. Friend. She didn't fancy him. He was just a friend. 'Matthew collected his stuff last night. I have a couple of estate agents coming round tomorrow. And Jo came for lunch yesterday. Oh and she rang me today.'

'How is she?'

Abby shrugged. 'Crying a lot. Not happy living with her parents.'

'Is she looking for a job?'

'Thinking about it.'

'You sound pissed off.' Nick flicked ash in the flowerbed. 'Is she hassling you?'

'She phoned twice today.' Abby hesitated, torn between wanting to talk about it and loyalty to her best friend. 'I think she's feeling a bit insecure.'

Nick nodded. 'You look tired.' He took one last drag on his cigarette and stubbed it out.

'Thanks! I got loads of sleep last night.'

'It's stress. It's not easy breaking up with someone. Especially when you've got their kid and you have to move and your best friend wants babysitting all the time.'

'I know.'

Nick put his hands in his pockets and stared down at her. 'I guess I'd better go.'

Abby thought about asking him in for coffee. She desperately wanted to. She wasn't going to see him for a week. But what then? It was hard enough keeping her hands to herself on the doorstep. She'd stand no chance in the privacy of the house.

'Okay. Thanks for the lesson.'

'No probs. Same time next week?'
Abby nodded.
They locked eyes for a moment.
'Take care.' Nick leant down and kissed her lightly on the lips.
Abby closed her eyes. Her stomach shifted and her limbs went floppy. He moved away and she almost fell forwards.
'Bye,' he said and Abby let her eyes catch on his. Ask me to stay, his eyes were pleading, forget Jo.
Abby was so tempted. What would one night hurt? But one night would lead to another, and another and another. And then they would be in a relationship and it would kill Jo. She couldn't do it. Not even once. And at least this way she had his friendship – she would see him every week for her driving lesson.
'Bye,' she forced herself to say.
Nick gave a sad smile and reached out, rubbing her lip with his thumb. Abby felt her eyes closing and her body leaning in and quickly pulled herself together.
And then he was striding down the drive, towards his car. Abby watched him pull away and she touched her lips. She thought of his kiss and his touch and his face and his body and she went inside to try not to cry on Fiona's shoulder.

Chapter Twenty-Four

Abby was acting strangely, Jo was almost sure of it. She seemed distant, impatient almost. Maybe she was regretting splitting up with Matthew or something.

Jo sighed and rolled over in bed. It was eleven am. And she was bored. Bored, bored, bored. Her parents were at work, the house was in silence and it was spotlessly clean. Her mother wouldn't let her lift a finger. It was nice in a way, but it left her with a lot of time on her hands. Her hands. She checked them out. Maybe she could get her nails done. Problem was she was running out of cash. She was still getting her jobseekers allowance but it didn't go far. She did another sigh. She needed to get a job.

She had tummy ache. Maybe she should get breakfast. Though it wasn't a hungry tummy ache. More like period pain. Maybe she was due on. Her boobs were tender and she had a spot on her chin. Must be due on. Rolling out of bed, she hooked her bag off the floor and grabbed her diary. She counted back. Two weeks ago, second night of Matthew. Sex with Nick on the Saturday before. Ah there it was. Thursday 12th February. Big P for period. So she was due on. She flicked forward through the diary. On Thursday. Oh. Thursday just gone. She went still, finger glued to Thursday 11th. She was six days late. She was never late.

Her heartbeat picked up and she counted again to make sure. Definitely late. Could be the stress. Or it could be that she was pregnant. She lay back on the bed and thought about that. Pregnant. A baby. It was what she'd wanted for ages. Years if she was honest. But that was when she was in a relationship. How would Nick take it if she told him she was having his baby? And she was sure it *was* his baby. They hadn't used any contraception and the timing had been spot on. She and Matthew had used condoms every time they'd had sex. Nick was definitely the father.

Excitement mounting, Jo jumped out of bed and headed for the shower. She resisted the urge to pee. She'd save it for the pregnancy test she was about to buy.

She told Abby first. Jumped in the car and shot round there, pregnancy test in hand. Abby was just heading out the door.

'Where are you going? Oh, Abby, you're not going to believe this.' She abandoned the car on the curb and ran towards her friend. 'I'm having Nick's baby. Can you believe it? I'm finally pregnant.' She waved the test around and watched her friend go from pale to flushed.

'Congratulations.' Jo accepted her hug and wondered why she wasn't more enthusiastic. Maybe she was jealous. She'd always wanted a big family but she and Matthew couldn't afford any more children, and now it was too late. She didn't have a boyfriend anymore.

'I have to go and get Olly, Jo. Can I call you later?' Abby stepped back and looked at the test.

'Oh, don't worry. I'm going to go and see Nick now. He can take me out to lunch to celebrate.' She waved at Abby and got back in the car. And then she pointed the car towards Camberley, dialling Nick on her mobile as she went.

'Nick? I need to see you urgently. Are you free for lunch?'

'What's wrong?' He sounded distracted.

'Nothing bad. I have good news and it can't wait.'

'Are you sure? I'm pretty busy.'

'I'm sure. I'll be there in ten minutes.' Jo ended the call before he could argue.

Nick was waiting outside when she arrived. He was having a cigarette and he looked tired. His suit was crumpled and his eyes were crumpled. Even his hair was crumpled.

He stamped on his cigarette and climbed in the car. 'I can't be long. Just go to the pub up the road.'

Jo drove in silence, parked the car and they went inside. Nick bought drinks and they ordered lunch and then they found a table.

'So what's wrong?'

Jo sat back and smiled, enjoying the moment. 'We're having a baby.'

Nick went still. 'We?'

'We. You and me, we.'

'How?'

Jo felt a stab of irritation. 'We had sex. The night we agreed to do the swap. Don't you remember?'

Nick stared at her blankly. And then he slumped back in his seat. 'I remember.' He gave her a weird look. 'And you know you're pregnant already?'

'I'm six days late. You can do a test the day your period's due.' She beamed. 'Isn't it wonderful news?' And then she waited for the smiling to start. Nick loved babies and children. He was such a good dad. This was going to be so much fun.

'Right. And it's definitely mine?'

'Of course it is! Who else's would it be?' Jo said, heartbeat slowing and increasing in pressure.

'You're sure?'

'Yes!' Jo looked at his pale, tired face. 'Are you okay? You don't look well.'

Nick gave a weak smile. 'I'm okay. I haven't been sleeping well. Have you seen a doctor yet?'

'Not yet. I only found out this morning.' She moved back to let the barman put the food on the table. Yummy, Ploughmans. She piled cheese and salad onto her roll and took a big bite.

Nick watched her until the barman left and then he picked up a chip. 'What are you going to do?'

Jo watched him playing with his chips and frowned. 'What do you mean? Move back in with you. Live happily ever after. Have more kids. Eventually get married.'

'But we broke up,' Nick said. He put the chip back on his plate and took a long swig of his drink.

'I know we broke up. But now we're having a baby. Surely you want to be part of it. You don't want another child you never see do you? Anyway, I can't do this alone. I can't live with Mum and Dad and I can't work with a baby.'

Nick stared at her. Still pale. Still crumpled. Still not happy. Maybe he was in shock.

'I have to go back to work,' he said. 'Let me know when you've seen the doctor. Take care.' He stood up and picked up his cigarettes. And then he left the pub, meal untouched.

Jo watched him go while she finished her lunch. He really was stressed. Maybe he was busy at work. Perhaps he was worried about the expense of another baby. Yeah, that must be it. Poor thing. Maybe he should look for another job. She'd need him at home a lot more when the baby came anyway.

She finished her mouthful. And then she looked at Nick's lunch. Burger and chips. Shame to let it go to waste. And she *was* eating for two now. She picked up a chip and reached for the ketchup.

Chapter Twenty-Five

When the doorbell rang at seven o'clock that evening, Abby almost didn't answer it. She couldn't face more Jo. But then she realised it probably wasn't going to be Jo. Jo was more than likely tucked up in bed with Nick. Or shopping for bibs and breast pumps.

She pulled the door open without enthusiasm. 'Nick!'

'Hi.' He smiled sadly and Abby stood to one side to let him in.

'Are you okay?'

'No.' He shook his head vehemently. 'I'm very not okay.'

Abby looked at him suspiciously. 'Are you drunk?'

'I most certainly am not! And if I were would you blame me? My ex-girlfriend is pregnant. I'm going to have to marry her and live unhappily ever after. Our child will probably be just as spoilt and insipid as it's mother and I'll have to work a hundred and twelve hours a week just to keep them in Crème De La Mer face cream and I'll have a heart attack before I'm fifty.'

'Did you drive?'

'No! I may not be drunk but I *am* over the limit. I don't drink and drive,' Nick said indignantly and walked into the living room. He fell onto the settee and patted the space next to him. 'Come and talk to me.'

Abby sat down. She left a decent amount of space between them and Nick immediately reached out and pulled her closer.

'That's better,' he said. He leant his head back and closed his eyes. 'God, I am so depressed.'

'A baby is pretty exciting,' Abby said encouragingly.

Nick opened one eye. 'A baby with you would be exciting. A baby with Jo is fucking frightening.' He sighed. 'When did she tell you?'

'Before she told you.'

'Figures. How did it make you feel?' He had both eyes open now.

'Like shit.'

'Why?'

'Because.'

'Because why?'

'Because I don't want you to be with Jo.'

'Why?'

'Because she makes you unhappy.'

'Is that the only reason?'

Abby stared at him. And then she stood up and glared down at him, hands on hips. 'Why? Why do you want to know? You want to hear me say I'm jealous? That I want you for myself? Well tough. What's the point? You have to stay with Jo now.'

Nick watched her, eyes hooded, expression blank. And then he reached out and pulled her onto his lap. 'I love you,' he said, hugging her tight to his chest and kissing the top of her head.

'No you don't.'

'Yes I do.'

'Don't.'

'Do.'

'Nick!'

'What? It's true.'

'You're drunk and you're scared. And you know it's safe to tell me you love me because I can't expect you to act on it.'

'Bollocks,' Nick said mildly.

They sat in silence, Abby cradled on his knee, his arms wrapped round her, hand stroking her hair.

'Where is Jo now?' Abby asked. She tried to wriggle away and Nick's arms tightened.

'I told her to call me after she'd seen the doctor.'

'Is the baby definitely yours?' Abby asked. She knew it was – Matthew couldn't have any more children - but she wanted to see if he knew it too.

He shrugged again. 'Apparently. She's still not admitting anything happened with Matthew.'

'She could miscarry,' Abby said tentatively.

'I know. That's why I'm stalling.' He loosened his grip and banged his head back against the sofa. 'Shit, fuck, crap. Why? Why the hell did this have to happen? I had plans.' He gave her a stern look. 'I was going to wear you down. Eventually you'd have succumbed.'

'I would not!'

'Would.'

'Wouldn't.'

'Would.'

'Wouldn't.'

'Wouldn't.'

'Would. N't. Shit you stupid twat.' Abby smacked him over the head and he chuckled.

'I won.'

'Didn't.'

'Did.'

Abby put her nose in the air. 'I refuse to play your drunken games any longer.'

'Only because you lose.'

'Don't.'

'Do.'

'Don't. Oh fuck. Just stop would you.'

They fell silent again.

And then Abby looked at Nick and started to cry. He looked so tired. So defeated, and unhappy and trapped.

'Don't cry,' Nick said softly and turned her round so they were chest to chest, her knees either side of his lap. 'It'll sort itself out. I don't have to live with her.'

'You do.' Abby sobbed into his neck. 'She can't bring up a baby alone. She can barely bring herself up alone. Anyway, that's not why I'm crying. I'm upset for you. You're the one who's trapped. I wouldn't have had you anyway, remember?'

'Yes you would have. Eventually.' He pulled back and frowned down at her. 'I'm still teaching you to drive.'

Abby blinked. 'Okay.'

'I mean it. Just because I can't keep you safe by being with you doesn't mean I can't still teach you to drive.'

'I know.'

He frowned even harder. 'I was going to stop you running in the dark and cycling in the dark and walking home in the dark. How can I do that if I'm living with Jo?'

Abby grinned. 'You couldn't do it anyway.'

'I stopped you cycling to work,' Nick said with a smile.

'No you didn't. I still cycled. And I would again but I want to learn to drive.'

Nick smirked.

'And when I've passed my test I can cycle to work again.'

That got rid of the smirk. 'You will not!'

'Will too.'

'Will not.'

'Will too.'

'Then I won't teach you to drive.'

'Okay. I won't cycle,' Abby said with an angelic smile.

Nick narrowed his eyes. 'Are you humouring me?'

'Not at all. Just bending to your will.' Abby fluttered her eyelashes.

Nick smiled.

And then he closed his eyes and started to snore.

Chapter Twenty-Six

It took Nick a few minutes to work out where he was. And then he remembered. He was on Abby's sofa. He'd passed out drunk after telling her he loved her. And Jo was pregnant with his child. Jesus! No wonder he'd got drunk.

'How are you feeling?' Abby appeared in the doorway, Olly on her hip. She was wearing jeans and t-shirt and looked utterly edible.

'Hello, Nick.' Olly beamed at him.

'Hi, Olly. How are you?'

'I got wobbly tooth.'

'No he hasn't. He keeps saying that since he saw Tilly.'

Nick grinned and started to stand up. His head exploded and lights flashed behind his eyes. 'Christ!'

'Asprin?' Abby asked.

Nick nodded.

She appeared a few minutes later with coffee and Asprin. 'I just need to run Olly to nursery. I'll be back in twenty minutes and I'll make you some breakfast. Okay?'

Nick nodded again. It hurt to talk.

Abby disappeared and Nick took the asprin. He drunk the coffee and waited for the pounding to subside. It didn't subside but it did fade enough for him to get up and walk. He went up to the bathroom and climbed into the shower. Ten minutes of scalding hot water and he started to feel a bit better. He did his teeth with Abby's toothbrush and dressed in yesterday's clothes.

After firing off a quick email to the office to say he'd be in at lunchtime, he went downstairs. Abby was in the kitchen; bacon and sausages sizzled under the grill and eggs were crackling in a frying pan.

'You're an angel,' Nick said and dropped a kiss on the top of her head.

Abby rapped his knuckles with her spatula. 'No kissing.'

Nick held up his hands and went for a cigarette. When he came back in his breakfast was on the table and Abby was already eating hers.

'Feeling better?' she asked.

'Much. I'm sorry about last night.'

Abby went still. 'Which part?'

'The part where I banged on for hours.'
'You remember?'
'I remember that I told you I love you.'
Abby swallowed. 'You were drunk.'
'I was drunk,' Nick agreed, 'but I knew what I was saying. I do love you.'
'You hardly know me.'
'I know you better than you think?'
'No you don't.'
'Do.'
'Don't.'
'Do.'

Nick grinned. He ate a piece of sausage. And then he stopped talking for a while so that he could eat. When he'd finished he sat back with a sigh. 'That was wonderful. Thank you.' He got up and started coffee and then loaded everything into the dishwasher. Abby took over the coffee making while he finished and then they took their mugs outside.

'You're back at work tonight aren't you?' Nick asked when they were settled with their coffee and cigarettes. It had been raining again so they were sitting on plastic bags.

'Yep.'
'Is Matthew staying?'
'I hope so.'

Nick went quiet for a moment. 'You remember when I first came to stay and you told me you couldn't go without sex?'

'I told you I didn't like going without sex, not that I couldn't.'
'Would you sleep with Matthew?'
'No!' Abby said and then she sighed and inhaled some nicotine. 'Look, Nick. Let's be realistic. You're going to get back with Jo. I'm not going to stay celibate forever. I like sex. And I'm not waiting eighteen years for your kid to grow up before you leave. I don't even want you to leave them for me. Family is too important.'

'Your parents split up.'
'Exactly! And I'm completely screwed up because of it.'
'You are not screwed up.' Nick scowled.
Abby grinned. 'I am screwed up. I've spent years in a loveless relationship because I'm too chicken or too lazy to wait for love. I meet someone I could love and almost sleep

with him probably because he's my best friend's ex so I know nothing can come of it. I'm an emotional cripple.'

'You are not.'

'Yes I am.'

'I love you.'

'Nick!' Abby stubbed out her cigarette and drained her coffee. And then she stood up. 'Go home.'

'No.'

'Please.' She turned to look at him and he saw tears glistening in her eyes. 'It can't happen. Stop torturing me and go.'

He was on his feet and by her side in seconds. 'But it's true. I promise not to tell you again. I'll even stay away if that's what you want, but I want you to know I'm telling the truth. I do love you.'

'Fine. I believe you,' Abby said flatly, eyes not meeting his.

He put his hands on either side of her face and tilted her head but still she wouldn't look at him. So he kissed her. Lightly, on the lips.

'No!' she said but her eyes were finally looking into his. 'Please, Nick. Go home.' And she started to cry in earnest. She wiped at the tears with her sleeve. 'Shit! I can't believe how much I keep crying. I never cry.' She scowled at him. 'You make me cry. And you make my nipples go hard.'

Nick bit back a smile and stroked her hair behind her ears.

'Please. Go.'

Nick sobered. 'Okay. If that's what you want.'

'It is. And I don't want you to teach me to drive either.'

'Tough. You're not cycling anymore.'

'It'll be light in the evenings soon.'

'I don't care. This isn't negotiable, Abby. I *will* teach you to drive.'

'Fine.' She crossed her arms and looked sulky.

Nick sighed. 'I'll see you on Tuesday.'

'Fine.'

He leant over and kissed her forehead. She leant into him for a beat and he resisted the urge to pull her into his arms. There was no point. She was right. All he was doing was torturing them both. He pulled back and looked down at her. Her eyes came open and she stepped back.

'Take care,' he said.

'You too.'

Nick turned and walked through the house and out the front door. He felt like he was going to throw up. Empty and bereft and sick to the stomach. And the worst thing of all was knowing how Abby felt. He knew without a doubt that she was crying her heart out right now and there wasn't a single thing he could do about it.

Chapter Twenty-Seven

Abby took the night off work and arranged to go out with Fiona and Becky on Saturday evening. She had lieu days owing from Christmas and desperately needed a night of oblivion. She was very tempted not to invite Jo – she really couldn't handle hearing her go on about Nick and her pregnancy all evening – but in the end she couldn't do it, she couldn't go out and not invite her best friend.

They started at The Prince Arthur at seven thirty. Matthew was babysitting and he was staying the night, so Abby didn't even have to go home if she didn't want to. They started on shots. Becky got the first round in – blue After Shocks. Then Abby got green ones. Jo stuck to sparkling water.

'Right.' Becky raised her glass and stared round the table. 'Nobody is allowed to talk about children tonight.' She looked at Fiona and Abby. 'Or pregnancy and ex-boyfriends.' She looked at Jo. 'Right, after three.'

She counted to three and they downed their drinks. Fiona went off to get the next round, Jo went to the toilet and Abby smiled at Becky. 'Thanks.'

'No problem. I can imagine how crazy she's driving you. Has she been on the phone non-stop?'

'Seven times today.' Abby leant forwards and banged her forehead on the table. 'I'm going to move away. I swear it and I won't tell her where I'm going. I'll just go and she'll be phoning and I won't be there.'

'Where are you going?' Jo followed Fiona over and set two Tequilas on the table. 'And why are you head-butting the table?'

'Nowhere and I don't know.' Abby downed her drink without waiting for the others and got up to get more. She needed to get drunk and she needed to get drunk quickly.

She leant over the bar, vying with a row of impatient punters for the barman's attention. 'Can I get you a drink?' an amused, and male, voice said beside her.

Abby turned round. *H-ello!* Not bad! Good body, dark curly hair, amazing smile. She gave her sexiest smile. 'You can. I'll have a Vodka and Red Bull please.'

She watched him order her drink. Nice voice. Very polite. He looked older too, a rarity in itself. The pub was mostly full of teenagers.

'Thank you.' She took the drink with a smile. 'I'm Abby.'

'I'm Chris.' He stuck out his hand and Abby shook it solemnly.

'I'm very pleased to meet you,' she said.

Chris grinned. 'Likewise.' He looked at her hand. 'Unless you're married.'

'Not married.' Abby sipped her drink and eyed him over the rim of the glass. 'Middle-aged, free and single, that's me. Though I have a three-year-old son.' She watched his face, waiting for him to lose interest.

Chris faked a gasp. 'You're not a virgin? Oh my God! Really?' He grinned. 'What's his name?'

'Oliver, Olly.'

'So you're a single parent?' he said, looking far from disinterested.

'Yep. I'm a statistic.'

He smiled. 'You're a very beautiful statistic.'

'Thank you. So tell me. What do you do?'

'I'm a policeman.'

'Really!' Abby looked at him with renewed interest. She had a thing about policemen. And bouncers. 'Do you like it?'

'Mostly.' He tipped his glass to his mouth, eyes never leaving hers. 'Who's babysitting your son tonight?'

'His dad. My ex.' Abby caught Fiona's eye. She did a thumbs up and Abby looked away quickly. 'Are you with friends?'

Chris nodded towards a couple of men sitting at a nearby table. 'George and Richard. Old college buddies. I take it you're with the three women who are staring at me.'

'Yep.' Abby followed his gaze and her friends smiled at them. 'Do you want to meet them?'

'Okay,' Chris said and followed her over.

Abby introduced him to everyone.

'I'd offer you drinks but I think we're leaving,' he said. George and Richard were putting their jackets on and waving him over. He turned to Abby. 'I have to go but I'd like to see you again. Would you like to go to dinner next week?'

'Okay,' Abby smiled. Chris pulled out his mobile phone and Abby put her number in for him.

'I'll call you,' he promised, before joining his friends.

Abby sat down.

'Not bad!' Becky said.

'Very nice.' Fiona.

Abby looked at Jo. She stared back blankly. 'Do you think I'll have a boy or a girl?'

Abby went back to the bar.

Luckily Jo left a little while after Chris. Abby was feeling fairly drunk by then and was at that point where it could go either way. She could become giggly and relaxed and happy or she could accidentally shove a beer bottle up Jo's left nostril.

'Thank God for that,' she said when she got back from walking Jo to her car. Becky or Fiona had been to the bar in her absence and she had another shot lined up. She downed it quickly and then sat back in her chair. 'What are you two looking so serious about?'

Her friends exchanged glances and immediately Abby knew. The little hairs on the back of her neck stood up and the relaxed feeling drained away. 'Where is he?'

'At the bar.'

Abby squared her shoulders and sat up straighter. 'I don't care. I am young, free and single and I don't care if Nick is at the bar. I'm here to enjoy myself and that's what I'm going to do.'

'Okay. But he's with a woman,' Becky said and Abby span round. She was right. He was at the bar and he was deep in conversation with a woman Abby didn't recognise. She looked to be close to Nick's age and she was fairly attractive. Slimish, blonde, okay-looking. Abby's first reaction was to barge over and find out what was going. Her second was to punch someone. Her third, and probably most sensible was to wait and see what happened. Becky's hand on her arm gave her enough pause to wait it out. That didn't mean she took her eyes off the couple and when Nick finally looked away his eyes went straight to hers.

And he grinned. He actually smiled. Abby turned back to her friends in disgust. 'Did you see that?'

Fiona chuckled. 'Obviously, it's perfectly innocent. Relax, Abs.'

'He's finished his drink,' Becky said from her prime position facing the bar. 'They're leaving. He's looking over here, wave at him, Abs.'

Abby got stiffly to her feet and went to the toilet. She forced a tiny dribble of wee then she washed her hands; every single inch of every single finger and then she made sure they were completely dry before slowly walking back to her friends.

'He's gone. He said to say bye,' Fiona said.

'And he introduced us to his sister,' Becky added.

Abby snorted. 'I'll bet.' And then she went to buy some more drinks.

She did actually relax after that and when she waved goodbye to her friends and headed for home, she was feeling fairly happy. She had a date. She'd achieved her evenings' objectives. And maybe she could finally—

'You won't find a taxi down here,' a familiar voice said beside her and Abby's heart jumped into her mouth.

'Jesus! You frightened the life out of me,' she snapped without stopping. 'What are you doing here? I thought you left ages ago.'

'I came back. Suspected you'd be dumb enough to walk home alone,' Nick said mildly.

'I came back. Suspected you'd be dumb enough to walk home alone,' Abby echoed in a piss-taking sing-song voice.

'Very attractive,' Nick said.

'Very attractive,' Abby said and this time Nick stopped, grabbed her by her shoulders and shoved her up against the nearest lamppost. His mouth closed over hers and his hands tangled in her hair. She tried to push him away and he pressed even harder against her, kissing her almost savagely. And she felt her resistance melt away. His tongue explored her mouth, hard and hot and persistent and she barely noticed when he picked her up and started walking.

But then he dropped her and she was on her feet again, still in his arms and still joined at the lips. She was aware of walls on two side and realised they'd moved away from the street. And then Nick's mouth left hers and she mumbled a protest. He ignored her, pushing her jacket off her shoulders and wrenching the straps of her top down her arms and then his lips were round her nipple, his tongue was working magic and his hands were unfastening her jeans. He slid them down her thighs, pulled her knickers off and kissed his way down her belly. His hands slid to her buttocks and suddenly she was being lifted in the air and his mouth was against her and around her and inside her and he was pinning her to the wall, his hands supporting her weight, his mouth holding her in place. She leant back, letting her head fall back and felt the pressure building inside her.

Nick moved his hand slightly and slid a thumb inside her. His tongue was darting and wriggling and circling, first against her and then his thumb swapped places with his tongue and then they were both inside her and both against her. Rubbing and flicking and the pressure built and grew and then Abby felt her body go rigid. Then just as suddenly she felt herself being lowered. Her body arched in protest, so close, so close and then she felt Nick sliding inside her, slowly, slowly, rubbing gently against her as he moved her with pulse-slamming speed down the length of him. And then he was buried to the hilt and she could feel his stomach against hers and he was pressing against the exact right place inside her and she cried out. Her head slammed back against the wall and she broke beneath his mouth, her body going into spasm, jerking and writhing in his hands and she was whimpering, practically sobbing.

Nick waited until the last spasms started to fade before he pulled back and thrust harder inside her and then he was crying out his own orgasm, jolting against her, hands biting into the soft flesh of her hips as he claimed her lips in a last kiss.

Chapter Twenty-Eight

Jo couldn't get an appointment until the following Monday, but that was fine. She knew she was going to end up back with Nick. That was the important thing. And it would be different this time. He'd appreciate her a lot more once she had his child. He'd stop expecting her to find a job and the digs about what she did all day would stop.

The doctor's appointment was a bit of an anti-climax. She'd taken a sample along with her so he confirmed the pregnancy. He gave her a load of information about pregnancy and what she should and shouldn't do and told her to come back and see the midwife when she was eight weeks pregnant.

Jo rang Nick as soon as she left the surgery. 'I've just seen the doctor. I'm due on the 19th of November.' She told him all the details, her excitement masking Nick's lack of reaction. It was only when she wound down that the silence registered. 'What's wrong?'

'Nothing. So it's definite then? You're definitely pregnant?'

Jo sighed. 'Didn't you listen to a word I said? Are you busy or something?'

'Yeah. It's actually not a good time. I'll call you tonight.'

There was a short silence and then Jo smiled into the phone. 'How about you don't call me? How about you talk to me face to face? I haven't finished unpacking yet you know. I could be moved back in by the time you get home.'

'No!' She heard Nick exhale. 'Look, we'll talk tonight. I'll ring you.'

He hung up and Jo climbed into the car. Poor Nick. He really did sound stressed. She must remember to speak to him about changing jobs.

Nick didn't get much work done that afternoon. He thought about the situation with Jo. He thought of living with her again – not a happy thought, and then he thought of her bringing up their baby alone – an even unhappier thought. It would be nice to actually live with one of his children. He hated living apart from Tilly. And living with Jo wasn't so bad. She was pretty easy-going and it was nice having the house clean and meals waiting for him every evening.

His thoughts slid to Abby. He closed his eyes and he could see her naked and gorgeous, writhing seductively on his bed. They'd gone back to his house Saturday night and made love all night. They hadn't spoken, not about anything important and when they'd parted with a kiss after two hours sleep on Sunday morning, they knew it was over. They had no choice. He because of the baby. Abby because of her misguided loyalty to Jo. He groaned and closed his eyes. He couldn't have Abby. He may as well let Jo move back in. Accept the inevitable. And it would be nice to have another child. He loved babies. And Jo would probably make a good mother.

He rang her to let her know and when he got home at seven she was already there. The house was sparkling and his dinner was on the table within minutes of his arrival.

He sat down to eat and Jo took the seat opposite.

'God it's good to be back. Aren't you happy? This is going to be so much fun.' She sat back and rubbed her flat stomach. 'Everyone is so excited. I just phoned the girls and told them I was back. And my parents—'

'You told Abby?' Nick cut in, mouth full of pork chop.

'Of course.' Jo looked startled and then she smiled. 'She's got a date on Thursday. With a policeman she met on Saturday.' Nick felt his heart stop beating for a moment. And then Jo continued with a frown. 'She didn't seem particularly excited though. She was more interested in us. That's Abby all over though. She's such a good friend.' She gave a dreamy smile. 'Do you think cheese triangles count as soft cheese? The doctor said I should avoid soft cheese.'

Nick finished eating and got up to put his plate in the dishwasher.

'You don't have to do that. Leave it for me,' Jo said.

Nick shrugged and finished clearing up and then he grabbed a beer and went outside for a cigarette.

Abby was dating. He lit his cigarette and inhaled deeply. The smoke hit the back of his throat and he closed his eyes, savouring the feeling. Why was he even surprised? She was single. She was free to do what she wanted. He got his mobile out of his pocket and phoned her at home. She answered on the sixth ring, sounding breathless.

'You're dating?' he asked before he could stop himself.

A seconds silence and then, 'You let Jo move back in?'

Nick sighed. 'I had no choice.'

'Right.' He heard rustling and the flick of a lighter.

'Are you outside?'

'Yes. You stress me out. I needed a cigarette.'

'You stress me out. I can't believe you're dating.'

'What do you expect me to do? Sit around and wait for your kid to grow up?'

Nick closed his eyes and inhaled some more. 'I didn't expect you to meet someone so soon that's all.' And then the realisation hit him and he fought to keep his voice even. 'You met him Saturday?'

'Yes.'

'Before you spent the night with me?'

'Yes.' Then before he could say anything, she continued. 'I met him at the bar. He asked me out for a drink. We didn't touch, we didn't kiss.' He heard her exhale. 'And don't have a go at me for not telling you. You never gave me the chance.'

'How could you? How could you sleep with me knowing you had another bloke lined up?'

'It wasn't like that, Nick. To be honest, I completely forgot about Chris. I don't know the man. I spoke to him for five minutes and he took my phone number. I wasn't to know he'd even phone.'

'Of course he'd phone,' Nick muttered. He heaved a sigh. 'I just can't believe you're dating already.'

'Why not? Why hang around? I met the bloke, he asked me out. What am I supposed to say? "Sorry, Chris, I need a few weeks to get over a relationship I never started with my best friend's ex whose baby she's having and will probably get back with." Yeah right.'

'His name's Chris?'

He heard Abby suck on her cigarette. 'Yes. His name is Chris.'

Silence stretched between them, broken only by inhales and exhales.

'You don't have to teach me to drive you know. I'll understand if you want to stop,' Abby said eventually.

'I'd love to stop. I'd rather stay away from you completely but I said I'd teach you and I will.'

'No you won't. If that's how you feel, forget it.' She sounded hurt and Nick instantly felt guilty. But then she continued and he wanted to snap her neck instead. 'Maybe I'll get Chris to teach me.'

'Like hell you will. I'll be there tomorrow.' He ended the call and stubbed his cigarette out.

'Do you want a coffee?' Jo stuck her head out the door to ask.

'No. I'm going to the gym,' he snapped and went inside to change.

Chapter Twenty-Nine

Abby left Olly playing with Fiona and went outside to wait for Nick. She was on her second cigarette when he pulled up.

'Evening,' she said, putting the cigarette out and eyeing him warily. He looked furious. 'Are you okay?'

'I'm fine.' He got in the passenger seat and waited for her to get behind the wheel.

Abby started the engine and pulled away. First try. No stalling. She moved to second and smiled. This was fun.

'Remember your mirrors,' Nick snapped.

'I checked my mirrors,' Abby said calmly.

'No you didn't.'

'Yes I did.'

'Don't argue with me. I saw you. You didn't check them.'

Abby checked her mirrors, indicated and dropping down through the gears, pulled over to the side of the road. And then she got out of the car and started walking back towards the house. She heard Nick come up behind her and then his fingers were biting into her arms and she was pulled to a stop.

'Where are you going?' he demanded.

Abby pulled away and glared up at him. 'Home. I don't have to take your abuse. Go home and yell at Jo.'

'I don't want to yell at Jo. And I wasn't yelling. I was reminding you to look in your mirrors.'

'I looked in my mirrors!' Abby shouted and then she blew out a sigh and continued, voice quiet. 'This is a bad idea, Nick. Maybe we should stay away from each other for a while.'

He scowled. 'No.' And then he stuffed his hands in his jeans pockets and closed his eyes briefly. 'I'm sorry. I'll stop yelling. Just get back in the car.' He opened his eyes. 'Please.'

They locked eyes for a moment and Abby walked back to the car.

'I don't want you to date,' Nick said quietly and Abby froze. She turned slowly to face him.

Her first instinct was to tell him what he could do with his preferences but he looked so forlorn that she instantly melted. 'I know you don't,' she said gently, 'but I have to. I don't want to sit in every night thinking about you with Jo. I'd like another baby of my own someday.' Nick stared at her, eyes sad and she reached out, almost without realising, and touched his arm.

He stiffened and then suddenly he relaxed and reaching out, pulled her into his arms. He held her tight, his chin resting on the top of her head. She leant against him, loving the feel of him, big and hard and warm against her. God, she wished Jo would meet someone else. Why the hell did she have to get pregnant? And then she thought that maybe it was because she and Nick weren't meant to be together. A firm believer in fate, she believed all things happened for a reason. She obviously wasn't meant to be with Nick for some reason. Maybe because she'd provoke him so much one day that he'd smother her with his pillow. She smiled against his chest and he pulled back slightly. 'Are you laughing?'

Abby nodded with a smile. 'I was thinking that everything's conspiring to keep us apart and maybe it's because if we got together you'd end up killing me.'

Nick stroked her hair behind her ears and grinned. 'You're probably right. I'd definitely keep you gagged a lot of the time.'

'Yeah?' Abby raised an eyebrow and Nick chuckled.

And then his expression got more serious and Abby lost her smile. She looked into his eyes and felt herself getting dizzy.

'Don't,' she whispered. 'We can't.'

Nick gave a rueful smile and stepped back. 'Sorry.' He cleared his throat. 'Shall we continue?'

Abby got back in the car and they carried on with the lesson. They were out for almost two hours and she was feeling really confident by the end of it.

'That was so much fun,' she said.

Nick smiled. 'You did really well. I can't believe how quickly you've picked it up. Are you sure you haven't driven before?'

'I had a motorbike when I was at college. An MZ50. Does that count?'

Nick lit cigarettes for them both. 'It's probably helped.' They walked up the pathway to the front door.

'How is Jo?' Abby asked.

'Haven't you spoken to her today?'

Abby shook her head and looked guiltily. 'She left three messages and sent eleven texts but I couldn't face her. I ended up switching my mobile off. She's doing my head in.'

Nick leant back against the wall and looked down at her. 'I know. She's getting completely obsessed by the pregnancy. She's already playing the baby music through her MP3 player. She's downloaded stuff that supposedly makes the baby advance more quickly.'

'Christ! It's boredom. She needs an interest. And she's not even twelve weeks yet. Imagine if she miscarries.'

They both went quiet. Abby looked at Nick and realised he too was relishing the thought. God, they were evil.

She put out her cigarette. 'I'd better go and relieve Fiona.'

Nick nodded.

'See you next week.'

He nodded again. And then he kissed her cheek. 'Take care.'

'You too.' Abby watched him walk away and then she went inside.

Fiona was in the living room. 'You were ages. I hope you were driving all that time.'

Abby flopped down next to her. 'Driving, arguing. He was being such an arsehole to start with. He's really pissed off about my date with Chris.'

'Do you blame him? He's lumbered with Jo again and you're starting anew. Picture him starting to date.'

Abby thought about it and felt herself flush. 'No way! I'd kill him.'

'Quite.'

'But it's not my fault he's back with Jo. He can't expect me to sit around and cry forever.'

'I know. Neither of you are at fault. It's just crappy circumstances.'

Abby told her about her fate theory.

Fiona chuckled. 'There is no such thing as fate. And I think you'd be great together. I'm pretty sure he wouldn't kill you either.'

Abby grinned. 'Pretty sure?'

'I couldn't swear to it. You can be very provocative.'

'True.'

Fiona heaved herself to standing. 'I'd better get home.'

'Thanks for babysitting. Though Nick would probably yell less with Olly on board.'

'I doubt it. It doesn't sound as if much could curb his temper at the moment.'

Abby walked her friend to the door and waved until her car disappeared from view. She made herself a coffee, thinking that maybe Fiona could teach her to drive. Or Matthew. But then she'd never see Nick and that thought made her feel even worse.

In the end, it was another two weeks before Chris and Abby actually managed to go out. He'd had his shifts changed and then Abby picked up a throat infection and spent most of her four nights off work in bed. They'd had some good long chats on the phone and although she could barely remember what he looked like, Abby found herself looking forward to their date more and more. She desperately needed some light-hearted relief.

Chris picked her up at seven-thirty on the Thursday night. Matthew was babysitting and was staying the night too. It made sense and he didn't mind. He didn't even seem to mind that Abby was dating.

'Good evening,' Abby said when she opened the door to Chris. He was better looking than she remembered. Not as tall as Nick, or as broad, but cuter, almost better looking in a softer kind of way. She gave herself a mental slap. She was *not* going to think about Nick tonight.

'Hi.' Chris smiled and then he offered his arm. 'Are you ready?'

Abby took his arm and followed him to his car. She wasn't very good with cars but whatever it was, it was nice. Big and sleek and shiny and silver. The police force must pay more than she'd thought.

'Do you live alone?' she asked. He held her door open and she slid into the passenger seat.

'Yeah.' He looked surprised. 'Why?'

'Just wondered. Do you rent?'

'No. I live in Church Crookham, in a house I inherited from an Aunt.' He started the engine and pulled away from the curb. 'Why d'you ask?'

'Just curious.' Abby shrugged. And then she looked him over. 'Are you an only child? How old are you?'

He didn't answer for a moment and Abby wondered if she'd annoyed him. Oh God, supposing he'd just lost a brother or sister? How awful. Christ, she was so tactless. And then she thought that Chris and Christ were very alike. The only difference being the T.

'Yes I'm an only child. And I'm thirty-one.' He flicked a look in her direction. 'Do you always ask this many questions?'

'Yes, usually,' Abby said, thinking *this is nothing, wait until I really get started.*

He didn't comment and Abby decided to keep quiet for a bit. Obviously he wasn't in the mood for answering questions. Maybe he was never in the mood for answering questions. She shot him a sideways look. Maybe he had something to hide.

'Don't you like being asked stuff?' she asked.

'I don't mind.' He looked amused and Abby decided that she'd imagined his pique.

They pulled into a car park a few minutes later. 'I wasn't sure what you liked, so I thought pub food was safest. Is that okay?' he asked. They were at the Queens Head in Dogmersfield.

'I like anything I don't have to cook myself. This is great.' Abby smiled and they went inside.

Chris was very well mannered. He held all the doors open for her, pulled out her chair, he even let her order first.

'Right, my turn to ask questions,' he said when the waiter left with their order.

'I think we should take turns, actually. You asked most in the pub when we met.'

Chris looked sceptical but didn't argue. 'Okay. Me first. Why did you split up with your ex and how long were you together?'

'Just over four years. And we split up because we weren't in love.' *And because I fell in love with my best friend's boyfriend. No I didn't. I do not love Nick.* 'That was two questions. My turn. How many women have you slept with and what's your longest relationship?'

Chris, who'd just taken a sip of his newly delivered beer, spluttered. 'Hey – you're getting too personal.'

'I'll answer anything you ask me. I'm not scared.' Abby grinned and Chris laughed.

'Fine.' He went quiet for a moment. 'Eleven. I've slept with eleven women. And my longest relationship was with Emma. Ended a couple of years ago, lasted for five years.' He grinned. 'My turn. Have you ever had a threesome?'

'Yes. My turn. Have you?'

'Hey, wait up. Not enough information.' Chris sat up straight, eyes wide, pupils dilated. 'This threesome. Two men, two women? One of each?'

'It's my turn first.' Abby sipped her drink, taking her time, prolonging the moment. 'Have you ever had a threesome?'

Chris looked sorrowful. 'No. Not through lack of trying though. So? Men? Women?'

'Two men.'

'Did you like it? How long ago was it?'

Abby gave him a stern look. 'Wait your turn. Have you ever hired a prostitute?'

'No. Did you enjoy it?'

'Yes. Very much. What's the most perverted sexual act you've carried out?'

Chris grinned. 'My ex before last liked being put on a collar and lead and being whipped.'

'Really? And did you enjoy that?'

'My turn first. When did this threesome happen?'

'Last summer.'

'I hate to admit it, but yes I enjoyed it. She had a lovely backside. Who was the threesome with?'

'Matthew, my ex and his friend Jared. What's your second most perverted act?'

Chris paused, obviously thinking. 'The same girlfriend, she was really into public sex. I handcuffed her to the bike sheds at the station. We had oral and anal sex. Do you still see Jared? Did you actually have sex with them both?'

'I see him sometimes. And yes. My turn now, two questions. Have you ever had a sexual experience with a man? Do you have any videos of yourself having sex?'

'No and no. Have you ever been with a woman?'

'I've kissed a woman.'

'Really?' Chris sat forward and Abby knew, without a doubt, that he had an erection.

'Yes. I didn't really like it though. I like muscle too much. Have you got an erection?'

Chris looked totally shocked. And then he gave a bark of laughter. 'I don't believe you! Yes I have an erection.' He looked her over. 'Are you wet?'

'Oh yes.' Abby sat back while the waiter put their meals in front of them.

They locked eyes.

Abby looked down at her meal. And then she looked up at Chris. 'I'm not hungry anymore.'

'Me either,' he murmured.

'Pay the bill. I'll go out to the car,' Abby said and walked quickly outside.

Chris followed a couple of minutes later. He opened her door and then he slid behind the wheel. And a few minutes later they were pulling into a driveway.

'Nice house,' Abby said. They were in a cul-de-sac in Church Crookham.

'Thanks,' Chris said and grabbed her hand, pulling her inside. He shut the door and pulled her into his arms. He kissed her and Abby fell into the kiss. He was an amazing kisser. His hands roamed her back and he deepened the kiss. Abby went straight for his fly and he kicked his trousers off. Abby took him in her mouth and he moaned. 'God, you are so amazing.' And a couple of minutes later he grabbed her arms and pulled her up. 'No more, I can't bear it.' And he pulled her into a nearby room, kissing her again, pushing her up against the dining room table. He pulled her top over her head and pushed her jeans over her thighs. She was left in bra and thong and he looked her over with a long exhale. And then he removed her underwear and hoisted her up so she was sitting on the table. He kissed her breasts and then her neck and then her mouth and she slid forward so he was against her.

'Condom,' she whispered, desperate to have him inside her.

'Bugger. Hold on.' He disappeared for a minute and re-appeared, already tearing the wrapper of a condom. He slid it on and walked back over. His hand went to the back of Abby's head, pulling her mouth to his. His other hand went to her buttocks and he slid inside her and Abby gasped with the suddenness of it. He was big, very big and she bit back a cry when he moved fully inside her. It felt good though, too good and she held on to him for dear life as he thrust over and over.

He kissed her hard, his lips bruising her mouth and all the time he gyrated against her and she was shaking against him, so aroused she could hardly bear it.

He let her slide to the floor and turned her gently around so she was leant over the table and then he was inside her again. His hand reached round and cupped her, his index finger doing something really amazing against her and suddenly she was screaming her orgasm and he was bucking even harder into her and then it was all over and he collapsed against her.

'Are you okay?' he asked when she could finally breathe again. He kissed her shoulder and straightened, pulling her up with him.

'Yeah.' Abby gave a shiver and smiled weakly. 'I've never done that before. Slept with a complete stranger I mean.'

'Really?' He looked surprised and Abby didn't blame him. He probably thought she was a complete tart. And she was. Here she was, in love with Nick, sleeping with a practical stranger on their first date. It didn't feel like betrayal though. It was so different to what she and Nick had shared. That had been making love, chemistry fuelled passion. With Chris it was pure and simple sex. It had been good, amazing even, but only because he was good at what he did. There were no emotions involved.

Though she did like him. She looked at his sceptical expression and smiled. 'Believe it or not, I've only slept with five men. That includes Jared by the way.'

Chris's eyes went a shade darker. 'Jared's a lucky bastard. I don't suppose you'd do it again? The threesome? With a woman this time?'

Abby smiled up at him and felt herself getting warm again. 'Nothing's impossible,' she said, voice husky and Chris groaned.

'Christ. You are so unbelievably sexy,' he said and kissed her again.

Abby got home at nine the next morning and she could barely walk.

Matthew and Olly were in the kitchen and Olly ran straight into her arms. 'Mummy, I missed you. Daddy got out of bed and there was a big spider in the bath. It was this big.' He held his arms as wide as he could and made straining noises.

'Wow.' Abby switched the kettle on and listened as he chatted about the spider and how many clouds were in the sky and how long he'd weed for and what he'd dreamt about and then he went through to the playroom and he was still chatting.

'Good night?' Matthew asked with a smile when she finally got to sit down.

'Oh yes.' Abby sipped her coffee and thought about going outside for a cigarette. God, her legs hurt.

'It's not like you to shag on the first night,' he said.

Abby stared at him. Was it that obvious? Did he mind? He didn't look as if he did. He was smiling, expression amused. 'I know. I don't know what happened.'

'Is he that nice?'

Abby sipped some more coffee and thought about it. 'Yes he is. He's a really nice bloke. Not my usual type – too nice if anything.' She put her mug down and sighed. 'Bloody good sex though.'

Matthew gave a little grimace. 'And how are things with Nick. You missed your driving lesson this week didn't you?'

'We did it last night. I couldn't do Tuesday because I was working and I missed last week because I was ill. It was okay. Though it was pissing down again. I really don't like driving in the rain. Nick didn't say a lot, he's very pissed off about Chris.'

'Don't blame him. If I still wanted you for myself, I'd be pissed off too.'

Abby grinned. 'No you wouldn't. You don't have a jealous bone in your body.'

'Hm. I wouldn't be too sure about that.'

Abby gave him a sceptical look but decided to let it go. 'Did you get the magazine article in on time?'

Matthew got up and put his plate in the dishwasher. 'Yep, it was pretty good I think. I should hopefully hear back next week.' He looked at his watch. 'I have to go. I'll pick Olly up at nine on Sunday.' He paused at the door and looked back. 'Are you seeing the cop again?'

Abby nodded. 'Saturday. I'll ask Becky or Fiona to babysit.'

Matthew gave her a long look and then he left.

Chapter Thirty

Jo was loving living back with Nick. It was so nice to have her own house again. And to have privacy during the day. And she adored being pregnant. She'd lie in bed and think about the baby and dream about what he or she would look like. The only fly in the ointment was Nick. He was being so grumpy, and totally unenthusiastic about the baby.

Abby wasn't much better though she had been better since she'd started seeing Chris. That was another thing Nick had been funny about. He'd asked how Abby's date had gone – the first proper sentence he'd uttered in days. They were sat at the table. Nick eating, Jo reading her latest pregnancy book and drinking herbal tea.

'It went really well,' Jo had replied. 'And they went out again last night. She was totally knackered though, I don't know how she's going to get through work tonight. Did you know the sex of the baby is already decided?'

'Why was she so knackered?' Nick asked with such an edge to his voice that Jo looked up from her book.

And then she smiled. 'Why do you think?' Oh bugger, now she'd lost her place on the page. She skimmed down, trying to find the baby sex bit.

'She slept with him? On their second date?'

Jo looked up again. 'What's wrong with you? They slept together on their first date actually. So what?'

Nick shrugged and his expression turned from strange to blank. Jo wondered, suddenly, if he was jealous. But then she dismissed the idea. He just wasn't the jealous type. 'I'm just surprised that's all. She just split up with Matthew. And I hadn't pegged her as a slut.'

'Nick!' Jo spluttered on her tea. 'Don't be so nasty. Abby is not a slut. It's about time she had some fun.'

'Like you did you mean?' Nick looked at her with narrowed eyes and she felt her stomach clench.

'I don't know what you're talking about,' she said, trying to keep her voice even. If she yelled, he'd yell and then she'd end up crying. She hated being yelled at.

'Yes you do,' Nick said evenly, tone completely at odds with the fury on his face. 'You're both sluts.' He sighed and gave his dinner a desperate look. 'I need a cigarette.' And pushing his untouched meal to one side he got up and went outside.

Jo breathed a sigh of relief and turned back to her book.

Nick lit his cigarette and then he dialled Abby on his mobile.

'Hello?' A man's voice said and Nick immediately thought of the cop.

'Who is this?'

'Matthew. Is that you, Nick?'

Nick sighed. 'Sorry mate. Yeah. Is Abby there?'

'She's asleep. She's working tonight and she had a heavy night last night.' He chuckled.

Nick sucked down half his cigarette. 'I heard,' he said curtly and hung up. He paced a bit, trying to get his temper under control. He just wanted to hit something, someone. *Anything*. God, she was such a bitch. How could she be sleeping around already? Was she that obsessed by sex? Or maybe she really liked this man. Maybe he'd end up moving in and then they'd get married and then when Nick split up with Jo – he had to believe that would happen – she'd be off limits. Not that he'd want her now anyway. Slag.

He realised he was smoking the filter and lit another cigarette. And then he paced some more. He just wanted to speak to her. Find out why she'd done it. Was it because she was in love already? Or was she doing it to get him out of her system? Maybe the guy was just irresistible. He checked his watch, seven forty-five. She'd be asleep for almost another two hours. He took another deep drag and almost burnt his fingers. Christ, these cigarettes got shorter and shorter.

He thought about lighting another one and then decided to go to the gym instead. Pound some of his frustration away before he spoke to Abby.

Chapter Thirty-One

When Abby came downstairs at nine thirty-five, Matthew was watching football and eating Pringles. Abby took a couple from the tube and sat down next to him. 'God, I wish I didn't have to work tonight,' she said.

Matthew glanced over. 'You look like crap. Nick phoned by the way. He said he couldn't get through on your mobile. I told him you turn it off when you sleep. He sounded really pissed off and when I said something about your heavy night he said, "I heard". Are you sure nothing happened between you?'

Abby, whose heart had started to race at the first mention of Nick's name, sighed. He'd been pissed off enough at her having a date, God knows what he was thinking now. 'I never said that.'

Matthew switched the TV off. 'You did sleep with him?'

Abby nodded and leant back against the settee. 'Not until we split up. But yeah.'

'And? What happened?'

'Jo was pregnant. It was after she found out. I'd resisted up until then. I didn't want to do anything to hurt Jo but then I realised it was never going to happen – not with a baby on the way and I was drunk and I bumped into him.' She shrugged. 'It was just the one night.'

'But he wanted something more?'

Abby stood up. 'I have to go to work. It's irrelevant now, Matthew. He's with Jo. I'm seeing someone else. It was never going to happen.'

'Why? Because of Jo?' Matthew followed her out to the porch. 'Where are you going? Where's your bike?'

'I've got a lift.' Abby picked up her bag and opened the front door. She threw him a puzzled look over her shoulder. 'I've not ridden my bike to work since Nick moved out, didn't you notice?'

'No,' Matthew gave an apologetic shrug. 'Is Nick giving you a lift?'

'No, his nephew. Nick only agreed to teach me to drive if I stopped cycling to work.' Matthew opened his mouth and Abby ploughed on, 'Forget it, Matthew. I don't want to talk about it. And if Nick rings back tell him it's none of his business.'

135

'Yeah right. Like I'm going to say that to Nick.' Matthew rocked back on his heels and crossed his arms over his chest. 'You're mad. Completely mad. You and Nick are perfect for each other.'

'No. We are not.' Will pulled up at the curb and Abby moved off. 'We're terrible together and he's having a baby with my best friend. Let it go.'

'You're pathetic,' Matthew called after her.

'Sticks and stones,' Abby called back and then she got in the car and Will pulled away.

She'd been at work for ten minutes when her mobile started to ring. Nick's name popped up on the display and she considered ignoring it. But she had to talk to him sooner or later. Best get it over with. She pressed the button to take the call, annoyed to realise she was nervous.

'If you're ringing to yell at me, don't bother,' she said.

'Why? Just tell me why?' he said, just below a yell.

'Because I can. I'm single, remember. I'm over sixteen and he wore a condom.'

'Didn't it mean anything? You and me, I mean?' He sounded sad now and that was far harder to take than his anger.

'Yes it did. But it can't happen. You're with Jo.' Abby looked up and realised that all three of her workmates were staring at her. She got up and walked through to the kitchen. 'Nick, you need to get over this. I'm dating now. We're going out again on Friday. I like him. It's not like it was with me and you but its fun and that's what I need right now. I don't want to fall in love. I just want to enjoy myself.'

'By being a tart?'

He was back to angry and Abby sighed. 'Yes. By being a tart. Please don't give me this crap, Nick. I've had estate agents and strange people traipsing all over my house all week. I'm having to sell the house I love and move somewhere horrible. Olly wee'd in my handbag today and I'm premenstrual. I don't need this today.'

There was a pause and Abby felt tears prick the back of her eyes. She swallowed the lump in her throat and blinked a few times.

'I'm sorry,' Nick said. He still sounded furious but was obviously making an effort to hide it. 'Why'd he wee in your bag?'

'Because there's a monster in the downstairs toilet, and a dinosaur in the upstairs toilet.'

'Right. Silly question.'

Another long silence.

'I have to go and do some work,' Abby said.

'Okay,' Nick replied and Abby couldn't stop a tear escaping. She felt sick. Really, really sick. He sounded so down and it was all so unfair.

'You realise that half our attraction is because we can't have each other?' she said in an effort to lighten the mood. 'If we were both free and single we'd probably hate each other.'

'Who said I don't already hate you?' Nick said and Abby smiled. Tears were falling freely now, but still she smiled.

'I love you,' she said and then she stopped smiling. 'Shit, sorry. No I don't.'

More silence. Then, 'Abby, you're right,' he exhaled loudly, 'I hate it, but you're right. You're right to date. I can't leave Jo so it's unfair to expect you to sit around and wait for me. And it wouldn't be you if you did, you wouldn't be the Abby I love.'

'Don't,' Abby whispered.

'I'm sorry. I won't phone anymore. We'll just meet for your driving lesson and I'll be really bossy and horrible and then you can hate me and it'll be easier,' he said, voice full of forced joviality.

'Who said I don't already hate you?'

There was another silence and Abby thought that Nick was probably smiling.

'I'll see you on Thursday,' he said after a while and Abby nodded even though he couldn't see her.

'Okay.'

They hung up and Abby grabbed some kitchen roll, blowing her nose and trying to stem the flow of tears. And suddenly Judy was there and she was hugging her and she let herself cry, really cry. Hiccups and snot and shudders and everything.

'Is it Nick?'

Abby nodded and sniffed. She blew her nose on her already sodden piece of kitchen roll and tried to compose herself.

'He's upset about your date? I take it you enjoyed yourself?' Judy led her to the window and they lit cigarettes.

Abby filled her lungs gratefully. 'Yeah. It was good.' She exhaled and inhaled again. 'He's not Nick though.'

'Are you sure you're not just wanting what you can't have?' Judy asked a little hesitantly.

Abby smiled. 'I thought of that but I don't think so. He drives me crazy. Really, really crazy but there's just this amazing chemistry between us. With Chris it's fun. He's sexy and sweet and funny, but he just doesn't have the same effect.'

'That would be too easy, huh?' Judy gave a rueful smile and flicked her cigarette out of the window. 'Best get back to work.'

Abby did the same and they went through to the office.

Her four night shift went surprisingly fast. She slept Thursday morning and in the afternoon she cleaned the house from top to bottom. Some very interested buyers wanted to see the house that evening and the estate agent had suggested, very gently, that it might help sell the house if it was a little more presentable.

And then it was time for her driving lesson. Matthew arrived to babysit – he'd offered when he heard people were going to be looking round the house. Nick knocked on the door at six and before Abby even got to the kitchen door, Matthew was letting him in.

'Nick, hi,' he said, standing to one side and watching Nick walk in.

'Hi, Matthew. How are you? Abby.' Nick greeted them both, his inscrutable gaze settling on Abby.

'How's Jo?' Matthew asked him, closing the front door and following them into the kitchen.

'Nick!' Olly came running from the playroom and stopped just short of Nick. 'I got a new Power Ranger. He's blue and I called him Pokemon. D'you want to see him?'

'In a minute.' Nick smiled and ruffled his hair. Olly beamed back and then ran back to the playroom.

'Jo's fine,' he said to Matthew. Abby watched them in fascination. Nick was stood in the doorway, stance casual, arms crossed, leaning against the door frame. Matthew was leant back against the worktop, arms also crossed. Neither looked particularly enamoured with the other.

'Good, good. I hear you're having a baby. Very exciting news. You must be very happy.' Matthew tried to sound jolly but failed dismally. He looked, and sounded, defensive and provocative, and Abby hid a smile.

Nick scowled. 'You know I'm not happy. And you've got a bloody cheek casting stones at me when you shagged my girlfriend.'

Matthew looked perplexed for a minute and then he heaved a sigh, expression back to pissed off. 'And you didn't do the same?'

Nick didn't falter. 'No I didn't. Abby wasn't your girlfriend at the time.' He shot Abby a "what'd you tell him for?" look.

'And you wouldn't have done it if she had been?' Matthew gave a dry laugh.

Nick forced his eyes away from Abby, and said irritably, 'What's your problem? You want me to leave Jo to have the baby on her own? You think I want to be with her?'

'All I care about is Abby. I don't give a shit about Jo or your baby or you doing the right thing,' Matthew said and pushed away from the counter. 'I'm going to give Ol his bath. Enjoy your driving lesson.' He kissed Abby's cheek and left the room, his entire body rigid with rage.

Abby watched him go and then turned to face Nick. He was staring at her, expression unreadable. 'What the hell did you say to him?'

'Nothing. I admitted to sleeping with you. Everything else he's figured out himself.'

Nick grunted. 'He's very protective of you.'

'What did you expect? We were together for a long time. We're good friends.'

'He's got a bloody cheek after the way he's treated you.'

Abby shrugged, 'Maybe he knew he wasn't hurting me.' And then she looked intrigued. 'That's the first time he's admitted to sleeping with Jo. Did you know for definite? Jo didn't come clean did she?'

'No. It was so bloody obvious though. Did you even doubt it?'

'No, I suppose not.

'Are we driving tonight or what?' Abby asked, and Nick straightened up.

'After you,' he said and stood to one side.

The driving lesson was uneventful. They drove to Basingstoke and back and Abby enjoyed herself despite the atmosphere. Nick was all business, no chat. They were home two hours after they left and Nick didn't even stop for a cigarette. He got straight in the driver's seat and cranked the engine over. 'See you next week.'

'Fine,' Abby said with the same lack of enthusiasm and he pulled away.

As soon as Matthew left she phoned Fiona. 'Can you teach me to drive?' she asked without as much as a "hello" first.

There was a silence. And then, 'What's happened?'

'Nick's being really cold and horrible and I just think it would be easier if I didn't have to see him at all.'

Another silence. A shorter one this time. 'I don't see why not. Will he mind?'

'We'll soon find out.'

'Is Matthew still there?'

Abby brightened slightly. 'No, he just left. It was really quite funny when Nick got here. I thought the two of them were going to have a punch up. Matthew did his macho protective thing and said he knew about Nick and me and told Nick all he cared about was me.' She thought about that for a moment. 'It was actually sweet when you think about it. Matthew can be so lovely. Oh and he admitted to sleeping with Jo.'

'Uh-huh. And how do you feel about that?'

'No different. I guess I already knew.'

'It was pretty much a foregone conclusion,' Fiona agreed. 'How did it go with the people looking round the house?'

Abby blew out a sigh. 'They like it. The estate agent thinks they'll come back with an offer.'

'That's good, Abs. The house is too big for just you and Ol. It would be easier for you if you had somewhere smaller.'

'I know. It's just so much hassle. I keep thinking I should start sorting stuff out, clear the loft and the garage, but I just can't face it. I can't believe how much crap we've accumulated in just a few years.'

Fiona made sympathetic noises. 'Give me a shout if you need any help.'

Abby said thank you and they exchanged goodbyes. She thought about starting on sorting out the playroom but one look at the mess in there and she closed the door instead.

Tomorrow. She'd start tomorrow.

Chapter Thirty-Two

Jo went round to see Abby the next morning.

'I hate Nick,' she said as soon as the front door was opened. 'Christ. You look like shit. Are you okay?'

Abby stood to one side and nodded. 'I'm okay. Just feeling a bit fragile. I think it's because it's my first night off – I always seem to feel worse for my first nights sleep.'

Jo led the way into the kitchen and flicked on the kettle. 'Sit down. I'll make coffee. Is Olly at nursery?'

Abby sank down onto a chair and laid her head on the table. 'Yeah. If I zonk out, wake me at twelve.'

'What's wrong? Do you feel sick or tired? Or both?'

'Both.' She lifted her head and raked both hands through her hair. 'I feel exhausted and dizzy and nauseous.'

'Are you sure you're not pregnant?' Jo asked jokingly, pouring coffee and not looking at her friend.

There was no reply and when she turned round to put the mugs on the table, Abby was looking into space. 'Abby?'

No response.

'Abby?' Jo said more loudly and sat down next to her friend.

Abby focused slowly and if anything, looked even paler.

'Oh Jesus. You're not are you?'

'No! I can't be.' Abby shook her head vehemently. 'Definitely not. Besides, I feel too pre-menstrual. No I can't be.'

Jo started to tell her that she'd felt the same way but something stopped her. Abby looked close to hyperventilating already. It might just push her over the edge.

'Let's talk about something else,' Abby said with a determined look on her face. 'Why'd you hate Nick?'

Jo sighed heavily. 'He's being such a wanker you wouldn't believe it. I started suggesting names last night and he told me I was only nine weeks pregnant and I was completely obsessed and that I needed to relax. And then he told me that thirty per cent of pregnancies end in miscarriage.' She looked at Abby, fear creeping over her again. 'Is that true?'

'I don't think so. Maybe at first but every day you're pregnant it's less likely.' Abby looked sympathetic. 'Has Nick shown any interest at all?'

'No. None.' She shook her head and then shuddered. 'He's horrible. He's so cold and unfriendly. Sometimes it's almost as if he hates me. I thought it was just work or something to start with but then he started yelling at me about loads of stuff, so maybe it's not work.' She looked at the table, the scratched and worn surface blurring beneath tears. 'I think it's me. I think maybe he's feeling trapped because of the baby or something.'

'Oh, Jo.' Abby put out a hand and stroked her arm. 'I'm sure that's not it. What's he yelling at you about?'

'Everything. Last night he came in and yelled because I'd cleared up some of his papers. And then I didn't answer the phone quick enough and he yelled again. And then I asked him about names and he said about miscarrying. It's okay most of the time because he works such long hours and he's hardly ever there.' She looked up and tried to smile. 'Maybe he'd just had a bad day or something. It's normally not that bad.'

Abby stroked her arm some more and she sat up straighter. 'I'm sorry. I shouldn't be so miserable. I should be happy. I've got everything I wanted. Hey. I know, let's go shopping!'

Abby gave a sad smile. 'I can't, Jo. I have to start sorting stuff out. We got an offer on the house this morning and the couple are really eager to move in. They've got no chain and they want to be in within the month.'

'Oh my God! Can't you say no? Do you have to move?' Jo looked round, feeling panicked for her friend. It was such a mess, such a jumble of stuff, such a mammoth task. 'You haven't even found somewhere to move yet.'

'I'm checking out some places tomorrow. There's a really nice two bed up by the station without a chain.'

'Two bed?' Jo said, feeling rather faint all of a sudden.'

'It's all I can afford if I want to stay in Fleet. And I want to stay in Velmead catchment if possible. I went to Heatherside and I hated it and none of the other schools are as good. Besides it's only for me and Olly. Why'd we need three bedrooms?'

Jo felt herself get sleepy at the school part. Despite being pregnant, she couldn't imagine ever getting excited about schools. School was school as far as she was concerned. As long as the uniform was a nice colour she didn't much care about anything else. And then she thought about the two bedrooms and shuddered. 'You'd just best hope you're not pregnant,' she said.

Abby closed the door behind her friend, her words resounding in her ears. Pregnant? God, but it made sense. She went through to the kitchen and checked the calendar. Her last period was on the 6th March. She was almost two weeks late. She dropped into the nearest chair and buried her head in her hands. Oh God. This couldn't be happening. She couldn't be having Nick's baby too.

She looked at the clock. Twelve ten. She had five minutes to get to nursery. She belted through the garage and grabbed her bike and got to Olly with seconds to spare. She stopped in Fleet on the way back and bought sandwiches and a pregnancy test from Boots. And then they went home and she settled Olly with his cheese and tomato sandwich before heading to the toilet to pee.

The blue line came up immediately. Very dark, very definite. She was very pregnant. Well, six weeks. She wrapped the stick in toilet paper and dumped it in the bin. And then she sat on the toilet lid and buried her head in her hands. Oh Christ. She was pregnant. Pregnant with Nick's baby. She needed to talk to someone desperately. She needed a hug. She thought of Jo. No! Nick. NO! Becky wouldn't be able to keep quiet and Fiona was out for the day. And then she thought of Matthew. She could trust Matthew. And suddenly she wanted him there so badly.

She went through to the kitchen, phoned him and asked him to drop round. And then she sat next to Olly and forced herself to eat. And all the time the words swam round in her head. Pregnant. Pregnant. Pregnant. Pregnant. Another baby. Nick's baby. Two bedrooms. Jo. Pregnant. Pregnant.

She swallowed the last of her sandwich and took Olly through to the playroom. She put a Power Rangers video on for him and then she heard a key in the door and Matthew came belting through.

'What's wrong? Are you okay? Is Ol alright?'

'I'm here, Daddy. I'm 'kay.' Olly gave Matthew a hug and Abby watched him slump with relief. And then he looked up at her. 'What's wrong?' he mouthed over his son's head.

Abby let him finish greeting Olly and then they went through to the kitchen. She switched on the kettle and rested against the worktop. Matthew leant his hip a few inches away and folded his arms over his chest.

'I'm pregnant,' she told him and watched his face go pale. Then red. Then it went a normal colour but wore a confused expression.

'But how?'

'Well it can't be yours. Even if you were still functional we haven't done it in weeks.'

'So it's Nick's?' Matthew said slowly. 'Oh shit, Abby. Didn't you use condoms?'

'Yes! Well, maybe not all the time. But most of the time!' She sighed. 'Does it really matter? It's a bit bloody late now.'

'What are you going to do? Are you sure? That you're pregnant I mean?'

'I just did a test. And I'm not going to do anything.'

'What?' Matthew looked surprised and then his brow creased up and his eyes narrowed. 'You can't just ignore it, Abby. It's not going to go away. You have to tell Nick. Or get an abortion or something.'

'I'm not getting an abortion.' Abby crossed her arms and lifted her chin. 'You know how I feel about abortion. And I'm not telling Nick. At least, I'm not telling him the baby's his,' she amended quickly. 'I'm telling everyone it's yours.'

Matthew's mouth dropped open and he looked utterly shocked. And then his face turned red and he took a step closer. 'No way! Why the hell should I take the blame?' he said through clenched teeth.

Abby stood her ground. 'Because you love me and we're friends. Nobody will be surprised – we were together at more or less the right time. If we did it on the last night before the swap and I got pregnant straight after my period – not impossible, it could've been yours. You offered to move back in. I refused. People will think I'm stupid, they won't blame you.'

'No! No way! What about the birth? What about afterwards? I'll be expected to pay maintenance for two kids and what about visitation? I'm hardly going to have Nick's baby to stay!'

'You'll be paying maintenance for Olly, nobody will know if you're paying extra for the baby. And we can make something up about visitation. You'll stay with Olly when I work anyway, so you'd see the baby then.' She thought about that and suddenly she felt nervous. 'You will still stay won't you? I can't work otherwise?'

Matthew stared at her, the colour gradually receding. And then he sighed and gathered her in his arms, holding her tight against him. 'You're a fucking disaster, woman,' he said against her hair and Abby immediately burst into tears.

'Hey! I was joking,' Matthew said quickly and Abby smiled into his chest.

'No you weren't.' She pulled away and wiped at her eyes. 'I'm sorry. Shit! I can't believe this.'

'Neither can I. Why the hell can't you just tell Nick the truth?'

'And what? He'll leave Jo for me? I don't think so. And if he did, then what? Jo would fall to pieces.' She shook her head and turned to make coffee. 'It's best this way and if you won't agree to let me say the baby's yours, I'll pretend I had a one night stand or something.'

Matthew gave her a long look and then he shrugged. 'Sod it. Tell 'em it's mine.'

Abby finished making the coffee. 'What's going on? You've given in too easily.'

Matthew took his mug and sat down. 'I think Nick will work it out.'

Abby froze. 'You're going to tell him aren't you?'

'No!' Matthew sat a little straighter. 'Of course not. But he loves you. He'll work it out eventually.'

'No he won't. He can't.' She shook her head so hard it made her dizzy. 'And I'm not telling him until I'm twelve weeks. I'm not telling anyone until then.' She rubbed her eyes and wished it were bedtime. 'And to make everything worse, I have to give up smoking again.'

Matthew groaned. 'Oh God no. Shit, am I glad I don't live with you anymore!'

'Hey! I'm not that bad.'

'You were a nightmare with Olly. I didn't think I was going to survive it. I can't believe you actually started smoking again after that.' He gave her a disgusted look and finished his coffee.

'It was stress,' Abby said flatly. 'I wouldn't have got through the lack of sleep without nicotine. God, I hope this one sleeps better. Do you remember how awful Ol was? He didn't sleep through the night until he was two and a half.'

Matthew smiled. And then he stood up. 'I have to go back to work. Will you be okay?'

Abby nodded. 'Yeah. Thanks, Matthew. I feel better now.'

'I actually felt better before I saw you,' Matthew said in a dry voice, 'but I'm glad I helped.'

Abby walked him to the door. 'I'll see you on Monday?'

'Yep.' Matthew kissed her forehead and gave her a quick hug. 'Call me if you need anything before then.'

'Thanks.' Abby watched him walk down the drive. 'Matthew,' she called.

He stopped and looked back at her.

'I love you.'

He grinned. 'I love you too, babe.'

Abby found it very, very hard to keep quiet about the pregnancy. She didn't know if it was because it was her second time round or because of the lack of sleep or just because of the different mix of DNA, but she felt terrible. Not just in the morning, but all day. Eight days after she found out she was pregnant, immediately after her first full night of sleep after working for four, she was violently sick as soon as she got up. And from then on she was sick every morning. It wasn't quite as bad if she worked – eating through the night seemed to help, but she still felt sick, and was often sick later in the day instead. She went to see the doctor when she was eight weeks pregnant and he gave her some anti-sickness tablets. They helped, though they didn't get rid of the nausea. She had no energy and she felt weak and out of sorts all the time.

The fact that nobody guessed she was pregnant was nothing short of a miracle. How could people be so blind? Or maybe they were just so self-involved they didn't notice. And then she thought that maybe she looked pale and drawn and sick all the time and that was why nobody had realised. But if she looked so terrible, surely she wouldn't have attracted Nick in the first place?

She hadn't seen Nick. Not once. She phoned him the day she found out she was pregnant and told him she was finding it too hard seeing him every week. She explained that Fiona was going to teach her to drive instead and thanked him for starting her off.

He was depressingly agreeable.

Jo said things hadn't improved at home. Nick was still being an arsehole. He'd started showing some interest in the baby, but as far as his attitude to Jo went, nothing had changed. Thankfully, she hadn't mentioned pregnancy again.

Abby had successfully given up smoking. Not that she'd doubted she would. Very aware of her faults, Abby knew that lack of determination wasn't one of them. The sickness had made it harder – she'd not suffered one day of sickness with Olly.

Most surprising was that none of her friends had noticed that she'd quit. Granted she hadn't been out drinking or socialising, but they came to see her and Fiona took her out driving at least once a week. Her colleagues at work had noticed of course but she told them she was trying to save money. They'd also noticed how ill she looked but put it down to her "heartbreak" over Nick.

She was due to vacate the house when she was twelve weeks pregnant. She'd looked at the two-bed house and ended up putting in an offer. It was accepted and everything was going through at a scarily quick pace. When she found out she was pregnant she'd considered moving out of the area so that she could have three bedrooms but then on balance she decided against it. If they were still in the two bed when the baby got bigger she could always sleep downstairs. Or the baby could share with Olly. She decided to wait and see what happened.

The house *was* nice. It was in a block of four houses and was the last one you came to. It was surrounded by gardens and very private. The back door (French) was next to the front door and it had a garage. The garden was a decent size for a two bed and it was in good condition. The current owners, a married couple with two children had decorated recently and the garden was lovely. It even had a two storey wooden playhouse and double swing set that they were leaving behind.

She'd been packing madly. The garage was full of stuff she planned to sell at a car boot sale. Everything they didn't use every day was in boxes. Matthew had been a great help and had practically moved back in – he was sleeping in the spare room – so he could be on hand if she needed anything. He'd started his job for the magazine and was loving every minute of it. His boss had loved the swapping story and was hoping for a follow up. The way things were going, he'd be able to start a regular column just on the fallout of the swap.

Abby had told Chris what was going on and told him it was best if they stopped seeing each other. He was disappointed but said he understood. It was sad – Abby thought they'd probably have enjoyed themselves for a while – but she'd been too ill to want anything sexual anyway. It was the first time she'd ever lost her libido. She and Matthew had been active right through until Olly's birth and had only waited two weeks afterwards.

Still, at least she didn't have to shave her legs. There was always a positive side. And from now on that was how she was going to live her life. Look for the positive. Be a my-glass-is-half-full not half-empty kind of person. A positive-full-glass person. A posiflasson.

Chapter Thirty-Three

When Abby was ten weeks pregnant, two weeks before moving day, Matthew loaded his car to bursting point, and the two of them headed off to Farnborough to do a car boot sale. Olly was with Matthew's mother for the day, the sun was shining and Abby hadn't been sick for the first day in a week.

The car boot sale was held in a multi-storey car park. The bottom floor was mainly under cover and the second floor was on the roof. If it was raining and you wanted to be guaranteed an indoor pitch you had to get there by seven or eight in the morning. There were a lot of regulars and Abby had never managed to get there earlier than them. In the end she decided that they left their cars overnight and got lifts over in the morning. Luckily it was a nice day so they arrived at half past nine and lined up in the car park alongside the other sellers.

The car boot sale started at nine thirty and the women came round at quarter past nine collecting money. Matthew paid the eight pounds and got his raffle ticket and ten minutes later they started going in. Abby knew the car boot sale drill and they were unpacked and set up within ten minutes. People were already milling around – the public could get in earlier than the official start time of eleven if they paid five pounds rather than fifty pence. Some of the other car booters were also wondering around, probably on the prowl for a bargain.

Abby put some prices on things she hadn't already priced. She marked things up cheaply – the object was to get rid of the stuff, she didn't want to end up lugging it home again. She priced books at five pence and above depending on value and condition. Games were twenty pence. She put Olly's toy Hotpoint cooker up at five pounds. It was a really cool toy, the buttons made the rings lights up and make different noises and it had an upper and lower cooker and loads of accessories. It even had a timer that went off when the cooking noises finished. And it looked like the real thing. It had cost almost twenty pounds and Olly had only ever used it as a car park. There was a puppet show too. Thirty pounds from the Early Learning Centre. Olly got it for Christmas and he'd never played with it. Abby put a ten pound tag on it. If she didn't sell it she'd put it in the local newspaper or on Ebay.

A man with hair growing out of his ears stopped and asked if they had any DVDs. Someone else asked for Power Rangers. And then someone wanted old action men. They sold a bag of old Thomas the Tank Engine trains for three pounds – Olly preferred the ones that went on the track. Things got quiet after that and Abby wished desperately that she could have a cigarette. She looked at the man at the stall next door. He was wearing a string vest under a beige shirt and he was smoking. Abby edged closer and tried to breathe in some smoke.

'Abby!' Matthew pulled her back. 'Secondary smoke is just as bad. Do some more pricing if you need to do something.'

'I've done everything. Do you think they'll let them in soon?' They could see the queue to get in – it wound all the way round the outside of the car park.

Matthew checked his watch. 'Ten minutes. Relax would you.' He looked her over. 'You're starting to show already.'

Abby looked down. 'I know. I look fat. And I've got a spot.'

Matthew followed the direction of her finger. 'There's nothing there. And you don't look fat. You look pregnant.'

'Only because you know.' She shifted position and looked at the beige man again. He'd nearly finished the cigarette. One long drag – Abby found herself inhaling with him – and he stubbed the cigarette out. There'd been at least another three or four good drags left on it and Abby itched to pick it up and finish it. Christ, she needed to get a grip. The man probably had herpes or something.

'Stop staring,' Matthew hissed and Abby gave a start. The man was looking at her, well leering actually. She looked away abruptly.

Their other neighbour dropped an ornament and glass smashed all over the place. She moved her table to cover the mess and that was that. Diversion over.

Luckily people started coming over shortly after that. And then more, and more, and pretty soon they were taking money and they didn't have time to talk to each other.

A gaunt woman wearing a gothicy t-shirt with the slogan "If God's not available talk to me" looked at the cooker. 'How much is it love?'

'Five pounds,' Abby said, thinking *read the bloody label*!

'Does it really work?'

'No. It's a toy.' Abby pressed some buttons to demonstrate.

'Ah. What a lovely cooker? Wouldn't hold much though,' another woman said. She had her grey hair in pigtails with lots of different coloured ribbons tied in them.

'Does it get very hot?' This from an old woman with a roller in the back of her hair.

'No, but there's some broken glass over there if you want to hurt your child,' Abby said under her breath. Matthew nudged her but he looked amused when he answered the woman.

'It's a toy. It doesn't actually work,' he said patiently.

'Excuse please. How much for the duvet?' A plump Indian woman asked. She was holding a single 12.5 tog duvet.

'Two pounds,' Abby said.

'Will you take twenty pence?' the woman asked.

The duvet was in perfect condition. It was clean and relatively new. The labels weren't faded and it was made by a leading brand. Abby thought two pounds was more than reasonable. 'Sorry. No. It's two pounds.' She'd rather give it to a charity shop than sell it for twenty pence.

The woman threw it down on the ground and waddled off. Abby folded it back up and put it back on the bin liner.

Two children were playing with Olly's old Fisher Price garage. They'd taken the cars out of the plastic bag and were running them down the ramps. Another child ran his scooter over the road mat they'd laid on the ground. Abby looked around for their parents but nobody was paying them any attention.

'Excuse me, darling. 'ow much is this?' A woman with two front teeth missing held up a photo frame. It had a twenty pence sticker on it.

'Twenty pence,' Abby said.

'I'll take it.' She started counting out money and Abby took the twenty pennies.

''ave you got a bag, darling?'

Abby got her a bag. The woman tossed the photo frame into it and picked up a candle stick. And then she picked up a vase. And then she put it all back so Abby's display was messed up and you couldn't see half the stuff anymore.

The scooter kid was crashing into the wallpaper table now.

'Crash,' he said and the table rocked slightly.

'Crash,' he said again and Abby grabbed the vase as it almost flew off the table.

'Crash,' he said again and Abby put her foot under the table and in front of his wheel.

'Oy. What you doin'?' he asked, dirty little face scrunched up in outrage.

'Can you go and crash somewhere else please? You're knocking my stuff over,' Abby said. She looked around. Still no sign of any parents.

The little boy stared at her. And then he poked his tongue out. 'Its crap stuff anyway,' he said and wheeled away. Abby watched him ride past the broken glass and waited for him to fall in it. But no, too many other people to torment.

A man stopped and looked at the puppet show. 'Are there any puppets?'

Abby pulled out the finger puppets to show him.

'Does it fold up?'

Abby showed him how to fold it flat. And then she showed him the storage and the story cards and the way the curtains moved across.

He looked thoughtful for a few minutes.

'Will you take five pounds?'

'No. Sorry. I can't take less than ten pounds.'

The man moved away.

The chubby Indian woman came back. 'You take one pound for the duvet?'

'Sorry. Two pounds.'

She waddled off again.

The puppet show man came back. 'So *what* is your best price?'

'Ten pounds,' Abby said with great patience.

'But it says ten pounds on the tag,' he said, brow furrowed with confusion.

'Yes, I know. It says ten pounds because that's how much it costs.'

He walked off again. And then he hesitated and came back. 'Will you take seven pounds fifty?'

'No! I will only take ten pounds.'

'You can take offers you know.' Matthew said at her side.

'It's the principle. That puppet show cost thirty pounds new and it's in perfect condition. It's worth ten pounds.'

Matthew threw his hands in the air. And then he went still.

'What?' Abby followed his look and saw Jo pushing through the crowd, Nick behind her. 'Oh, shit.' She quickly pulled at her top, trying to loosen it over her stomach.

'Stop it! You're drawing attention to it,' Matthew hissed.

'Abby! Matthew! Fiona said you'd be here. Have you got any baby stuff?' Jo gushed, rooting through the stuff on the table and messing it all up again.

Abby gritted her teeth and tried not to look at Nick.

'Nick, mate. How are you?' Matthew said and shook Nick's hand. He pinched Abby's waist. 'At least say hello,' he said in her ear.

'Hello, Nick,' Abby said obediently, shooting him a quick smile. And then she actually looked at him – really looked at him – and her eyes got stuck. He looked terrible. Actually he looked gorgeous, but for him he looked terrible. He looked older, more tired and a lot less happy. Abby guessed that the strain of living with Jo was taking its toll and she suddenly felt incredibly sorry for him.

She may be pregnant and about to move into a shoebox but at least she wasn't saddled with someone she didn't love. 'How are you?' she asked gently.

'Good. You?' he gave her a long look and then his eyes flicked over her.

She automatically pulled in her stomach and when his eyes met hers he was smiling. 'You look really good,' he said.

'Thanks,' Abby said.

'How's the driving going?'

'Good. I've booked my theory. It's in two weeks.'

'Well done. Good luck. And how's the cop?' he asked very casually.

'We're not seeing each other anymore,' Abby told him. 'I decided against it.' She shrugged and changed the subject before he could delve further. 'How's Will's training coming along?'

Nick smiled, genuinely this time. 'Good actually. I think he may be in with a chance though don't tell him I said so.'

'Why not? He'd be so pleased.'

'Don't want him getting complacent,' Nick said and then Jo butted in.

'I feel like I haven't seen you for ages, Abby. How's the packing going? When are you moving? Next week isn't it? You've put on weight haven't you?'

Her eyes fixed to Abby's middle and Abby ground her teeth. 'I'm moving in two weeks.'

'Oh I know why you've got fat. You've quit smoking haven't you? Substituting the fags with chocolate are we?' she teased.

'Abby is not fat,' Matthew said before turning back to the customer he was serving.

'You've given up smoking?' Nick looked stunned. 'Well done, I'm impressed.' He looked at her midriff.

'It's Nick's birthday on Tuesday,' Jo said, examining a DVD on the table. 'We're going to dinner on Wednesday. Do you want to come? Nick's going out with his friends on his actual birthday.' She scowled in his direction.

'I'm back at work on Wednesday. Sorry,' Abby said gratefully, thinking she'd rather dye her nasal hair purple. She looked at Nick. 'Happy Birthday for Tuesday.'

'Thank you,' he replied looking really uncomfortable. Abby guessed car boot sales weren't his thing.

'Will you take one pound and ten pence for the duvet?' the Indian woman was back.

'No. Its two pounds,' Abby said.

'What does this do?' A woman with a pink t-shirt bearing the words "I love swearing" asked, pointing to the cooker.

Abby demonstrated.

'Oh, it's a toy then?' The woman looked disappointed and wondered off.

The cooker was about thirty centimetres tall. How could anyone think it was real?

'Have you still got your baby stuff?' Jo asked. Matthew was selling someone a set of books and Nick was watching Jo and Abby.

'Yes.'

'Can I come round and look through it?'

'Er no,' Abby said and watched the Indian woman walk back over.

'Will you take one pound and fifty pence for the duvet?' she asked.

'No. Its two pounds,' Abby said.

Nick smiled.

'Why?' Jo asked.

'Because it's worth two pounds.'

'No. Why can't I look through your baby stuff?'

'Because I don't want you to.'

'But why? It's not as if you're having another baby. You haven't even got a boyfriend,' Jo said looking totally confused.

Matthew put an arm around Abby's shoulders. 'She doesn't have to have a boyfriend to have a baby.'

'Yeah. Maybe I'm getting artificially inseminated,' Abby said.

'One pound and seventy five pence for the duvet?'

'No! Its two pounds,' Abby almost yelled. The Indian woman picked up the candlestick. It was priced at ten pence.

'Will you take five pence for the candlestick?' she asked.

'Why would you get artificially inseminated?' Jo asked in confusion.

'I'm pregnant, Jo,' Abby snapped and then she turned to the Indian woman. 'You can have the duvet and the candlestick for two pounds.'

Jo was standing with jaw almost on the floor. The Indian woman looked thoughtful. Abby slid a look at Nick. He was staring at her and he looked furious. Furious? Abby stared at him in amazement. What was he furious about?

'I will take them,' the Indian woman said as if she were doing Abby a massive favour. 'Do you have bag?'

Abby took the two pounds and put the duvet and candlestick in a bin bag.

'You keep them? I come back later?'

'Fine, whatever.'

Off she wobbled.

'Why didn't you tell me?' Jo asked. 'How pregnant are you?'

The man who'd offered five pounds for the puppet show came back over. 'Will you take eight pounds?'

Abby shook her head. 'Ten pounds.'

The man stared at her.

'I'll give you ten pounds for it,' said a lovely looking woman with a toddler on her hip.

'Okay, thanks.' Abby smiled at her.

'I'll give you ten pounds fifty,' the eight pound man said.
They both stared at Abby. The toddler looked at Nick.
'Eleven pounds,' the woman said.
'Daddy?' the toddler asked and Nick smiled.
'I don't think so,' he said.
The woman shot him an embarrassed smile. 'Sorry, everyone's daddy at the moment.'
Nick grinned at her and she stared at him, eyes wide.
'Twelve pounds,' the eight pound man said and held out a ten pound note and a two pound coin.
The woman was still staring at Nick and didn't notice.
Abby took the money. Silly tart didn't deserve it anyway. The man took the puppet show and wondered off. The toddler started to scream, 'My puppet show, my puppet show.'
The woman finally yanked her gaze off Nick. 'Oh! Did he buy it?'
'Yes. Twelve pounds. Sorry about that.' Abby smiled at her.
'So how pregnant are you?' Jo said and everyone stared at Abby.
'What's pregtent?' the toddler asked.
'Having a baby,' Abby told him.
'You're having a baby?' another voice said and suddenly Becky and Fiona were there too.
'Congratulations,' Becky said.
'Who the hell is the father?' Fiona hissed in her ear mid-hug.
Matthew put his arm round Abby's neck and pulled her in close. 'It's my baby of course. Who else's would it be?'
'You slept with the policeman didn't you?' Jo said. And then she looked annoyed. 'When's it due anyway?'
'I'm ten weeks,' Abby said. 'I'm too pregnant for it to be Chris's.'
Fiona looked at Nick. He stared back and then he looked at Abby.
'Excuse me. How much for the cooker?' A woman asked.
'Five pounds,' Matthew told her.
'Is it gas or electric?'
Abby rounded on the woman and Matthew quickly jumped in, 'It's a toy,' he said.
'Oh. So it doesn't actually cook?'
'No, it doesn't cook. It's pretend.'

The woman started to walk away. 'Does it get hot?'

'No!' Abby said.

'Right.' She turned away and then turned back. 'Have you got any doilies?'

Abby closed her eyes.

'So are you back together?' Jo asked.

'No,' Abby said.

Matthew squeezed her shoulder.

'Why not?' Jo looked at his arm and raised an eyebrow.

'Because we broke up. We're not getting back together just because of the baby. That would be stupid,' Abby said.

Fiona and Becky sucked in their breath.

'Why would it be stupid? Me and Nick got back together,' Jo said, looking genuinely confused.

'Is everything okay?' A man wearing a yellow vest walked past.

'Fine, thank you,' Abby said. She guessed he worked for the car boot sale people. Either that or he was just very strange. Or very friendly.

'Who do you think gets the money we paid to get in? Do you think they pay rent for the car park?' Abby asked Matthew.

He grinned but didn't answer.

'Have you got any jewellery love?' A Mr T clone asked.

'No,' Jo snapped at him. 'This is ridiculous.' She looked round in disgust.

'Go home, Jo. We can talk later,' Abby told her.

'But . . .'

'Come on, Jo. Abby's right. Now's not the place,' Nick took her arm and pulled her away.

'Phone me when you get home,' Jo called over her shoulder and then they were swallowed up by the crowd.

Abby slumped with relief. Matthew gave her another squeeze and took his arm away.

'Are you okay?' Fiona asked.

'Are you keeping the baby?' Becky asked. 'Where will you put it?'

'Of course she's keeping it.' Fiona told her. And then she looked at Abby and sighed. 'We'll leave you to it. I'll call you later.' She kissed Abby's cheek and dragged Becky away.

Abby and Matthew stood in silence for a few blissful moments.

'Well that was fun,' Matthew said with a grin.

'Oh yes. Wasn't it just.'

Matthew sobered. 'Nick suspects. I reckon you'll hear from him today.'

Abby scowled at him. 'I'm not telling him. Don't start on me again.'

'How much is the telephone? Does it work?' someone asked and Matthew turned to serve them.

They sold most of their stuff and went home over a hundred pounds richer. Even the cooker had sold. For the full five pounds.

'I hate car boot sales,' Matthew said when they finally got home.

'I don't usually mind them. When I can smoke and we don't end up having to announce that I'm pregnant in front of ten million people.'

Matthew smiled.

And then he unloaded the car and went to collect Olly. Abby shuffled up to bed, trying to work out how she could squeeze eight hours sleep into the six hours left before work started again.

Chapter Thirty-Four

Abby moved house on the last Friday in May. Matthew and his dad hired a van and moved the furniture while Becky and Abby moved the smaller stuff in Becky's car. Matthew's mother looked after Olly.

It took all day but by eight-thirty Becky and Matthew's dad had gone home and the new house was in some sort of order. Olly's bedroom had been cleaned, his bed and wardrobe put together and his pictures put on the wall. He was fast asleep in bed, his favourite Power Ranger with his head on the pillow next to him. He hadn't been bothered about moving at all. He liked his little bedroom with its Harry Potter wallpaper and blue carpet. He liked having Abby's bedroom so close and he loved the playhouse in the garden.

Abby had spent most of the afternoon trying to fit her furniture into the one room downstairs. She'd managed it eventually and it actually looked really good. The room was nicely decorated – the floor was wooden and the walls were a mixture of pink, blue and yellow. It was a weird combination but actually worked very well with her assorted furniture and patchwork settee.

The living room looked out onto the garden and wrapped round the kitchen with a dining area just outside the door. The dining area sloped down under the stairs and Abby had used the smaller space for Olly's toys.

The kitchen was tiny and Abby had reluctantly left her dishwasher behind. The tumble dryer sat on the work surface and the chest freezer was outside in the shed. It was inconvenient, but it would do. At least she had a house. And a two bed at that. Imagine if they'd had no equity in their old house. She'd have ended up in a one bed flat in Aldershot or something. That would have been fun with two children!

'Are you okay?' Matthew came downstairs, screwdriver in hand. He'd just finished putting the bed back together and was bare-chested. It had been scorching hot all day and was still very stuffy.

Abby nodded. 'Tired.'

'It's a nice house,' Matthew said.

Abby burst into tears.

Matthew pulled her into his arms. 'It's okay. You'll get used to it.'

'I know. I don't know why I'm crying really,' Abby said, but still she cried.

Matthew rocked her in his arms until she reached the hiccupping stage.

'Would it help if I stayed?' he asked.

Abby nodded and pulled back. 'But where will you sleep?'

'On the sofa.' Matthew shrugged, unconcerned.

'Don't be silly. You can share the bed.'

'Are you sure?'

Abby hiccupped and then she smiled. 'Yeah. I trust you.'

She felt much happier knowing Matthew was there. Silly really – it wasn't as if she was scared or anything. It was just a little strange and she was probably hormonal. She decided that was it. Definitely hormones.

She'd taken her following shift off work to give her time to settle into the new house. She spent the weekend unpacking and sorting things out. Olly spent most of the time in the garden – he loved his new home.

On Monday morning Matthew came over and took Olly to nursery and then he and Abby headed over to Frimley Park Hopsital for her twelve-week scan.

'It's really nice of you to come with me,' Abby told him on the way over.

Matthew shot her a sideways look. 'I'm a nice guy. Plus how else were you going to get over here?'

'I could cycle.'

'True. Anyway I don't mind. Plus everyone will ask me how it went and I'll be able to tell the truth if I'm actually with you.'

'I'm really nervous,' Abby said. She looked out of the window and tried deep breathing. 'I wish I could smoke.'

'Well you can't. And why are you nervous? You've done this before.'

'Not alone I haven't. What if there was something wrong with the baby? I'd have to deal with it on my own.'

Matthew sent her a soft smile. 'No you wouldn't.' He reached out and squeezed her hand.

Abby smiled gratefully and did some more deep breathing.

She'd been told to have a full bladder for the scan so she'd drunk a pint of water before they left. She was also sipping from a bottle as they drove. And she was busting for the toilet already.

They told the receptionist they were there and took a seat in the waiting area. 'I need a wee,' Abby said.

Matthew grinned. 'You went through this last time, remember?'

'I know but it's worse this time. My bladder's not as strong. I'm nearly thirty now.'

Matthew just smiled.

By the time they went in Abby could hardly walk. She climbed on the bed and lay down. The nurse put jelly on her tummy and started running the scanner over her and Abby squeezed her legs together.

'Are you okay?' the nurse asked.

'I need the toilet,' Abby said.

The nurse smiled. 'Yes, you do have a very full bladder. Ah, here's the baby. And here's the heartbeat. Lovely and strong. Let's see if we can get baby to move.' She wiggled Abby's stomach about a bit and she automatically crossed her legs. The baby gave a little kick and the nurse stopped wiggling.

'Can you see the leg? And there's an arm there – see baby's sucking its thumb.' She pointed out a few other limbs and Abby felt her eyes fill with tears. It was her baby. Tiny and real and alive on the screen. Kicking away inside her stomach. Matthew squeezed her hand and she smiled up at him.

'Well. Everything looks wonderful,' the nurse said and handed Matthew a photograph. 'You need to make an appointment for your twenty-week scan.'

Abby stood up and thanked her.

'Good luck, dear,' the nurse said and Abby fled. Out of the door and down the corridor and into the toilet. She did the longest wee in the history of weeing and then headed back to Matthew.

'Feel better?' he asked.

'God, yes!'

They made the next appointment and walked back to the car.

Abby studied the photograph all the way home. It was her baby. And Nick's. She wondered if it was a boy or girl. And if it would look like her or Nick. Olly was totally Matthew's. He had nothing of Abby's.

'Are you okay?' she asked Matthew realising that he hadn't spoken all the way home.

'I'm fine. I just feel a bit sorry for Nick,' Matthew said.

Abby felt some of her happiness evaporate. 'Why?'

'Because he should have been there. It's his baby.'

'He just had a scan with Jo. He's had his turn.'

Matthew shot her an exasperated look. 'You know that's not the point. It's just not fair. You're screwing Nick over and you're fucking yourself up and why? To protect your whiney spoilt little friend.'

'Hey! You slept with my whiney spoilt little friend.'

'More fool me,' Matthew snorted. 'You've got your priorities so wrong. *You* are the most important person here. Not Jo.'

Abby leant her head back on the seat. 'Thank you,' she smiled.

Matthew sighed. He'd done this conversation too many times and Abby was surprised he even bothered anymore.

Next on her list was to tell work. She thought of all the ways to do it on the way to work. Should she tell Sid in private? Ask for a word with each of them in turn? Announce it gently to all of them – ask for a meeting perhaps? In the end she just walked in, put her bag down and said, 'I'm pregnant. I had a scan on Monday. Everything is fine. The baby's Matthew's. I'm almost thirteen-weeks along.'

Everyone went silent. Nobody moved for at least forty seconds and then they all moved at once. Sid and Judy came round the partition and sat on the desks opposite.

'Are you okay?' Judy asked.

'Will you be leaving?' Sid.

'Oh, hen. Are you okay? Will you get back with Matthew?' Sally.

'Definitely not,' Abby said.

'That explains why you've quit smoking,' Judy said.

'Are you still moving? Did you move already?' Sid asked.

'I moved on Friday.'

'Be a bit squashed won't you, hen?' Sally said.

Abby shrugged. 'We'll be fine.'

'What did Nick say?'

'Nothing,' Abby said, trying to keep the bitterness out of her voice. He really hadn't. She'd expected to hear from him after her announcement at the car boot sale, but she hadn't. Not a dicky bird. She'd heard from all three of her friends – had ended up meeting them later on, but not Nick. Fiona said he'd probably just decided to accept the baby was Matthews, but Abby knew him better than that. Obviously he didn't want to acknowledge the possibility that it could be his.

'Are you sure it's Matthew's?' Sally asked.

Abby thanked God that she'd never told anyone about Matthew's infertility. 'Yes, I'm positive.'

'Jesus,' Sid said.

'It never rains but it pours,' Sally said.

'Amen,' Judy said.

Chapter Thirty-Five

Abby had passed her theory with flying colours and her test was booked for the twenty-first of June. It was a Monday and Matthew – thank God for Matthew – was taking the afternoon off work to take her over to the test centre. His mother was looking after Olly. Fiona was away and she wasn't insured on Becky or Jo's cars. So it was all down to poor Matthew. Again. Luckily he was turning out to be a much better friend, than he'd been boyfriend.

Only at one forty-five, just an hour before her test was due, Matthew phoned. 'Abby you're not going to believe this. My bloody car won't start. I've called the RAC but they'll be at least half an hour.'

Abby sat down on the floor. 'Oh fuck!' she said. And then she banged her head back on the wall. 'Don't worry, Matthew. It's not your fault. I'll just have to reschedule.'

There was a silence.

'What?' Abby said.

'Why don't you try Nick?' he asked tentatively.

Abby sat up sharply. 'Did you plan this?'

Matthew sighed. 'No! Of course I didn't. But it makes sense. You're on his insurance and he wants you to pass. Just ring him.'

'I might not be on his insurance anymore.'

'It won't hurt to ask.'

'Fine,' Abby snapped and hung up.

And then she chewed her nails and tried to still the flapping butterflies in her stomach. Should she? Shouldn't she? She looked at her watch. Forty minutes before she had to be there. She picked up the phone again and dialled Nick at work.

'Nick, speaking,' he said and Abby lost her breath.

'Hello?'

'Hi. It's me.' Abby cleared her throat. God she sounded weird. 'Abby.'

'Oh. Hi. What's up?' He sounded confused and pleased and wary all at the same time and Abby had to swallow the lump in her throat before she could continue.

'I have my driving test in forty minutes and Matthew's car has died.'

'Right,' Nick said slowly.

'I'm not insured on anybody else's car.'

There was a short pause and then he said, 'I'll be there in five minutes. Wait outside.'

Abby packed up Olly's stuff and went outside. Matthew was meant to be dropping Olly off at his mum's but obviously that hadn't happened. Maybe they could drop him off with Jo or something.

'I'll watch him while you take your test. It doesn't take long,' Nick said, fastening Olly into Tilly's booster seat. 'You'd better drive. It's been a while since you drove my car.'

Abby agreed and a few minutes later they were driving towards Farnborough.

'How are you feeling? Remember your mirrors. That's it, good girl. Are you still feeling sick?' Nick asked.

Abby looked at him in surprise.

'Eyes on the road. Jo tells me everything,' he said, not sounding particularly overjoyed at this.

'Sorry.'

'Not your fault. She has nothing better to do than gossip. And spend money on the baby.' He sounded resigned and Abby resisted the urge to touch his arm.

'I'm feeling great now. The sickness has completely gone.'

'And how's the new house? I almost went to pick you up from the old one.'

'It's fine. I like it now actually. And it's a lot easier to keep clean, being half the size. And Olly loves it. He likes the garden and he loves our next-door neighbour. She's an ex-school teacher and spends hours talking to him. She's offered to babysit actually but I don't really feel I know her well enough yet.'

Nick nodded. 'Probably wise. You can't be too careful.'

'How's Tilly?'

'Good. She's learning to write and she keeps sending me letters. Watch out for the motorbike. She can swim without armbands now. And she can ride her bike without stabilisers.' He went quiet and Abby slid a look at him. He looked sad. 'It goes so quickly.'

Abby thought of the new baby but she didn't say anything. He still didn't seem particularly enthused, though she was sure that would change. It had to with him adoring kids the way he did.

They arrived at the test centre a few minutes later and ten minutes later Abby left Nick and Olly in the waiting room and followed the examiner outside. Surprisingly, she wasn't too nervous. Maybe because she had too much else to worry about or maybe because she knew it wouldn't be the end of the world if she failed.

But when the examiner told her she'd passed, Abby burst into tears. 'Sorry,' she said, 'I can't believe how happy I am. I wasn't even nervous. Thank you so much.'

The examiner, a fairly old man with long eyebrows, smiled gently. 'You drove well, my dear, you deserved to pass.' He patted her hand.

Abby followed him inside and beamed at Nick and Olly.

'You passed,' Nick stood up with a massive smile and Abby flew into his arms. She couldn't help it. He hugged her and then he pulled back and smiled down at her. 'Well done! I knew you could do it.'

Abby just grinned. She couldn't seem to stop herself.

'Mummy drive now?' Olly said and Abby forced herself to hug him instead of Nick.

'Yes! Mummy can drive,' she said and hugged him until he squealed.

Nick drove them home because Abby was too manic to concentrate. Abby desperately wanted to invite him in for a drink so it was probably just as well that Matthew was there. He was stood in the driveway, hands in pockets.

'I passed!' Abby squealed and let him swing her in his arms. 'How long have you been waiting? Where's your car?'

'At the garage. They couldn't get it started. I got a taxi over.' He looked at Nick. 'Hi, Nick. Thanks for taking her.'

'No problem,' Nick said. 'Do you want a lift somewhere?'

'No, but thanks. The garage should be delivering a courtesy car any minute.'

'Will Abby be able to use it for work?'

'Yes,' Matthew said and Abby looked up in surprise. He sounded unusually tense.

Nick nodded. 'I'll tell Will.' He jangled his keys in his pocket and looked at Abby. 'I'll leave you to it then.'

'Okay,' Abby said and stared at him, feeling helpless. She didn't want him to leave but what was the point in him staying? 'Thanks for taking me.'

'Anytime. Take care.' He looked deep into her eyes and she felt her knees buckle but then he looked at Matthew, said goodbye and got back into his car. He waved at Olly and then he started the engine and pulled away.

Abby heaved a sigh and turned to Matthew. 'What was . . .' she started to say and stopped. 'What's wrong with you?'

Matthew looked furious. 'You. You're what's wrong with me. Imagine if the baby was mine. Imagine if I was gutted that we weren't together. How do you think I'd feel watching you and Nick together?'

'But the baby's not yours and you're not gutted,' Abby said, feeling as if she were the only drunk person in the middle of a very grown-up, sober dinner party.

'I might be.' Matthew scowled. 'That's not the point anyway. It shows lack of respect when you fawn all over Nick like that.'

'Bollocks,' Abby said and then looked at Olly but he was collecting stones off the driveway and was oblivious. 'And I wasn't fawning all over Nick.'

'And I hate the way he acts as if you're his. Like "will Abby be able to use it" as if I can't look after you properly.' He was really getting into stride now, though his impression of Nick was pretty crap.

Abby bit back a smile. 'I don't need either of you to look after me. I was perfectly happy to cycle. And I was happy for you to be happy for me to cycle. Me and Nick would have ended up falling out big time over his protectiveness. It was nice short term but I couldn't live like that.'

'But you'll use the car for work now?' Matthew asked, sounding a lot calmer. Abby had obviously said something right.

Abby shrugged. 'If that's okay. It's not much fun cycling in the dark, especially when I'm knackered and I have to pass loads of drunk people.' Matthew nodded, expression a little sad. 'What's wrong?' Abby asked softly, touching his arm.

'I'm jealous,' he said. He gave a wry laugh. 'Stupid huh? I don't want you for myself but I hate the way you and Nick are around each other. You really love him don't you?'

Abby sighed. 'I don't know anymore. I'm starting to think that maybe I just want him because I can't have him. How well do I really know him? If you added all the time we've spent together it'd be nothing. I hardly know the bloke.'

Matthew stared at her for a beat.

And then a car pulled into the drive. It was the courtesy car and Abby took Olly round to the house while Matthew sorted out the paperwork.

Chapter Thirty-Six

'Do you think Abby got pregnant just because I am?' Jo asked when Nick got home that evening.

'What?' Nick stopped and stared at her.

'Do you think—'

'I heard what you said, I just didn't believe it. Don't be so fucking stupid. Of course she didn't. Do you really think she'd have planned to get pregnant? In her situation?'

Jo watched the play of emotions on his face. Angry, indignant, protective. 'Maybe. Maybe she did it to trap Matthew.'

'They're not getting back together.'

'Doesn't mean she doesn't want to,' Jo said and then she sighed. 'You're in love with her aren't you?'

'Don't be ridiculous,' Nick snapped and stormed upstairs.

Jo reached for the utensils jar and got the potato masher out. Maybe she was imagining things but Nick had been acting so weird lately. It had got worse since they found out Abby was pregnant and worse again when she passed her driving test. It could be coincidence but Jo didn't think so. She only had to mention Abby and pregnancy, or Abby and Matthew and he went off on one.

And strangest of all, she didn't really care that much. Nick was hardly ever around and when he was he was working. Jo was finding it increasingly easy to ignore him. And she was so happy. She couldn't remember ever feeling this happy. She was going to have a baby and she couldn't wait.

She finished mashing the potatoes and served them with chicken and cabbage. And then she called Nick. He joined her at the table a few minutes later. He was wearing jogging bottoms and vest.

'Going somewhere?' Jo asked.

Nick poured himself a pint of milk. 'Gym. I'm helping Will.'

Jo watched him cut his chicken. The muscles on his arms bunched up and moved around. He looked bigger. Not surprising really; he'd been going to the gym almost every day. 'Do you go to the gym just to get away from me?' she asked.

Nick paused with fork inches from his mouth. 'No,' he said shortly and carried on eating.

'But you're not happy.'

Nick looked at her.

Jo opened her mouth to ask if it was because of Abby and then she stopped. What if she did push him for a reply? What if he admitted he loved Abby? Or that he didn't want to be with Jo for whatever reason? She didn't want to be alone. So what if she was happiest when Nick wasn't around. If they split up she'd have to move back with her parents. Or to a smaller house. And when the baby came she'd be a single parent. Surely being with a miserable Nick was better than being alone.

She turned to her food and dropped the subject.

Chapter Thirty-Seven

Abby was nineteen weeks pregnant when she met Chris again. She was driving Matthew's car and was on her way home from work. It had been a busy night and she'd managed forty-two minutes of sleep. All she could think about was bed as she drove along, fighting to keep her eyes open and the car on the right side of the road.

And then she heard nee-nawing and when she checked her mirror there were flashing lights. She groaned and pulled over. Just what she needed! She stayed in the car and watched the policeman in her side mirror, winding down her window when he approached.

'Sorry to stop you ma'am. You're driving . . . Oh, Abby!'

Abby gave him a second look and felt a smile spread across her face. 'Chris! How are you?'

'I'm fine.' His gaze flickered back towards his car. 'You were weaving a bit back there, Abby. We thought maybe you'd be drinking.'

'Sorry.' Abby blew out a sigh and climbed out of the car. 'I'm on my way home from work and I've had no sleep.' She looked back at his car. Another policeman was sitting in the passenger seat.

Chris started writing something on a pad. 'How have you been?' he asked. 'Have you got your driver's license with you?'

Abby leant back in the car and got her wallet out of her bag. She handed over her licence. 'I'm fine.'

'Still—'

'Pregnant? Yes.' Abby smiled, he could hardly miss her bump now.

'Back with—'

'Matthew. No.'

Chris looked up from his pad with a grin. 'Seeing anyone else?'

'Nope.'

They smiled at each other and Abby felt herself waking up. She'd forgotten how nice he was.

'Are you?' she asked and Chris shook his head, smile still wide.

'What if I asked you out to dinner?'

'Before or after you fine me for drink driving?'

Chris pulled a face and Abby chuckled.

'I would love to have dinner.'

And that was that. She drove home, wide awake now. She'd been breathalysed, warned to drive more carefully and asked out on a date. Not bad for a mornings work and it wasn't even 7.15am yet.

'You're going on a date?' Jo looked stunned. She and Abby were at the gym. They were on the bikes and Jo was on effort level two, cycling on the flat. Abby was on level eight and was mid-hill.

'Yep. Tomorrow night. I'm really looking forward to it.'

'But you're pregnant.'

'Ye-es.' Abby wiped her face with her towel and relaxed slightly as the resistance on the bike dropped. 'So what?'

'Doesn't he mind?'

'Apparently not.'

'What about Matthew?'

'What about him?'

'Won't he mind?'

'Why would he. We broke up, remember?'

'I know. But you're having his baby. And what's the point in dating? Chris is hardly going to marry you. You're carrying someone else's baby.' Jo was pedalling really slowly, face red with effort. Abby looked her over in disgust. Life was so unfair. Here was Jo, supremely unfit – she'd only joined the gym because Abby had, and she hardly ever came – and she was still really skinny. Even in pregnancy she hadn't put on any weight. She just looked the same but with a pregnant stomach. Abby, on the other hand was piling the weight on. She'd been visiting the gym every day and it had helped but she was really having to watch what she ate.

'I don't want to marry Chris. I want some fun. And if he doesn't mind me being pregnant, what does it matter?'

'So it's just about sex?' Jo said, suddenly reminding Abby of Matthew's mother.

'Yes. Basically,' Abby said and stifled a smile before concentrating on getting up the next hill.

Matthew's reaction came as quite a shock to Abby.

'But you're pregnant.'

Abby, who was getting ready to leave for work, looked over at her ex. He was sat on the settee, posture relaxed, face set to disgusted.

'And? You sound like Jo.'

'You can't go shagging around when you're pregnant.'

'Says who? And don't be crude. It's not "shagging around". Chris is a nice bloke. I really like him.'

'What about Nick?'

Abby zipped her bag shut and stood up. 'What about Nick?'

'He's not going to be pleased.'

'So? It's fuck all to do with him.'

Matthew sighed and turned to look at the TV. 'You're making a mistake.'

'I'm just having some fun, that's all.'

'We'll see.'

Abby stared at him for a minute. He ignored her and continued to watch the TV. She gave a mental sigh and left for work.

Fiona was the only one who didn't disapprove. Even Becky sounded shocked. Abby figured it was because Fiona was the only one who'd had children. Everyone else thought bump equalled no sex. Luckily, Fiona was also happy to babysit.

'One of us should be getting it,' she said when she arrived and Abby thanked her. 'You look great by the way.'

'Thanks.' Abby smoothed her loose fitting dress and looked at her friend. 'Why aren't you getting it?'

Fiona pulled a face. 'Edward's been working loads of hours. When he does finally come to bed he zonks in seconds.' She shrugged. 'I've got my Rabbit, I'm okay.'

Abby chuckled.

'Oh and I'd best warn you. Jo's planning a surprise birthday party.'

'For me?' Abby asked in surprise.

'For both of you.'

'What about you?' Fiona's birthday was four days before Jo's. Abby's a week before that.

Fiona shrugged with a grin. 'I wasn't mentioned.'

'Well I want a joint party with you,' Abby said.

The doorbell rang.

Abby went to answer it, Fiona on her heels.

'Hello, Chris,' Fiona said.

'You remember Fiona?' Abby asked.

Chris smiled and kissed Fiona's cheek. 'Of course. How are you?'

'Fine, thank you. You?'

Chris looked Abby over. 'Very good.'

'We were just planning a birthday party. We're both thirty at the end of the year,' Abby told him.

Fiona grinned. 'Yeah. Abby'll be thirty-eight weeks pregnant. It'll be a hell of a party.'

Abby grimaced and put a hand on her stomach. 'Bugger. I'd forgotten about that. What rotten timing.'

'Yeah. That's the problem with unplanned pregnancy,' Fiona said with a smile. Her eldest had been unplanned. That made four out of five surprise pregnancies. It made you wonder really. How many kids out there really were planned? From what Abby could gather, if you wanted to get pregnant it didn't happen. It had taken Fiona almost a year to conceive her second. When Jo was trying to get pregnant nothing had happened. Why was that?

'Hello? Earth to Abby,' Fiona said, passing a hand in front of her face.

'Sorry, sorry.' Abby forced herself back to the present. 'Shall we go?' she said to Chris and a few minutes later they were in his car.

'So how are things?' he asked once they were moving.

'Fine.' Abby leant her head back and turned to look at him.

'Things okay with Matthew? Did he mind you coming out tonight?'

'Actually, yes.'

'You sound surprised.'

'Well he didn't mind before.'

'You weren't pregnant before. Does he want you back?'

'No.'

Chris sent her a sideways look. 'You are carrying his child. You can't blame him for getting funny.'

Abby didn't comment. It probably wouldn't be wise to tell him the baby was actually Nick's.

'Are you still smoking?'

'Nope. I gave up when I found out I was pregnant.'

They drove in silence for a few minutes.

Abby watched him manoeuvre round a roundabout. He was wearing a short-sleeved shirt and he had really nice arms. Tanned and muscular with really thick wrists.

He glanced over. 'Are you okay?'

'I was just thinking that I'm actually not that hungry.'

'Really?' His eyes darkened and Abby smiled.

'We could just go to your place?'

A muscle tightened in his jaw and he nearly crashed into a parked car.

'Jesus, Abby,' he said but when he reached the next roundabout he went right round it and ten minutes later they were pulling up outside his house.

They had sex three times before he drove Abby home at eleven. She felt wonderful. Relaxed and satisfied and happy. And sleepy, she was almost asleep when he walked her to the door.

'I feel really bad. You only ate toast and we hardly talked all evening,' Chris said as he watched her unlock the door.

Abby kissed his cheek. 'I had a wonderful time. Thank you.'

'You're very welcome. I'll call you tomorrow.'

Abby watched him drive away before she went in to find Fiona.

'I'm in here.' Abby followed her voice into the kitchen and found her making coffee. She held a mug out. 'Good evening?'

'Very.' Abby led the way into the living room and sat down with a groan. 'My thigh muscles are killing me.'

Fiona grinned. 'Good. That's what I like to hear. Where did you go? Was he romantic? He seems the type.'

'We went straight to his house and no, he wasn't romantic.' Abby sipped her coffee and grinned. 'He didn't get the chance, I jumped him the minute we got through the door.'

'Was it good? How'd you work round the bump? Doesn't he mind you being pregnant?'

'Didn't seem to. And we worked round the bump very easily, thank you.'

Fiona leant back and smiled. 'Isn't it weird how some men seem to love pregnant women and others hate it. Edward never wanted it as much when I was pregnant.'

'Matthew did. He found it very sexy.'

'Matthew finds everything sexy.'

'This is true.'

'Who's best?' Fiona drunk some coffee and smiled at her friend. 'Out of the three of them I mean?'

'Matthew and Nick?'

'And Chris.'

'Nick,' Abby said without pause.

'Really? But I thought it was brilliant with Chris.'

'It is. But it's just sex. It was different with Nick.' Abby leant her head back and closed her eyes. And then she blew out a big sigh. 'Maybe it would be different now. Maybe I imagined it was that good and if we did it again I'd be really disappointed.'

'Do you think about it a lot?' Fiona asked quietly. Abby opened her eyes and was surprised at how sad she looked.

'No. Not anymore. What's the point?'

'True,' Fiona said and then she scowled. 'I hate Jo,' she said vehemently.

Abby chuckled. 'It's not her fault.'

'Of course it is. If she was a normal woman and she had a bit of self-respect she wouldn't have got back with Nick. She must know he doesn't really want to be with her.'

Abby shrugged. 'I don't think she cares. She likes the lifestyle and she doesn't want to live with her parents or by herself.'

Fiona looked thoughtful. 'Maybe we should find her another man.'

'That would work but who'd want her?' Abby said and then she grinned.

Fiona grinned back and they laughed.

'God, we're bitches,' Abby said.

'I know.' Fiona stood up and took her mug through to the kitchen. 'I'd better get home. When are you seeing Chris again?'

Abby followed her to the door. 'He's ringing tomorrow. His shifts have been changed for the next week and he's not sure when he's off again.'

Fiona rummaged in her bag and pulled out her keys. 'I'll call you later in the week.'

'Okay.' Abby hugged her friend and watched her walk to her car. 'Thanks for babysitting.'

Fiona waved over her shoulder and a few minutes later drove away.

Chapter Thirty-Eight

Jo invited Abby and Chris to dinner four weeks after they'd started seeing each other again. They'd only managed a handful of dates – Chris' night shifts never seemed to fall on the same nights as Abby's.

'Are you sure you want us round? You've only met Chris once. Does Nick know you've invited us?' Abby asked.

Jo looked up from her doughnut. They were sitting in her kitchen, drinking coffee. Olly was playing in the garden and it was the first time they'd met for over a week. 'Of course Nick knows. And I want to get to know Chris. That's the whole point.'

'Hm.' Abby pushed the doughnut box away.

'Why are you hm-ing? I thought he was nice.'

'He is nice. He's lovely.'

'Anyone'd think you didn't want to come to dinner,' Jo complained. She licked the sugar off her fingers and picked up a chocolate covered ring. 'Are you sure you don't want another doughnut?'

Abby pulled a face. 'I'd love another doughnut but I'm putting on too much weight. And we'd love to come to dinner, thank you.' She sipped her coffee. 'Are you sure Nick's okay with it? Won't Tilly be here?'

It was Jo's turn to pull a face. 'Of course she will. And when I okayed it with Nick he just grunted. Which is positive. Usually he just ignores me.'

It wasn't the first negative comment she'd made about Nick and Abby put her mug down with a bang. 'You are joking?'

Jo shook her head. 'Nope. Seriously, he hardly even talks to me anymore. He's slept in the spare room for the past few weeks, says I keep him awake fidgeting.'

'But you're having his baby.' Abby looked outraged and Jo felt better just for having her support.

'I know.'

'Have you spoken to him about it?'

Jo shook her head and polished off her third doughnut.

'Why not? You should.'

'I told you, he doesn't listen.'

'Make him listen. Shout at him. Throw something. Don't give him a choice.'

Jo smiled. 'I'm not you, Abs. I hate confrontation and I'm a wimp. I hate it when Nick shouts. I always cry when we argue. What good would that do?'

Abby rolled her eyes, a faintly disgusted look on her face. 'Better than doing nothing. Don't you mind? Why don't you leave him?'

Jo looked up, surprised. 'And go where? Back to my parents?' She shook her head. 'I'm happier here. I hardly see Nick, it's easy to pretend everything's okay.'

They drank their coffee in silence for a few minutes.

'Don't you miss sex?' Abby asked.

Jo thought about it. 'A bit. I miss the closeness rather than the actual sex. I was never like you, Abs. Sex isn't that big a deal to me.' She blinked back tears and forced a smile. 'Mostly I miss having someone in bed with me.' She pushed the memory of Matthew away. With Matthew sex had been a very big deal.

Abby rushed around the table and hugged her friend. 'Oh, Jo. This should be such a special time for you. It's not fair. Do you want me to talk to him?'

Jo pulled back, the tears stopping as quickly as they'd started. 'Would you do that?'

'Of course I would.'

'You're such a good friend,' Jo said.

Abby kept hearing those words all the way home. Was she a good friend? Surely if she was a good friend she wouldn't have slept with Nick. Should she have told Jo what had happened? What good would it have done though? None. No, she was right to keep quiet. Though it would have been more right to not have done it at all.

The baby kicked and Abby automatically put a soothing hand on her stomach. Her heart contracted as it always did when she thought of the baby. It had been exactly the same with Olly. It was such a special feeling, one you couldn't imagine until you'd experienced it.

The gravel crunched as Abby cycled over the driveway. She leant her bike against the wall and went inside. She dialled Nick at work.

He answered on the fourth ring and her heart did a double somersault.

'Nick, it's Abby. I need to talk to you.'

'Is everything okay?' His voice was full of concern and Abby felt herself getting angry again.

'No. I want to talk to you about Jo.'

There was a long silence. Complete silence. And then a train sounded in the distance and Nick sighed down the phone. 'Lunch? Twelve thirty? The Prince Arthur?'

Abby resisted the urge to tart herself up. Just as well really, she only just arrived on time as it was. Nick was already waiting – he'd managed to get a table on the pavement enclosure.

'Hi. Are you okay to sit out here? It's a bit warm but I though it'd be better for Olly. Hi, Olly. How are you? Have you been to nursery?' Nick stood up as they approached.

He pulled out a chair for Abby. She ignored it and sat down opposite.

'I'm on holidays. I've got no more nursery until Saturday,' Olly chirped merrily.

'September,' Abby corrected automatically.

'They've broken up already?' Nick sat down and passed her a menu.

'Yep.' Abby got a couple of cars out of her bag and settled Olly under the table to play. 'Why are you being so vile to Jo?'

Nick looked up from his menu. He looked surprised, then irritated, then flat-out annoyed. 'I'm not being vile to Jo. What's she told you?'

'That you don't talk to her. You don't even sleep in the same bed anymore. Why did you bother getting back with her? She'd be better off without you.' Nick looked away and Abby felt her eyes widen. 'Oh my God. That's what you're trying to do, isn't it. You're trying to force her to leave. That's disgusting, Nick. And gutless and . . .'

Nick put his menu down on the table. 'Give it a rest, Abby. I am not forcing her away. I'm working twelve-hour days. I'm knackered. The mortgage has just gone up, Jo's spending a fortune on baby stuff – it's a nightmare. She wants the baby's room decorated, shelves put up, special flooring put down. There just aren't enough hours in the day. At night she fidgets and moans and gets up for the toilet every ten minutes. I need my sleep – all five hours of it. And why the hell am I explaining this to you? It's none of your damn business.' He stood up, chair scraping noisily on the paving stones. 'What d'you want to eat?'

Abby stared at him for a beat. 'Nuggets for Olly. I'll have scampi and chips please.'

'Drink?'

'Lemonade please.'

Nick stalked off and Abby sat back in her seat.

'Is Nick grumpy, Mummy?' Olly piped up from under the table.

'He's just tired, baby.'

Olly poked his head out and stared at her for a minute. 'Which car do you like best?' He held up his cars, one green, one red. 'The blue one or the yellow one?'

'The yellow one.'

'Silly,' Olly said with a big grin. 'They're green and red. I was tricking you.'

'Oh, silly mummy,' Abby said.

Olly ducked back down and started crashing the cars. And a couple of minutes later Nick was back.

He put the drinks on the table and sat down. 'Do you mind if I smoke? Didn't Olly want a drink?'

'He's got his beaker.' Abby watched him light a cigarette. 'Would you have been the same with me?'

Nick took a long drag on his cigarette and stared at her through the smoke. 'Excuse me?'

'Moody, quiet. Sleeping in the spare room.'

Nick continued to stare. He inhaled some more. And then some more. And then he grinned. 'I wouldn't have slept in the spare room.'

'But you'd have still been stroppy and horrible?'

Nick lost his grin. He inhaled and then exhaled noisily. 'I don't know, Abby. Probably not. But it'd be different. You work. You appreciate how tiring it is and you have some concept of money and cost and stuff. Jo is so spoilt. She spent eight hundred pounds on her credit card last month. And that was without food.'

Abby grimaced. 'Can't you take the card away?'

'I'll have to if she carries on, but she said it's for baby stuff. She got a really expensive pram. It's not just that. You know I don't want to be with her. It's very hard to act happy and cheerful and chatty.' He stubbed out his cigarette. 'And then she invites you and Chris to dinner. As if I want to spend the night watching you slobbering all over your boyfriend.'

Abby bit back a smile. 'I won't slobber, I promise. And Jo's just trying to get to know Chris. She doesn't know it'll bother you.'

'It doesn't bother me,' he snapped. And then he gave a sheepish half-smile. 'Okay, so it does bother me.'

'What's slobber, Nick?' Olly asked from under the table.

Nick and Abby exchanged a smile. 'Dribble,' Nick said.

And then there were more car noises and the sound of metal hitting metal.

'How's it going with Chris?' Nick asked. He was smiling but his eyes were sad.

'Okay.' She didn't want to hurt him anymore than she had to. 'It's not going to last forever. I'm pregnant for Christ sake. But we're having fun. He's a nice bloke.'

Nick held her look. 'I'm glad. That you're happy I mean.' He paused while their food was placed on the table. 'Thanks,' he said to the barman and then they were alone again. 'Do you think it could last? Maybe he'll want to marry you or something.'

Abby grinned. 'I don't think so. I couldn't marry a policeman.'

'Why not? It's not as if you regularly break the law or anything.'

Abby shrugged. 'I'd just worry about laws I don't know about. And what if I do want to turn to crime? And what if I fell in love with him and he was stabbed or something?' She speared a scampi with her fork and dunked it in tomato sauce. 'How's Will doing by the way?'

Nick watched her eat for a moment. 'Good. He's doing really well. I'm having to keep training on the sly to keep ahead of him. Can't have my nephew lifting more weights than me.'

Abby smiled. 'Fair enough. I thought you were looking . . . ' she looked at his shoulders, 'bigger.' Much bigger actually. And he'd been perfect to start with. She quickly shoved another mouthful of fish in her mouth.

Nick's eyes smiled, his mouth slightly turned up at the corners. 'How's the scampi?'

Abby swallowed. 'Lovely.'

Nick grinned for a moment longer. And then he turned his attention to Olly. Abby watched him settle Olly in a chair and cut his nuggets up.

'Are you getting excited about the baby?' she asked Nick.

Nick handed Olly a fork and sat back. 'No,' he said and then he sighed. 'That sounds horrible doesn't it? It's just the expense, and Jo, and the hours I'm working.' He shrugged. 'I'm sure I'll get more excited closer to the time.'

Abby nodded, thinking it was unlikely. God, imagine if she'd told him he was her baby's father too. And asked for maintenance. He was pretty bloody lucky really. Matthew was paying maintenance for Olly. Abby was dreading the day he realised Nick was going to get away with it. He seemed to be hoping she and Nick would end up together eventually which was probably why he wasn't worried at the moment. Things were going to be tough though. Especially while Abby was on maternity leave. She'd arranged a break from her loan, which would help, but after the first six weeks she'd be surviving on a hundred and fifty pounds a week.

She looked at Nick and wondered if he'd be excited if he knew she was carrying his child. Probably not. Thank God she'd never told him.

'Look, Nick, my chicken nugget looks like a spaceship. And this one looks like the moon. Uh-oh. The spaceship just crashed into the moon.' Olly shoved the moon and the spaceship in his mouth and smiled at them, cheeks bulging.

Nick smiled back and then looked at Abby. 'Is Matthew excited?'

'About the baby?' Abby stroked her stomach. The baby kicked her hand and she chuckled. 'Yes, he is actually.' And he wasn't even the father. Sometimes it was so hard to keep quiet.

'Uh-oh. The android and the spaceship just crashed,' Olly chuckled.

Nick and Abby stared at him, open-mouthed.

'What's an android, Olly?' Nick asked.

'It's a pink helicopter with whirly things on top that cut your arms off. And it goes into space and kills aliens. Aliens with one eye that stays open even when they sleep,' Olly made whirly actions with his arms. 'And when your arms come off they shoot blood everywhere.' He stopped whirling and looked down at his dinner. 'My tomato ketchup looks like blood.' He picked up a nugget dunked it in his sauce and popped it in his mouth. And then he picked up his fork and started eating the sauce neat.

Nick shook his head, expression bewildered. He finished his meal and sat back, flicking a quick look at his watch. 'I have to go in a minute. I've got back to back meetings this afternoon.' He gave her a long look. 'What will you report back to Jo?'

Abby grinned. 'What makes you so sure I'll be reporting back?'

Nick raised an eyebrow and she chuckled. 'I'll talk to her about money. Don't worry – I'm kind of on your side even though I think you're a moody bastard.'

'Thanks. I think,' Nick said and then he got up to leave. 'Take care of yourself. See you tomorrow for dinner.'

'If I can get Matthew to babysit again,' Abby said with a grimace. That was the problem with working nights. She already needed Matthew to babysit four nights out of every eight. It was getting wearing asking him to babysit extra days too.

'Can't you put Olly to bed at ours?'

Abby stared at him. Searching for reasons to say no, finding none and realising it was actually a good idea. 'Okay, thanks.'

'No worries. Bye, Ol.'

Olly waved goodbye, mouth full of chips and tomato sauce.

And then they were alone again.

Chapter Thirty-Nine

Matthew picked Olly up at nine thirty on Saturday morning. He was taking him to see his family for the day.

'Are you going out tonight?' Abby asked him, 'Do you want a coffee?'

'No thanks. I told Mum we'd be there by ten and I need to stop in town first. I've got a date tonight. Why? Are you going out?'

'Only to Jo's. I can take Olly with me. They've invited me and Chris to dinner,' Abby said with a grimace.

'Really?' Matthew grinned and calling Olly, headed for the front door.

Abby kissed Olly goodbye and waved until they drove off.

She spent the day cleaning and catching up with the washing. She got her hair cut at five and then went home to shower and shave and exfoliate. She dressed in a short pleated pin stripe skirt and white shirt with oversize collar. And when she put her make-up on she was shaking so much she had to start over three times. What the hell was wrong with her?

Nick came to pick her up at six thirty so she could get Olly settled and into bed before Chris arrived at seven thirty.

'Wow. You look nice,' Nick said when she opened the door.

'What about me?' Olly demanded from her side. 'I look nice as well. Look, I've got Spiderman pyjamas on. Daddy took me to see Spiderman today. Mummy shouted at him cos it was scary but I wasn't scared. I'm a big brave boy aren't I?'

'You are. Very brave.' Nick smiled and picked him up and carried him out to the car. Abby locked the door and followed.

Olly talked about Spiderman for the entire journey, which was just as well. Abby was feeling so nervous she didn't think she'd have managed conversation. Stupid really. How many other times had she been alone with Nick? And so what if they were all having dinner. He'd got back with Jo before she started seeing Chris. She had nothing to feel nervous about.

Nick carried Olly into the house, setting him down in the hallway and yelling for Tilly. 'Where do you want to put him?' he asked Abby. Tilly came running out of the living room and dragged Olly up the stairs. 'Tilly wants him in with her but it's probably not a good idea.'

Abby tore her eyes away from his biceps. He was wearing dark blue jeans and a black short-sleeved shirt and it took her breath away just looking at him. 'Not if we want peace this evening.'

'Put him in the room next to Tilly's then,' Nick said and then he seemed to realise that they were still standing in the hallway. 'Do you want a drink?'

'Yes please. Something strong.'

Nick looked at her stomach and she sighed. 'I can have one.'

'I know. What do you want? Gin? Vodka? Wine?'

Abby rubbed her bump. 'All of them. And a cigarette,' she said and went upstairs to find Olly. He was in Tilly's bedroom and they were stood with linked arms in front of her microphone.

'I take Olly to be my awfully webbed husband,' Tilly was saying.

Olly stared at her, mesmerised. 'What's webbed? Can we play Power Rangers now?'

'Not yet. We're getting married,' Tilly said impatiently.

'And then can we play Power Rangers?'

'Okay.'

Abby knocked on the doorframe. 'Bedtime, Olly.'

'No! Don't want to go to bed.'

Abby stepped into the room and Olly ducked under her arm and sprinted away.

'We were just getting married, Abby. Can't he stay up a little while longer?' Tilly asked. 'Please, just five minutes.'

'No, he can't,' Nick said, coming up the stairs with Olly in his arms. 'It's grown up time. Can you go and do your teeth please, Tilly? If you're in bed in five minutes you can have a story. Deal?'

'O-kay,' Tilly said and slouched towards the bathroom.

'Can I have a story too?' Olly said, putting his face close to Nick's.

Nick looked at Abby.

She shrugged.

He held her look for a beat longer before turning to Olly. 'If you go to bed like a good boy.'

187

Olly forced a sigh. 'I will.'

'Say goodnight to Mummy then.'

Another sigh. 'Goodnight, Mummy.'

'Goodnight, baby.' Abby leant forward and kissed him, overly aware of how close it brought her to Nick. She held her breath and stiffened but his scent burned into her brain and she felt his jaw brush her hair.

'Your drink's in the kitchen. Cigarettes are there too,' Nick said with a smile and then he carried Olly into the spare room.

Abby banged her head against the doorframe. Idiot. Fool. What the hell was wrong with her? It was the intimacy. The domesticity and the children thing. It was like living with him again. Lunch in the pub was okay, she could deal with that. But this was too weird.

'Abby?' Jo asked, poking her head out of her bedroom. 'Are you okay?'

She was obviously halfway through dressing, was only wearing jeans and bra. Her bump was much smaller than Abby's. And her belly button looked normal too.

'Abby?'

Abby concentrated on focusing. 'Sorry. Nothing's wrong. I'm fine. I just need a drink.' She went downstairs. The clock in the hall said seven o'clock. Abby sighed. Christ, she wished the evening was over.

Jo changed her clothes four times before she finally headed downstairs. It was her first social event for months and she wanted to look nice. Maybe Nick would start paying attention if she made an effort. She thought of Abby and the way she'd looked when Jo interrupted her doorframe headbanging. Tired, vacant, weary. She looked in the mirror. And she smiled. She was glowing.

She got downstairs just as the doorbell rang. 'I'll get it,' she called and opened the front door. 'Chris?' she said. *Wow*, she thought. She had no memory of the night he and Abby met. 'I'm Jo. Come in.'

Chris smiled and stepped inside. 'I remember. We met in the pub. How are you?'

'Fine, thank you. What would you like to drink?' Jo led him to the kitchen, peering into the living room on route. 'I'm not sure where Abby is. Do you want wine or would you prefer beer?'

'A beer would be good,' Chris said and then he stopped. 'Abby?'

Jo followed his look to where the back door swung open. Abby was lying on the grass, cigarette in one hand, smile on her face. 'Hello. It's lovely out here. I think I just saw a star.'

'What's going on?' Nick came in behind them. 'What's she doing?' he asked when he saw Abby and then he gave a wide grin.

'It's not funny. She's smoking,' Jo said.

'Is she drunk?' Chris asked.

Nick looked at Chris, and Jo remembered her manners. 'Nick, this is Chris. Chris, Nick.'

Nick looked slowly away from Abby. 'Hi. It's nice to meet you,' he said and shook hands with Chris. And then he looked back at Abby. He shook his head slightly, smile twitching at the corners of his mouth.

Jo watched him walk outside. Abby was lying with her arms behind her head, feet crossed at the ankles. A glass jug was propped against her side, straw curling into her mouth. She turned her head slightly when she heard Nick approach.

Chris stepped outside and Jo followed closely behind.

'You weren't supposed to drink the whole jug,' Nick was saying, pulling the straw away and moving the almost empty jug out of her reach.

'I was thirsty. It's not alcoholic is it?' Abby started to sit up and immediately fell back. 'Whoa! Dizzy spell.'

Nick smiled and held out a hand. Abby took it and he pulled her up to sitting. She reached for the cigarette packet which was on the ground besides her. 'Cigarette?' she held one out to Nick.

He sat down next to her and took it from her. 'Yes, thank you. I'd like one of my cigarettes.'

Abby looked down in surprise. 'Oh. Sorry. I thought they were mine.'

'You don't smoke anymore. Remember?'

Abby was silent for a moment and then she sighed and leant back on her arms, head thrown back. 'Shit.' And then she looked upside down at Jo and Chris. 'Hello. When did you get here?'

'At half past seven,' Chris said without expression.

Abby stared at him. 'Of course you did,' she muttered and looked back up at the sky.

Jo moved closer. 'Are you okay, Abby?'

'I'm fine. Wonderful. Never better,' Abby said.

Jo looked at Nick. He raised an eyebrow. 'Why don't you sort out drinks? I'll just finish this,' he held up his cigarette, 'and we'll be in.'

'Okay.' Jo went inside and got Chris a beer from the fridge. 'Shall we go through to the dining room? It would have been nice to eat outside but I get bitten so badly that we don't bother anymore. Do you smoke?'

Chris followed her through to the dining room. 'No, never. Here, let me.' He jumped forward and pulled her chair out for her.

'Thank you,' Jo sat down and beamed up at him. Looks, and manners too. She watched him take the seat opposite. 'So, tell me about yourself. I know you're a policeman, but that's about it. Where do you live? How old are you? Are you going to marry Abby?'

Nick watched Abby watch him smoking. She was inhaling and exhaling every time he did. 'Fuck it,' she said in the end and lit a cigarette of her own. She inhaled with her eyes closed, savouring every second. And when she opened her eyes she realised that Nick was staring at her. 'What?' she snapped. 'So, I'm pregnant. I can't be perfect all the time you know.'

Nick grinned. He stubbed out his cigarette and stood up. 'Come on, we should go inside.'

Abby looked at his outstretched arm. 'Why?'

'Because Jo and Chris are in there.'

Abby stared at him.

'Chris. Your boyfriend?' Nick reminded her, trying not to look as amused as he felt. Abby sighed and fell back to lying.

'I'm not in the mood,' she said.

Nick sat back down. 'What's wrong?'

Abby stared up at him, eyes big and bright and sad and he felt his heart contract. 'Everything,' she said and put her arm across her eyes.

'Tell me,' Nick whispered.

'I can't.'

Nick opened his mouth to encourage her some more but then he realised that she was shaking. And then he saw tears running down her face and into her ears and he gathered her in his arms, pulling her head against his chest, her upper body on his lap. 'What is it, Abby. Please tell me. Maybe I can help,' he said, holding her tight against him, alternating between rocking her gently and stroking her head.

Abby shook her head and cried even harder. 'I just want to go to bed.'

Nick held her for a few minutes longer, desperate to know what was wrong but loath to keep asking.

Eventually, with big, shuddery sobs, she pulled away, straightening and wiping her eyes with her hands. 'I'm sorry. I'm okay, honest. Just overtired. Please could you take me home?'

Nick nodded slowly, mind racing. He didn't want to take her home. Not in this state and definitely not with Chris. 'Why don't you stay here tonight? It saves disturbing Olly.'

Abby stared at him, face pale and streaked with dampness.

'I might even cook you breakfast.'

'Fried eggs?' Abby whispered.

'Whatever you want,' Nick murmured back.

Abby nodded and then she gave a long shuddery sigh. 'Jesus, I can't believe what a mess I am. What the hell was in that drink?'

Nick grinned. 'Not much actually. A bit of Vodka and some Banana Liqueur. You just can't handle your alcohol anymore.'

'Really?' Abby looked surprised for a second and then she smiled. 'So I haven't poisoned my baby?'

'I think you'll probably be okay.'

Abby beamed.

'Come on,' Nick stood up. 'Let's go inside.'

Abby held out her hand and he hauled her to her feet. She stood for a moment on very shaky legs and Nick kept hold of her hand, leading her slowly inside. Laughter hit them immediately and then they heard Jo and Chris chatting, talking over each other, quickly and excitedly in the way only two people who have discovered a soul mate do.

Nick and Abby stopped and stared at each other; Nick looking for signs that it bothered Abby, Abby just looking surprised. And then she smiled and Nick smiled back, happy and relived that she didn't mind. And then he led her upstairs and onto the landing. 'Will you sleep with Olly?' he asked in quiet tones.

Abby moved a little closer. 'What are the other choices?' she asked, eyes smiling into his, caressing his face, catching on his lips.

Nick lost himself in her gaze and it was as if she was touching his face with her hands. 'I could take you home,' he murmured.

Abby's eyes closed slightly and she swayed against him. 'Too tired. Olly,' she whispered and then she fell against him and his arms instinctively went round her waist. She snuggled closer and when he lowered his mouth she pressed hers against it eagerly, greedily almost.

And just as suddenly she pulled away. She opened the door to the spare room and slipped inside. Nick watched, waiting for it to close and then she opened it a little wider and looked out at him. Her hair was tousled, her cheeks flushed.

'I love you,' she said as quickly as a child with her first crush and then she quickly slammed the door shut.

Nick smiled. And then he smiled even wider. She loved him.

'Nick?' Jo called up the stairs. Nick spared one last look at Abby's closed door and headed downstairs. 'What's going on? Where's Abby?' Jo asked when she reached him.

'She's gone to bed.'

'Really?' Jo looked towards the dining room. 'What about dinner?'

'What about dinner?'

'We invited Chris and Abby to dinner.'

'So? You can eat without Abby can't you?'

'Well yeah. But isn't it a bit weird?'

'No. Not at all.' Nick sighed. 'Look, Jo. I'm feeling pretty crap myself. I think I'll grab some toast and go to bed too. Apologise to Chris for me would you.'

Jo stared at him, aghast, mouth opening and closing. 'But . . . but.' And then she closed her eyes and Nick watched her face turn red. 'Fine,' she said and went through to the dining room.

Nick watched until she disappeared from view. She hadn't put up much of a fight. He realised then that she had a bit of a thing for Chris. He started to feel amused and then he remembered that she'd already taken one of Abby's boyfriends. And she hadn't even asked what was wrong with Abby.

Scowling, he changed his mind about going to bed. He wasn't letting Jo upset Abby again. Jo and Chris were giggling away in the dining room, empty glasses in front of them.

'I changed my mind,' he said sitting down. 'What's for dinner?'

Jo and Chris stopped laughing and turned to look at him.

'Is Abby okay? Jo said she'd gone to bed,' Chris said.

'She's very tired.'

'And drunk,' Jo said.

'She wasn't drunk. I hardly put any alcohol in her drink,' Nick said, reaching for the wine and pouring himself a glass.

'She was drunk enough to smoke,' Jo argued. Chris nodded, disapproving look on his face.

'Oh for God's sake. Give her a break. She's a single mum, about to have another child—'

'Do you really think the baby's Matthews?' Jo asked suddenly.

'Who else's would it be?' Chris asked.

Jo shrugged.

'Why don't we wake her up and ask her?' Nick said in a quiet voice. Jo looked at him and her expression grew wary.

'I was just asking,' she said.

'Well don't. She's your best friend. Show some respect.'

Chris cleared his throat. 'It's getting late. Maybe I should head home.'

Jo jumped to her feet. 'But you haven't eaten. I'll go and get the dinner.' She left the room and Chris smiled at Nick, obviously uncomfortable.

'Would you like some wine?' Nick asked, finishing his own and pouring some more.

'No thank you. I don't really drink.'

'Right. Are you working tomorrow?'

Chris nodded. 'Yes.'

They sat in silence. Nick tried to think of something else to say but was at a loss. What did Abby see in this guy? It must just be sex. The thought made him feel sick, very sick, so he concentrated on drinking more wine instead.

'How well do you know Abby?' Chris asked tentatively.

Nick stared at him for a beat. 'Fairly well.'

'Do you think the baby could be someone else's?'

Yes mine, Nick thought. Then he forced his mind elsewhere. He'd gone through this when she announced her pregnancy. The baby was Matthews. End of story. Chris was staring at him, expression increasingly worried, and Nick realised that he cared a lot. Jesus, was he planning on marrying her or something?

'Who knows,' he said with a shrug. Sod it, let him think badly of Abby. She certainly wasn't overly bothered about him. 'Do you want a drink?'

Chris looked from Nick to his empty glass. 'Yes please. Anything non alcoholic would be fine.'

Nick went through to the kitchen and poured him a lemonade. Jo was taking things out of the oven and arranging them on plates.

'Do you think Chris is serious about Abby?' she asked, 'can you take a plate through please?'

Nick picked up the biggest. 'No. I think he would like to be though.'

'Do you think he loves her?'

Nick thought of his face when Abby was lying on the grass. 'No.' He found it interesting, but not particularly distressing, that Jo was so interested in Chris and Abby's relationship. He took the plate through and a few minutes later Jo followed and they all started to eat. Conversation was stilted; Chris was clearly not very comfortable with Nick, and Jo was acting strangely, shy almost.

Nick made his excuses and went to bed as soon as they'd finished desert.

Chris made "leaving" noises but Nick could hear them chatting as he walked up the stairs. Dickhead. What on earth did Abby see in him?

Chapter Forty

Abby woke with a feeling of dread, memories of the evening before crashing into her consciousness like bricks into a skip. She'd drunk. And she'd smoked. And what about Chris? Had he turned up? She didn't remember seeing him but she was sure he'd been mentioned. She'd kissed Nick too. Oh God, and hadn't she told him she loved him? She groaned and covered her eyes with her arms.

And what about Olly? She heard yelling. Tilly's voice. And Olly's. They were playing Power Rangers from the sounds of it. There was a knock on the door.

'Come in,' Abby said, heart skipping beats because it could be Nick.

The door opened and Nick poked his head round. 'I brought you coffee,' he said and came into the room. Abby pulled herself to sitting.

'How much did I drink last night?'

Nick put the mug next to the bed and gave her a long look. 'Why? Do you feel rough?'

'No, not particularly.'

'You hardly drunk anything.'

'But I smoked?'

'Two cigarettes.' Nick smiled. 'You'll be fine, honestly. Don't worry.'

'Was Chris here? Did he stay?'

'Yes. He stayed for dinner.' Nick put his hands in his pockets and rocked back on his heels. 'He seems like a nice bloke.'

'Ye-es.' Abby sipped at her coffee and watched him over the edge of the mug.

'Is it going well then?'

Abby grinned. 'What's wrong? Did he go off with Jo or something?'

'Would you mind?'

'Oh my God,' Abby clapped her hand over her mouth. 'She didn't did she?'

Nick shook his head. 'I don't think so. You don't seem upset.'

'Why would I be? Me and Chris are hardly going to get married. I told you before, it's just fun.'

Nick looked at her, eyes searching, expression serious. And then he took his hands out of his pockets and shuffled his feet a bit. 'Is the baby really Matthew's?'

Abby spat her mouthful of coffee across the bed. 'What?' She grabbed tissues from the bedside table and dabbed at the spillage, mind racing, heart somersaulting at a sick-making rate.

'It could quite easily be mine. How do you know its Matthew's?'

'We used condoms.'

'Not every time we didn't.'

'The timing was wrong.'

'No it wasn't. I was awake all night thinking about it. I got Jo's book and worked it out. It could be mine.'

'Well it's not,' Abby said and started to get out of bed. 'Please can you go away? I want to get dressed.'

Nick stared at her. She could feel his eyes on the back of her head and she pretended to mop some coffee off her leg.

'Fine. But we need to talk about this, Abby.' He paused. 'I thought you'd have an immediate reason why it's not mine. I can't believe you'd have passed my child off as Matthews.'

His voice was rising and Abby quickly jumped in, 'I wouldn't. I told you, it's not yours. Now please, go away and let me get dressed.'

'This conversation isn't finished.' A few more beats passed and then she heard him move away. Abby waited until the door clicked shut behind him before throwing herself back on the bed. Oh my God. He knew. He *knew*. What the hell was she supposed to say? She must have had an explanation ready at the start. When she announced her pregnancy at the beginning, at the car boot sale. Nick had looked odd then. What excuse did she have ready for him?

'Mummy? Mummy?' Olly yelled from outside the door. The door handle jerked back and forth a few times and then the door flew open and Olly fell into the room. 'Can I go to the park with Tilly? Please? Can I? Can I?'

'No, honey. We have to go home. Daddy's coming to get you soon.'

'But I want to go to the park.'

'Maybe Daddy'll take you to the park.'

Olly thought about that for a moment. 'To the sand park?'

'I don't know, honey. You'll have to ask Daddy.' Olly pursed his lips and she quickly added, 'But I expect he will. If you ask nicely.'

Olly placated, Abby got up and dressed. She had a quick coffee with Jo and then walked home. She could have waited for Nick. Jo told her he'd taken Tilly to the park and would drive her home when he got back. Abby decided against waiting.

She screened all her calls for the next few days; letting them go to voicemail if the number was unknown. But it never was. And by the end of the week she still hadn't heard from him and she stopped worrying. Either he'd decided the baby wasn't his or he'd decided he didn't care. Abby started to relax again.

She and Matthew had been for her twenty-week scan on Monday – it was two weeks late, she was actually twenty-two weeks. And she was having another boy! She was ecstatic. It made the pregnancy feel so real. It wasn't just a baby kicking the crap out of her insides. It was a boy. Tom. She'd named him Tom. That was the advantage of having no father for your baby – you could choose the name all by yourself. She felt so much closer to him now that she knew he was a he. It seemed to kickstart the bonding. She didn't share this with Jo of course. Jo had decided against finding out the sex of her child and Abby thought she was already regretting it. She expected to hear from Nick once she'd told Jo about the scan. But there was nothing. No visit. No phone call. Not even a text.

Abby was torn between relief and something that felt very like disappointment. Ridiculous of course. What if she did confirm that he was the father? He still wasn't going to leave Jo. Not if Abby had anything to do with it.

And to make everything worse, work was a nightmare. Abby was so tired all the time and she was finding it increasingly difficult to stay awake and get the work done. And to make things even harder, Sid had left. His replacement, Tara, was shaping up to be a complete and utter bitch. She and Judy had buddied up and Abby was starting to dislike her with a vengeance.

Three weeks into Tara's new job, Abby was off sick for three nights. She'd picked up a tummy bug and was really ill with it. She got back to work the following shift, the first Thursday in September.

The other three were already there. 'Hello, hen,' Sally sang when she walked in, 'How are you? Feeling better? You look so tired. Are you getting enough rest?'

Abby gave a weary smile and fell into her seat. 'I'm fine. Olly came down with my tummy bug as soon as I got over it. It's been a bad couple of days. How are you?'

'I'm not being funny, Abby. But you or your son or boyfriend are always ill. What are you all eating?' Tara piped up from the other side of the partition, her shrill voice grating on Abby's nerves.

'We're not always ill . . .' Abby started to say and then she bit her tongue. Sally was smiling at her, expression sympathetic. Tara seemed to have taken a dislike to Abby and Abby only. She was okay with Sally, a bit abrupt sometimes, but at least she didn't pass judgement on everything she said. Abby was trying to ignore it – what was the point in arguing? All it did was make things tense. She'd decided Tara was still settling in and was giving her the benefit of doubt for now. 'How was your meal on Saturday?' she asked Sally instead.

They ploughed through the weeks emails and Abby updated her calls. There was some data entry that needed doing and Abby started it without prompting. Judy and Tara chatted the whole time. Sally did a couple of reports and then picked up her knitting. At two o'clock Abby ticked the final line and settled back in her chair. God, she really was so unbelievable tired. She closed her eyes and felt herself drifting off to sleep, the clicking of Sally's knitting needles and the constant drone of Judy and Tara's voices lulling her into dreamland.

And then she came abruptly awake when the droning voices suddenly turned to loud squawking. 'Abby? Abby?' Tara was saying.

Abby blinked her eyes open and sat up straight. 'What's wrong? Did I miss a call?' She looked at the plasma screen. Calls = 0. She looked at her inbox. No emails. And then she looked at Tara, bewildered.

'We are not paid to sleep you know,' Tara said.

We're not paid to sit and chat either, Abby thought but didn't say. 'I'm sorry, did some work come in?' she asked.

'No. That's not the point. We're here to work.'

'Okay.' Abby moved her chair closer to the desk, 'what work shall I do?'

'Look at old calls. Check the other shift's calls. There's always work to be done,' Tara said. She disappeared from view and Abby heard the sound of pages turning. She got up and went out to the toilet and when she came back in she walked past Tara and Judy. They were both reading magazines. Sally was still knitting.

She sat back in her chair and closed her eyes again.

'Abby!'

Oh for Christ sake. She opened an eye. 'I'm on my lunch break.'

She closed her eye again. Silence. She crossed her arms over her chest and put her feet up on the desk. She heard Tara's sharp intake of breath. Another pause and then she exhaled loudly. 'Fine. You've had eleven minutes. You've got forty nine left.'

'Seventy-nine. We're allowed two fifteen minute breaks too.'

'Not altogether we're not. We have to spread our breaks out so everyone gets their turn.'

Abby ignored her. She set her alarm to go off in seventy-nine minutes time and fought to get back to sleep. But she was too angry. She was seething, her stomach churning with bitterness and dislike. As far as Abby knew, Tara hadn't done any work since getting in five hours ago. Abby had worked for four hours straight. She always did more work than anyone else. True, she slept more, but she was the only one with a young child.

When her alarm went off she quickly turned it off and spent the remainder of the night playing solitaire. And when she went out to the toilet she slammed the door and watched Tara jerk upright. The bitch had been asleep. Eight and a half hours and she hadn't done any work. She'd chatted and read all night and then she'd slept. Sally was still knitting. Judy was reading. Abby was so angry she couldn't see straight. But what the hell could she do? The big boss was a woman too. Julie Arlington. She'd probably adored Tara. She'd chosen her over thirty-three others apparently. Tara had been very eager to tell them all about that.

Abby was first out of the door and she didn't say goodbye to anyone. She'd text Sally later to apologise. Right now she was too tired and too hormonal to talk. She got home at seven-fifteen praying that Olly was asleep and she could get ten minutes' rest before she had to do breakfast and all the other chores mornings entailed. He wasn't.

'Mummy! You came home,' he yelled and ran down the stairs. 'Did you go to work?'

'Yes. I went to work. Would you like a drink?'

'Yes please. And Cheerios. And can I watch Paw Patrol?'

Abby got him breakfast and turned the TV on to Nick Jr and then she flopped onto the settee and closed her eyes. She must have fallen asleep because the next thing she knew Matthew was waking her up.

'Abby? It's eight-thirty. I have to go to work. Are you okay?'

Abby forced her eyes open. 'No. I want to die.'

'I'll see you tonight,' he kissed her forehead, kissed Olly and left.

Abby lay there for another ten minutes, fighting to stay awake. In the end she was forced to get up because Olly did a poo and wanted his bottom wiped. Lovely! She brushed his teeth, got him dressed and then she cycled him to nursery. She fell into bed with a blissful sigh, thanking God that the summer holidays were over and Olly was back at nursery. While he'd been off she'd actually managed more sleep but it was very broken. She'd sleep on the sofa while he played and watched TV, only getting up when he was tired of entertaining himself or needed feeding.

She was woken at ten-thirty by the doorbell. It was Yodel asking her to take in a parcel for next door. She looked at the clock. Ten-forty. One hour and twenty minutes. She went upstairs and got back into bed. And then she watched the clock until twelve. She was so tired she felt sick and dizzy with it, but she just couldn't sleep. Maybe she was too tired. Or maybe it was because she only had an hour. Or because she was so wound up about Tara and Yodel. In the end she got up and had a shower. Finally she went to collect Olly.

They had a quiet afternoon and she had him ready for bed by six. She tucked him in and put a DVD on. 'Mummy's going to bed now. Can you be a really good boy and be quiet for me until Daddy gets here?'

'Yes, Mummy.'

'Goodnight, baby.'

'Goodnight, Mummy. I love you.'

'I love you too.' Abby kissed him goodnight and went next door to bed. She'd left the door ajar and she could hear the television. She relaxed and felt it lulling her to sleep.

'I need a poo, Mum,' Olly said from the doorway.

Ally helped him onto the toilet, watched him strain for two seconds and then she cleaned him up and put him back to bed.

Six twenty-five. She closed her eyes. She imagined she was lying on a lilo on the sea. Things got fuzzy and then the phone started to ring. Bugger! She'd forgotten to turn it off.

'Hello?' she said groggily.

'Hello. I understand you've recently been in an accident. Did you know that we can—'

Abby hung up and stumbling downstairs, ripped the phone out of the socket. She checked on Olly and got back into bed. Six forty-one.

She didn't need any enticement to sleep this time. The next time she woke up it was seven twenty-three. She sat bolt upright. What had woken her? Olly? She hurried through to his room. He was fast asleep, legs hanging over the bed guard. She straightened him up and went downstairs. Matthew was watching TV, pizza on his knee.

'Hi. You okay?' he asked.

'Fine. I'm going back to bed,' Abby mumbled and went back upstairs. She could never sleep properly until she knew Matthew was there. She didn't fully trust herself to wake if Olly needed her. She heaved a sigh. She could relax now.

Seven thirty. She closed her eyes. She listened to the TV. She pretended she was at sea. She counted sheep. She tried her antenatal relaxation techniques. She looked at the clock. Seven forty. Seven forty-seven. Seven fifty-three. She could hear someone yelling from the petrol station. A train went past and the house shook. And then a car alarm went off in the distance. A dog barked. Eight o'clock.

Abby rolled over and buried her head in the pillow. She made herself relax and tried to empty her mind. Her leg was itching. She ignored it for as long as she could and then she scratched it. Oh bloody hell. Now her thigh was itching. The baby kicked and did a couple of somersaults.

She rolled onto her back and checked the clock. Eight fifteen. Her back was aching now. She wedged a pillow behind it and cradled her stomach. Eight seventeen. She started to relax and felt herself drifting off. Yes! Oh bloody, bloody hell. Now she needed a wee. She got up and went to the toilet. She washed her hands and went back to bed. Eight twenty-six.

Eight thirty. Eight thirty-six. She thought about Tara. She had teenage children. She'd probably got eight hours sleep today. Oh why had Sid left? She couldn't handle much more of Tara. But what could she do? She couldn't leave, there were no other jobs that would fit in and pay so well.

Eight forty-one. Maybe she could become a childminder. But that took months to register and get started. And what if she hated it? What if Olly hated it? What if the house was too small? Maybe she could look for another night job. Yes. She would. First thing tomorrow. Eight fifty-eight. She rolled onto her side and put a pillow under her leg.

'Abby? Abby? It's nine forty. You've slept through your alarm,' Matthew was saying.

Abby got to work at two minutes to ten. Tara and Judy were already there. Sally had the night off.

'You look knackered,' Judy said when she sat down.

'Hm,' Abby said noncommittally.

'Didn't you sleep today?'

'Not much. I kept getting woken up.'

'I turn the phone off and unplug the doorbell,' Tara said.

'I can't turn the phone off. Olly might need me. And he's only gone for three hours so I only get to sleep in the morning and after he goes to bed,' Abby said conversationally. She would make the effort. Maybe Tara wasn't that bad. Maybe it was Abby being paranoid.

'If you can't sleep during the day you shouldn't work nights. That's why you sleep all night.'

Abby stood up and glared over the partition. 'I don't sleep all night. And I've worked nights for ages now. I manage fine.'

'You have to get enough sleep during the day. It's not fair on the rest of us if you sleep at night.'

'I hardly ever sleep at night. And if I do it's only for my lunch break. I sleep as much as I can but Olly is only three.'

'So? That's not my problem. You're here to work,' Tara said.

Abby opened her mouth to argue and then she clamped it shut. Fuck it. What was the point? The woman was an insensitive, self-obsessed, intolerant old cow. And why the hell wasn't Judy sticking up for her? They'd been good friends for years now. She looked at her friend. She was watching Tara, nodding slightly in agreement.

Abby sat down and logged onto her email. Sod it. Sod them. She was going to look for a new job. And then she thought of the baby. Nobody was going to hire her. She was twenty-eight weeks pregnant. She blinked back tears and went through to the kitchen to heat up her lasagne.

Food would help.

Luckily Olly went to Matthew's the next day and Abby got to sleep for five hours. Five uninterrupted hours. She woke up feeling a lot better but realised something had to be done. It wasn't good for the baby. She was too tired and too stressed. She worked out her maternity leave. She could leave eleven weeks before the baby was due. That was next week. But then she'd only get twenty-eight paid weeks after the baby was born. She'd hoped to work right up until the birth but now knew that would be impossible. Maybe she could leave six weeks before her due date. Compromise. But that was six weeks away. Six weeks was forever. Twenty-four nights of Tara. Two hundred and forty hours.

She desperately wanted to speak to Nick, but with his suspicions over paternity it just wasn't worth it. She couldn't deal with any more stress right now. And what could he do anyway? In the end she wrote to her employers to say she was leaving six weeks before the birth. With four days holiday outstanding she could leave in just over five weeks. She was an adult. A grown woman. She could cope with five weeks.

Chapter Forty-One

'I want her to die,' Abby said to Jo a couple of weeks later. 'Seriously. I really want her dead.'

'Abby, that's an awful thing to say.' Jo watched her carry two mugs of coffee over. 'She can't be that bad.'

'She is that bad. She criticises everything. She wakes me up after an hour every single night and then the other night she said that I was harming the baby by not getting enough sleep. I told her I was a single mother and I had to work and she said that I should have made more effort in my relationship or not have got pregnant in the first place. Can you believe it? The worst thing is knowing that Judy has been telling her stuff about me. Honestly that woman thinks she is so damn perfect. I told her the condom split and she asked why I didn't get the morning after pill.'

'The condom didn't split though did it?' Jo looked confused.

'No. I wasn't telling her that though.'

'Would you have got the morning after pill if it had?'

'No. I didn't get it after having unprotected sex why would I get it after a split condom?'

Jo sipped her coffee. 'Why did you have unprotected sex?'

Abby shrugged. 'Didn't really think about it. Stupid I know but I don't need Miss Perfect telling me that. What the fuck's it got to do with her anyway?'

Jo left an hour later, head reeling. Poor, poor Abby. Nick was in the kitchen eating lunch with Tilly when she got in.

'Everything okay?' he asked.

Jo shook her head. 'Abby's not happy.'

'Why? What's wrong?' Nick looked up from his sandwich.

'Work. She's got a new boss and she's making her life completely miserable. She won't let her sleep and she's a real bitch from the sound of it.'

'How long has she got left?'

'Two weeks. Eight more nights.'

'Is she getting any sleep?'

'Not a lot. Olly's playing up at night and she's really uncomfortable with the baby. She said she's having trouble sleeping. I think she's too wound up.'

Nick turned back to his sandwich. Jo made herself a salad and went through to the living room to eat in front of the TV.

Nick took Tilly round to Abby's the following afternoon. It was a really warm day and all the windows and doors were wide open. Olly was playing in the playhouse and came running across the garden, gibbering with excitement. He and Tilly scampered off and Nick knocked on the door frame. 'Abby?' He peered inside. She was lying on the settee, struggling to sit up.

'Hi, Nick. What's up? Is Jo with you?'

'Nope. Just Tilly. Jo told me you weren't doing too well. I stopped round to see if I could help. When are you working next?'

'Tonight. First night on. You shouldn't have bothered. I'm okay. Just a bit tired.' She rubbed her eyes and gave him a weak smile. He was shocked at how rough she looked. Her face was pale, eyes swollen. She looked exhausted.

'Go to bed, Abs. Seriously. Now. It's two o'clock. You could get a good couple of hours before tea time. I can look after Olly.'

Abby opened her mouth to argue and then she snapped it shut with a sigh. 'Okay, thank you. I wouldn't but I really am tired.' She yelled goodnight to Olly and disappeared up the stairs.

It was dark when she woke and she looked around, feeling completely disorientated. The clock said eight fifty. The house was in silence and she felt a brief moment of panic. But she'd left Olly with Nick. He'd be fine. She got up and dressed in warm clothes – it got really cold in the office at night. Olly was in bed, fast asleep. Abby washed her face and brushed her teeth and then she headed downstairs.

Matthew was on the settee watching TV. 'Feeling better?' he asked, sheepish look on his face.

'Much better thank you,' Abby lied. She actually felt like crap. The glands in her neck and throat felt swollen, her ears hurt and her back was agony. 'When did you get here?'

'Seven. Nick made me feel really guilty. He'd cut the grass, washed up, fed and bathed Olly.' Matthew cleared his throat and shifted his eyes round a bit. 'He also told me that if the baby's mine I ought to be looking after it a bit better.'

Abby froze and stared at him in dismay. 'What did you say? You didn't tell him did you?'

'I didn't say anything. I don't think he expected me to. But he knows, Abby. I'm sure he does.'

'Shit.' Abby sat down and buried her head in her hands. 'Why hasn't he said anything to me?'

'Maybe he's waiting until the baby's born. Maybe he doesn't want to upset you right now.'

'I can't handle this, Matthew. I'm going crazy. I feel like crap; I hate my job; I hate my new boss; I have no money and now this. What the hell is he planning? Oh my God, you don't think he's going to try and take the baby away do you?'

Matthew looked like he was trying not to laugh. 'Abby, calm down. Nick won't do anything to hurt you, I can promise you that. He said to tell you that he'll pick Olly up from nursery tomorrow, Tuesday and Thursday. I'll do it on Wednesday so you should be okay for sleep this shift. Then you've only got four nights left and Nick said he'd help out then too.'

'Really?' Abby started gathering her stuff for work, brain racing. She was grateful, so very, very grateful. She really was so unbelievably tired that she hadn't been sure how she was going to survive the next couple of weeks. She was worrying about money too so when she did get the opportunity to sleep she was too stressed.

She connected her iPhone to the car's bluetooth and dialled Nick on the way to work. 'Thank you for today, Nick. I really appreciate it.'

'No problem. You should have asked for help. I didn't realise things were so bad. Listen, Jo said you were worrying about money. Have you thought of taking a mortgage break?'

'Yeah, but my mortgage is too new. I'm taking a break on my loan and I've got my credit card repayments down to twenty pounds a month for the next nine months. With maternity pay and what Matthew gives me I'll just be able to cover my direct debits but we have to eat and I've only got a few hundred in my savings.'

Nick was silent for a few moments and Abby started to regret telling him everything. What could he do anyway? He was struggling himself.

'What about doing some work from home?'

'Like what? And I'd lose my maternity pay if I got found out.'

'Then don't get found out. I know two women at work who need someone to do their ironing. You could charge ten pounds an hour I reckon. And what about delivering leaflets? I had something in the post the other day and this guy who does property leaflets pays ten quid an hour. Though that's probably a bit riskier. He'd probably put it through the books. But you could do something like that.'

Abby thought about it, searching for drawbacks. But there weren't any. Apart from the fact that she hated ironing of course. But beggars couldn't be choosers. Two hours ironing would provide basic food each week. Another hour would pay for nappies and baby wipes.

Nick promised to talk to his contacts and tell her the outcome when he brought Olly home the next day.

Abby sailed through work that night. She ignored Tara completely and read an entire book. She did her grocery shop in her lunch hour and dealt with the majority of incoming emails.

She took Olly to nursery then slept until Nick came round at two thirty. 'He's had his lunch and we've been to the park.' He handed her Olly's folder and a piece of paper. 'Two numbers. Both need at least two hours ironing a week. I said you'd ring this afternoon. And if you want more I can get you more. There are a lot of women in my office who hate ironing and don't have time to do it.'

'Thanks, Nick,' Abby said gratefully.

'You look better today,' Nick said. Abby looked down at her nightie. Her hair was greasy and she hadn't brushed her teeth.

'Christ, I must have looked really hideous yesterday.'

'How's Chris?' Nick asked.

Abby stumbled mentally, struggling to adjust to the change in subject. 'He's fine. I haven't seen him for a while but we've spoken on the phone. We're not seeing each other any more, I ended it after dinner at your place. Didn't Jo tell you?'

'No. She didn't,' Nick said with a strange look on his face. 'I have to go back to work now. I'll see you tomorrow.' He smiled in a vague fashion and calling goodbye to Olly disappeared out the front door.

Abby went to shower, wondering what the hell was going on. Where were the kisses and the affection? He was acting like a good buddy now. Didn't he want her anymore? Abby looked down at her belly. She couldn't even see her feet. Why would he want her?

Chapter Forty-Two

'Will you marry me?'

Abby looked up from her Kindle. Matthew was stood in the doorway and had just come in. 'Oh my God. You're gay!' she exclaimed, snapping the Kindle cover shut.

Matthew pulled a face and sat down next to her. 'Of course I'm not gay. I wouldn't be proposing if I was.'

Abby screwed her face up, trying desperately to figure out what was going on. 'You can't be pregnant. You're not gay. I know! You've met a married woman and you think she'll sleep with you if you're married too.' She smiled triumphantly.

Matthew shook his head, expression serious. 'Abby, I love you. I want to marry you.'

Abby slowly lost her smile. She shifted in her seat, uncomfortable now. 'No you don't. Oh God, Matthew. Please don't do this to me. You know I don't want to marry you.'

'But you love me,' he said, tone almost defiant.

'Yes. I love Fiona. I don't want to marry her though. What's going on? You're not in love with me. You wouldn't have been unfaithful if that was the case.'

'I am in love with you. And I don't want other women.'

Abby shook her head. 'You will. You're not cut out for marriage. And you're certainly not cut out for another man's child.' He opened his mouth to argue and Abby rushed on, 'Besides, I don't love you like that. I don't want to marry you.'

'Because of Nick,' Matthew said bitterly. 'He won't leave Jo you know.'

'I know.'

'Even if he knew the baby was his.'

Abby wasn't so sure about that but she didn't argue. 'It's nothing to do with Nick. Even if there were no Nick, I wouldn't marry you. We're just friends.' She looked at him, confusion still creasing her brow. 'Are you sure you're not gay?'

Matthew scowled.

'Knock, knock,' Nick said from the doorway.

'Mummy!' Olly came flying across the room and then he noticed Matthew. 'Daddy!' He climbed onto Matthew's knee and gave him a hug. 'Why are you here? Are you sleeping here tonight?'

'No, son. I just came to talk to Mummy. Where have you been?'

'Swimming. Nick took me and Tilly. I swam without armbands. All the way across the swimming pool.' He made swimming motions and ran around the room a few times. Abby looked at Nick who shook his head slightly. Olly had recently started telling a lot of stories. Fibbing was probably the wrong word, it was more like the product of a very overactive imagination. The trouble was that you never knew what was real and what wasn't. He'd come home from nursery last week and told her that Mrs Ball, one of the nursery teachers, had shouted at him. Abby started to get wound up; what had her angel done? Why had Mrs Ball shouted?

And then Olly continued, 'A big dog bit my leg and there was blood squirting everywhere and Mrs Ball picked him up like this,' he pinched two fingers together and held them in the air, 'and the dog said sorry and woofed woof woof and then she shouted at me and the dog ran away and he got into a balloon and flew up, up into the sky. And then I got my gun and shot it and it fell down and the dog died. I need a wee now.' And he'd run off to the toilet leaving Abby's head reeling. She asked at nursery the next day and apparently Mrs Ball hadn't even been in nursery the previous day.

'How was he?' Abby asked Nick now. 'Do you want a coffee or a beer or something?'

'A beer would be good thanks. He was fine. He had a great time.'

'Matthew? Do you want a drink?'

'Beer please,' Matthew said.

Abby started to get up and Nick held up a hand. 'I'll get them. Don't get up. Do you want anything?'

'A glass of water please.'

Nick went through to the kitchen. Matthew scowled at Abby, 'bit bloody comfortable here isn't he?'

Abby rolled her eyes. 'He's been here a lot lately. Helping me out.' She shot Matthew an accusing look and he scowled even harder.

'It's his baby. He should be helping out.'

Abby shushed him just as Nick came back in.

'Are you taking Olly this afternoon?' He asked Matthew.

'Yes. He's staying overnight with me. Why?'

Nick looked surprised for a beat. 'Just wondered.'

Matthew opened his beer, tipped it into his mouth and stood up. 'I'll be off then shall I?'

Abby stood up and went upstairs to get Olly's bag. Ten minutes later they'd left and Abby was left with Nick and Tilly. Only, Tilly was in the garden, so really, it was just her and Nick.

'What's up with him?' Nick asked.

'Matthew?' Abby sighed and flopped back in her seat. 'He just asked me to marry him.'

'Really?' Nick looked stunned. Abby thought that she should be insulted but she couldn't summon up the energy.

'Yep.'

'What did you say?'

'No of course! You don't seriously think I'd say yes do you?'

Nick grinned. 'Just checking. You are having his baby after all.' He stopped grinning and his eyes nailed hers.

Abby looked away. 'Yeah well. I don't want to marry him.'

She heard Nick sigh. 'I'd better get Tilly back to her mum. I'll pick Olly up on Tuesday. I'm working from home all week so I'll take him home with me for a couple of hours. He can play in Tilly's room. I'll drop him back about three thirty if that's okay.'

'That'll be wonderful. Thank you, Nick. I'll make it up to you one day.' She stood up and followed him to the door.

He gave a little smile and looked her over. 'I'm counting on it,' he said. And then he called Tilly and left.

No kiss, no hug, nothing. Just the "look" and the innuendo. What the hell was going on?

When Abby got to work on Monday night Tara called her into an office for a "chat".

'A couple of things. Firstly, I need to know if you're coming back to work after you have the baby.'

'Yes. That is my intention,' Abby said. She could have told her it was none of her business. She didn't actually have to commit either way until much nearer the time. But she had four nights left. What was the point?

'Fine. We're getting a temp to cover the ten months so obviously we need to know asap if you're not coming back. Right. Also, I wanted to talk to you about the way you've reacted to my coming here. Obviously you were hoping to be made team leader—'

'You what?' Abby stared at her, aghast. 'I never wanted that. I'd hate to be team leader.'

'What? You'd hate earning more money?' Tara gave a superior smile. 'Anyway. I know you don't like me being here, you've made that perfectly clear. But at the end of the day, if you do come back—'

'Which I will.'

'If you say so.' Another smile that made Abby want to slap her stupid, ugly face. 'We need to get along. It's not been easy for me – you've made me feel quite unwelcome. If it wasn't for Judy, who by the way is very surprised at how you've been acting—'

Abby took a sharp intake of breath, unable to believe what she was hearing, and then she had a coughing fit because the breath did something funny and tickled her chest.

Tara waited patiently. 'So we'll make more effort to get along? Agreed?'

Abby sighed. 'Fine, whatever.' She couldn't even be bothered to argue. The bottom line was that she just didn't care. Four nights and she wouldn't have to talk to this woman for another ten months. Why waste her energy disagreeing?

They went back to work then and Abby concentrated on getting through the night.

Nick brought Olly back at four o'clock the next afternoon. Abby offered him coffee and they sat outside while he drunk it.

Abby told him about her chat with Tara the night before and then she watched him light his second cigarette off his first.

'Are you okay?' she asked. He looked alright, a little pale maybe, but he'd been working hard as usual.

'Not really.' He inhaled some nicotine and gave a rueful smile. 'Jo walked out last night.'

Abby's jaw dropped open and she stared at him. And then she stared some more. She couldn't speak. She was too shocked.

Nick chuckled without mirth. 'She's met someone else apparently. And she said I didn't love her anyway so what was the point in staying.' Nick looked at Abby, expression fierce. 'That's two kids I'll have that I hardly see.' He sighed and raked a hand through his hair. 'Do you know I thought your baby could be mine for a while? Stupid hey! But the dates tallied and we didn't use condoms every time. But then I realised that you'd have told me if it was mine. You wouldn't keep something that big a secret from me. And I felt guilty for even thinking it.' He put a hand over hers. 'You know I think too much of you for that.'

Abby swallowed. Hard.

'So anyway. There it is. I'm rattling around in my big house again. Forking out two lots of maintenance and missing seeing my kids grow up. God, I'm sorry, Abby. I know I should be grateful. At least I like my job and I have enough money.' He put his cigarette out and looked at her. 'Are you feeling any happier now you've sorted out your money a bit?'

Abby nodded and forced herself to speak. Not easy with a lump the size of a football wedged in her throat. 'Yes. Thank you for the numbers. They both sound really nice. I'm starting next week actually. And Sandra's husband has his own business and she asked if I'd be interested in occasional work doing typing and envelope stuffing and things like that. Apparently she's been doing it but it's too much for her. So that could be good too.'

Nick nodded. 'She mentioned that last week. She said you sounded lovely.' He drained his mug and stood up. 'I have to stop into the office. Do you want me to collect Olly tomorrow?'

'Not unless it's convenient. I've only got three nights left now, I can manage now the end is in sight.'

'I know. But it's better for the baby if you get more rest. I'll bring him back at three-ish.' He carried his mug inside, kissed her forehead and left without another word.

Abby went and got Olly a drink and then she built him a train track and all the time she was thinking, *bugger, shit, bugger, shit,* over and over and over. What had she done? Nick was free now. Available. And what was going on with Jo? Abby hadn't heard from her since Saturday but that was quite normal when she was working. Jo had got far more considerate lately and worried about waking her, so she usually left it to Abby to make contact. She'd met someone else? When? Who? How? She was just about to have a baby. Where had she been to meet a man?

It was a dream come true. Jo had left Nick. He was free. Abby could have him. Except she was carrying his baby and if he found out he would hate her. And how could he not find out if they got together. And she wouldn't want to keep it from him anyway. The only reason she'd kept quiet was Jo. And now Jo was gone. God, imagine if Nick hadn't mentioned the baby. Abby would have blurted it out, thinking he'd be ecstatic. She pictured his face. His expression as he recoiled in horror. And then she went upstairs and threw herself on the bed, sobbing madly because she realised what a monumental mess she'd made of everything.

Chapter Forty-Three

'So come on. Tell me about him. Who is he? Where'd you meet him? When do I get to meet him?' Abby teased her friend the next day.

Jo stroked her stomach, a contented smile on her face. 'His name's Pete. We met at the doctor's surgery. How are things at work?'

'Don't change the subject! I want to meet him! Are you living with him? What does he think about the baby?' Abby finished making coffee and dumped the mugs on the table. She sat down opposite Jo and leant forward as far as her tummy would allow. 'Does he mind?'

'Not at all. He's really excited about it. And yes, I'm living with him.'

'Where? God, Jo. How long ago did you meet him? I mean, it's all so sudden,' Abby squirmed impatiently. It was like getting blood from a stone. Jo was acting all dreamy and weird, almost as if she'd been taking drugs.

'I don't know. A while ago. And it's not sudden. When you know its right, you know its right.' Jo gave a little smile and watched her stomach moving around. 'This baby never stops moving.'

Abby gritted her teeth. 'Have you taken something, Jo?'

Jo looked up in surprise. 'My multivitamin. Why?'

'No reason.' Abby rolled her eyes. 'Have you talked to Nick? Since you left I mean. What are you going to do about visitation and stuff? Has he met Pete?'

'No. Do you think he'll want to?' Jo looked a little surprised and Abby whacked her own forehead with the palm of her hand.

'His child is going to be living with this man, Jo. Of course he'll want to meet him.'

'Oh. I hadn't thought of that,' Jo said, looking very upset all of a sudden. She looked at her watch. 'I have to go now,' she said and stood up.

'You just got here and you haven't touched your coffee.'

'I know. I'm sorry. I just remembered that I have to be somewhere,' Jo said and hurried out of the door.

Abby watched her go. If she had a car, she'd follow her. Something wasn't right. Yes, Jo was acting as if she was in love. But why the panic over Nick meeting Pete? Why the secrecy? Maybe Pete was married. Or he was a woman. Maybe he'd just got out of prison. Perhaps he was eighteen years old. But surely Jo would admit to any of that. She knew Abby well enough to know she wouldn't judge.

Or maybe, *maybe*, Pete didn't exist.

Abby couldn't let the thought go. It was like an itch she couldn't scratch. She phoned Nick while Olly was eating his dinner.

'What's up? Have you slept? Did Matthew collect Olly?' he said on hearing her voice.

'Yes. I got almost five hours. Listen, Jo was round this afternoon. I don't think there's another man. I think she's lying.'

Silence lay between them. Olly ate a pea. Then another one.

'Why? Why would she lie? Why would you think that?' Nick said eventually, tone giving away zilch.

'I said something about you meeting him and she panicked. And then she rushed off.'

Another silence. Three peas. Then, 'So? She wouldn't go it alone. Not if there was an alternative.'

'I think she has. I think we should follow her.'

'No,' Nick said firmly. No hesitation this time. 'Leave it be. I mean it, Abby. You've got enough to worry about.'

'Fine. Do you even know where she lives? She could be sleeping rough for all you know. She's acting stoned. Maybe she's on drugs.'

'Abby! Cut it out. I am not spying on my ex-girlfriend. End of conversation. She's entitled to her privacy.'

'Even if your child is at risk?'

'Jesus, you don't know when to stop do you?' Nick snapped and ended the call.

Abby smiled at the silent telephone. And then she dialled Jo's mobile. It was engaged. She finished feeding Olly and put him in the bath before trying again.

Jo answered this time, tone almost wary.

'It's just me. Where are you living?' Abby said.

There was a long silence. 'Nick just phoned and asked me that.'

'And? Did you tell him?'

'Yes. I'm living at Sean's.'

Abby lost the plot for a moment. That was too easy. 'Sean, your brother? Why are you living with him?'

'I'm not living with him. He's working abroad for six months. I thought I told you.'

Something stirred in the sludge at the back of Abby's brain. 'Maybe you did. I thought you were living with Pete.'

'I am. We're staying here while we look for something more permanent.'

'Why did you say "I" then? Are you going to buy or rent? What does Pete do? Where did he live before?'

Another pause. 'We're going to buy. He's manager of some computer repair business and he was living with his ex.'

'Did he leave her for you?'

A longer pause. 'No. Can we talk later, Abby? I'm in the middle of cooking dinner.'

Abby hung up and dialled Nick.

'Now what?' he sighed on hearing her voice.

'Charming!'

'I spoke to Jo. She's living at Sean's. This Pete guy is living there with her and they're looking for somewhere of their own.'

'Did you ask when you can meet him?'

The silence stretched between them. Abby watched Olly drowning his action man and thought that she really ought to get him out of the bath. His hands were turning wrinkly.

Just as she was on the brink of ending the call, thinking he'd walked away, he asked, 'Shouldn't you be going to bed? You're working tonight remember.'

'I'm bathing Olly. And it's my last night. Yippee! And don't change the subject. When are you meeting this "so called" Pete?'

Nick exhaled noisily. 'Stop bugging me and go to bed.'

'Wimp.'

'Excuse me?'

'Why aren't you insisting on meeting him?'

Nick hung up again.

Abby didn't sleep at all before work that night. She was too intrigued about Jo, too excited about finishing work and too uncomfortable with her bump. But for once she didn't care.

After tonight she could sleep all she wanted. She watched the clock progressing and wondered about Jo and Pete. She wondered if giving birth would be easier this time. And then she wondered where Matthew was. It was eight thirty and he still hadn't arrived.

She waited ten minutes more and then dialled his mobile.

It took ages for him to answer and Abby could hardly hear him for the background noise.

'Where are you?' she asked.

'At Richard's party. It's his birthday remember. What's up?'

'Are you leaving soon?'

A short pause. 'I wasn't planning to. Why?'

'I'm working tonight. You haven't forgotten have you? Shit Matthew, what is wrong with you,' Abby's voice raised to an almost shout. 'It's my last night.'

'I thought last night was your last night. That's why I picked Olly up today,' he said and then he huffed a loud sigh. 'I'll have to get a taxi over. I've been drinking since six.'

'Forget it. I'll ring Fiona,' Abby stabbed the off button and threw the phone across the room. And then she swore and waddled across the room to pick it up again.

Ten minutes later she had a babysitter but no car. Great! She got ready for work, calling Matthew every single nasty thing she could think of. Fiona arrived at nine thirty. 'Can't you call a cab? Won't Nick give you a lift? It can't be good for you cycling with that bump.'

Abby grinned. 'It won't hurt. I cycle every day. I can't afford a cab and I refuse to ask Nick. I'll be fine cycling.' She hugged and thanked Fiona and headed off to work.

'Hi, hen. Last night!' Sally sang when she walked into the office. She handed Abby a wrapped parcel and envelope. 'Just a little something from me.'

'Thank you, Sally.' Abby hugged her friend and sat down to open her present. It was a really cute babygro and a box of Roses. 'Yummy, you shouldn't have.' Abby immediately opened the chocolates and they both dug in.

'Good evening,' Judy said, walking in practically arm-in-arm with Tara. 'Saw the bike. Why aren't you driving?'

'A friend's babysitting tonight and I'm not insured on her car,' Abby explained, offering her colleagues a chocolate.

Tara shook her head. 'No thank you. It can't be good for the baby, you cycling this late on.'

'Exercise is good for the baby. Exercise is good full stop.' Abby said and Tara sat down without further comment. Sally grinned. Tara didn't look as if she did a lot of exercise.

Abby had a busy night closing or re-allocating all her open calls. She finished some data inputting and cleared her section of the desk. And then she read her book for the remainder of the night. She would have loved to sleep but Tara was watching her like a hawk. At five to seven, minutes before home time, Tara decided it was time to do her job.

She handed Abby a big envelope. 'On behalf of the company I'd like to say thank you for all your hard work and to wish you the best of luck. We hope everything goes well and we'll miss you. This is from the day shifts and other night shift too.'

She didn't meet Abby's eye once and Abby was hard pressed not to laugh. It must have killed her to say that. She made thank you noises and opened the envelope. A hundred pounds Mothercare voucher and loads of best wishes and lovely messages from her colleagues. All Tara had written was "Tara".

With a bone-crushing hug from Sally, a more restrained squeeze from Judy and a curt "goodbye" from Tara, Abby was on her way home. She climbed on her bike and started peddling. Her eyes were stinging from lack of sleep, her body fluid with the need for rest, but she was elated. No more work. Just sleep and the new baby and time with Olly. She smiled and indicated left, pulling out onto the main road. A filthy white van whizzed past, Abby wobbled and fought to balance and suddenly her back wheel slid away and she lost the fight. She fell to the road, her backside hitting the edge of the pavement causing a groin-cracking pain to shoot up her spine.

She sat there, stunned, for a moment. A few cars went past but nobody seemed to notice her sitting in the road. She put out a shaky hand and eased herself to standing. She felt okay – a little winded maybe. She lifted her bike up and moved it out of the road. And then she noticed the back tire. It was completely flat. Tears stung in her sleep-deprived eyes and she made herself take some calming breaths.

A few minutes later and she pulled her mobile out of her bag. She tried Matthew first. No answer. She started to dial home but realised Fiona could do little to help. She'd have to bring Olly and then the bike wouldn't fit in the car. Jo's car was too small and Becky started work at seven. With a sigh so big it lifted her hair, she dialled Nick.

Nick was furious. Totally, utterly, dangerously furious. He was going to take Abby's bike and he was going to burn it until it fit into his pocket. He knew he should try and calm down before he saw her but that would mean her standing on the side of the road for even longer.

She said she was okay but what if she wasn't? And even if she was, who was to say she would be the next time. She could kill herself. At the very least harm the baby. His baby. He overtook a car, returning the driver's insulting hand gesture with a beep of his horn. He pressed his foot against the accelerator and watched the speedo edge towards the hundred mph mark. When the hell was she going to come clean? He'd given her so many chances to tell him. He'd even begun to think he was wrong, that the baby really was Matthew's. But then he'd fed her the line about knowing better than to think she'd deceived him and he'd known for sure. Her reaction had given her away completely. She only had seven weeks to go and there was no way he was staying away for the birth. He was watching his son come into the world and he was taking him and Abby home with him.

And if she thought she was naming the baby Tom she could think again. His son wasn't a steam engine and he wasn't eighty years old either. And pretty soon Abby was going to know about it. And this would be the last thing she ever kept from him too. He'd been patient, understanding even, but there was no way he would put himself through something like this again. And this was the last straw on the cycling front too. No more. He was buying her a car and the bike was going to the dump.

He slowed down when he got to the main road. There she was. She was sitting on the pavement, her bike lying on the ground next to her. She was dressed in black jogging bottoms, trainers and a thick fleece coat and she was visibly shivering. Nick pulled onto the pavement and put his hazards on.

Abby stood up and watched him approach. Her face was dulux white, eyes almost purple - ringed with fatigue. Nick took off his coat and wrapped it round her. 'Get in the car,' he said curtly. He tried to sound normal but he was so mad he wanted to throw the bike through a shop window. He forced himself to open the boot. He calmly lowered the back seats and lifted the bike into the car. And then he closed the boot lid and got in the driver's seat.

He pulled away from the curb, too angry to speak but very aware of Abby sitting trance-like next to him. She was still shivering. He turned the heating up to its hottest setting.

Ten minutes later he parked the car next to Fiona's and followed Abby round to the house. Fiona was sitting at the table with Olly.

'Mummy! I missed you!' Olly yelped and then he saw Nick, 'Nick! I missed you as well. Look I've eaten all my toast and Fiona says that I've growed since she saw me last time.'

Fiona stood up, eyes on Abby, clearly worried. 'What happened?'

'I fell off my bike,' Abby said and burst into tears. Fiona immediately stepped forward and put her arms round her friend. Nick watched helplessly. Wishing he could give comfort but wanting to shake her until her ears fell off.

He felt Olly press against him, his little hand moving trustingly into his. 'Mummy's okay. She fell off her bike and she's a bit shaken up. She'll be okay when she's been to sleep,' Nick told him.

Olly nodded but didn't respond.

Nick watched Abby and Fiona hug for a little longer and then he took Olly upstairs to get ready for nursery. Fiona appeared just as he was rinsing Olly's toothbrush.

'I have to go home,' she said from the doorway.

Nick put the toothbrush away and straightened up. 'Why are you here? Where's Matthew?'

Fiona met his look, eyes steady, expression serious. 'He forgot Abby was working and had drunk too much to drive over. She phoned me just before nine, panicking.'

'And she's not insured to drive your car,' Nick said, stating the obvious.

Fiona nodded.

'She shouldn't be cycling.'

'I told her that last night. I wanted her to call a cab or phone you but she said she likes to cycle.'

Nick held her look for a beat longer before heaving a sigh and rubbing his eyes with the balls of his hands. 'She could have seriously hurt herself,' he said.

'I know.'

'Fiona?' Abby called from downstairs. 'Are you okay?'

'Just coming.' Fiona gave Nick a sad smile. 'See you later.' Nick listened to her walk down the stairs and moved to sit on the edge of the bath. He felt drained. The anger and worry and stress had him so tied up he couldn't see straight. He closed his eyes, burying his head in his hands, fighting for some semblance of control before he went back downstairs.

'Nick?' Abby's voice right in front of him had his head snapping back, eyes coming open. 'Are you okay?'

'No. I am not okay,' he said. 'You could have killed yourself. Or the baby. Or both.' Abby's eyes flared open and spots of colour appeared on her cheeks. 'What were you thinking? You're thirty-three weeks pregnant. You can't go cycling six miles on no sleep.'

Abby stepped closer, arms rigid at her sides, hands clenched into fists. 'I can do whatever I damn well please. I'm sorry you were inconvenienced by my call. Had I realised it was so much trouble—'

Nick sprung to his feet. Abby unconsciously moved away and he followed, backing her up until she came up against the wall. He didn't make another move, just stood in front of her, body skimming hers, arms at his sides. She stopped arguing immediately.

They stayed like that for a long time. Nick could hear Olly chattering away to himself, he heard a train pass by, traffic on the road. And all the time he was aware of the violence – firmly controlled, but there all the same. He'd never experienced anything like it before and was in awe of its power. He could feel Abby next to him. Her huge belly pressing into his stomach, her breath warm on his neck.

'I want to comfort you but I can't,' he told her calmly. 'I'm so damn angry I want to beat the crap out of you but I can't do that either.' She stayed silent, the rise and fall of her chest the only movement. 'I want you to check and make sure you're not bleeding. Check for bruises and get ready for bed. I'm going to take Olly to nursery and then I'll come back and check you're okay.'

Still no response. He pulled back slightly and looked down at her. 'Okay?'

Abby nodded, head down, eyes on the floor.

Nick put a finger to her chin and lifted her face until her eyes met his. They were bright, sparkling with moisture but she wasn't crying and he felt inordinately proud of her. Jo would have been in pieces the minute he'd started to speak.

He pushed away and went downstairs to get Olly ready for nursery. And after he'd dropped him off he was going to the dump. The bike was history.

Abby waited until she heard them leave and then she closed the door and undressed. She quickly did as Nick had ordered. No blood. Phew. Bruises? None yet but there was a huge red mark just above her buttocks. Other than that she looked okay. Fat and pregnant; but okay. She brushed her teeth and climbed into a t-shirt before falling into bed.

She closed her eyes and felt herself falling. She tried to force her eyes open. She had to wait for Nick to come back. But her eyes wouldn't open and then she floated away.

The first thing she noticed when she woke up was the silence. And then she noticed that it was light. She looked at the alarm clock. Two fifteen. In the daytime. Shit! Olly. She struggled to sitting, feet already reaching for the floor. And then she saw him. Nick. He was sitting in the chair by the door, elbows on the arms, fingers steepled in front of him.

Memories crashed into her head, one on top of the other. Last night at work. Saying goodbye. Getting on her bike. The white van. Falling. Nick. Quiet. The barely contained fury when he held her against the wall. She took a deep breath and met his look.

'I'm not bleeding.'

He acknowledged this with a slight inclination of his head.

'I've got a red mark where I landed but nothing else.'

Another whisper of a nod.

'I'm fine.'

Nick stared at her for a beat and then he lowered his hands. 'Let me see.'

'See what?' Abby said and then she faltered. He wanted to see where she fell. She opened her mouth to tell him no way but his eyes were still on her and his expression was so guarded, so scarily unfamiliar that she did as he asked. She stood up, turning round and lifting her t-shirt, thanking God that she was wearing knickers.

She felt Nick's eyes on her and scrunched her own eyes shut, waiting for him to speak. Not wanting to turn away until he was satisfied she was okay. And then she felt his hands on her hips and suddenly she was sitting on his lap, engulfed in his arms. He buried his face in her neck and blew out a sigh. 'You frightened the fucking life out of me,' he said and she relaxed into him, knowing the worst was over. 'I've dumped your bike and I'm buying you a car. And if you argue with me I'll lock you up until the baby is born.'

'You can't dump my bike!' Abby pulled away, panic pushing every other thought out of her head. 'How will I get Olly to nursery? What if I have to rush somewhere?' She felt her mind scatter, scrambling, all the repercussions of no bike flooding her consciousness.

Nick tapped her lightly on the head. 'I'm getting you a car.' Abby stared at him, open-mouthed and he did another sigh. 'How do you think you're going to get around with two children? Even if you get another seat on the bike, you can't use it until the baby can sit up. And there's no way you're using one of those trailers. You have no double buggy, no buggy-board. I know you're excited about the baby but from what I can gather you've done nothing about planning for it.'

Abby stared at him. He was right. 'Oh my God. You're right.' She clapped a hand over her mouth. 'I'm the worst mother in the history of worst mothers.' She took her hand away and listened. 'Where's Olly?'

Nick smiled. 'He's gone to play at Jamie's.' He checked his watch. 'I'm collecting him at three. And you're not the worst mother in the world. You're the most stressed, overtired mother in the history of mothers, but not the worst.' He paused. The bedside clock ticked four times before he spoke again. 'I've done a lot of overtime lately. I can afford to get you a basic runaround.'

'You're not buying me a car,' Abby said, sitting up straighter and crossing her arms. 'No way. I'll get the money for my own car somehow but I don't want you buying me one.'

'Tough.'

'I won't drive it.'

Nick rubbed his nose with the flat of his hand. 'Even you're not that stubborn. Though stubborn's probably not the right word. More like ridiculous. Stupid. Foolish.'

'Why? Why are you doing this? I'm not your responsibility. If you insist on doing something then lend me the money to buy *myself* a car. I'll pay you back when I go back to work.'

Nick glared at her, eyes narrowed, mouth pinched with anger. 'Why can't you just accept my help?' Abby glared back at him and he threw his head back. 'Fine. I'll lend you the money. I'll come with you to choose a car and you can pay me back.' He slowly lifted his head until his eyes met hers again. 'But you don't get on a bike again until after the baby is born. And after the baby is born you only cycle alone and for fun. I don't want Olly going on the bike with you anymore. It's not safe. And I want you to promise me that you'll never, *ever* take my son on the back of your bike.'

Abby's first reaction was to tell him to bugger off. If she wanted to cycle she would. And Olly was nothing to do with him – she could take him wherever she wanted, however she wanted. And then his words came crashing around her.

His son.

Chapter Forty-Four

Three weeks went by before Abby decided Nick wasn't going to push her about the baby. Not yet anyway. His mobile had rung seconds after he called the baby his and she hadn't seen him since. He'd dropped Olly back from Jamie's and left his car keys on the table with a note telling her she could use his car until they went car shopping. Abby had no way of knowing what, if anything, he was driving and she didn't intend to contact him to find out.

Matthew thought that Nick was biding his time. Giving Abby space because of the pregnancy and that he'd be back to claim them both before the baby came. Abby wasn't so sure.

After weeks of solitude, days spent sorting out finances and paperwork and doing odd jobs round the house, nights spent tossing and turning and worrying about Nick, Abby decided she needed a night out with her friends.

She picked up Fiona and Becky first. And then Jo. She guessed from the way Jo was waiting in the driveway that she was just as eager for a night out. Though with all the lights burning in the house, maybe it was just another way to avoid introducing them to the elusive Pete.

'Isn't this Nick's car?' Jo asked, heaving her bump into the passenger seat.

'Is Pete home?' Abby asked, eyes watching the living room window, hoping to see someone move inside.

'No. Why are you driving Nick's car?'

'He loaned it to me until I get one of my own. My bike got wrecked.'

'What's he driving?'

Abby looked at her friend before she pulled away. She sounded pretty nonchalant but it had to be weird – seeing your best friend driving your ex-boyfriends car.

'I've no idea. He dropped the car off weeks ago and I haven't heard from him since.'

'Maybe he's walking,' Fiona said from the back seat.

'No. He's definitely driving. He came over the other day and he had car keys,' Jo told them and Abby felt her insides twist. Why had he been to see Jo and not her? Especially if he knew both babies were his. Unless he'd been testing her? Maybe he wasn't sure the baby was his? Or maybe he knew it was his and hated her now? Abby sighed and tried to concentrate on her friend's conversation. She'd been over this. Over and over again while she lay in bed at night. Did he know? Didn't he know? What was he going to do? Tonight she wanted to forget all about it.

They started off at the Oatsheaf and bumped into Matthew at the bar. He bought them all drinks and followed them to the arm chairs in the front window. 'How are you doing?' he asked Abby. They were behind the others and the pub was noisy enough that they couldn't be heard.

'I'm okay.'

'Still haven't heard from him?'

'Nope. He's been to see Jo though,' she said bitterly. Matthew gave her waist a squeeze and pulled out a chair for her.

'He can't avoid her as well. He has no reason to.'

'Hm. Why are you out anyway? You're supposed to be bonding with our son.'

Matthew grinned. 'Our son is sleeping. Mum insisted I went out and got drunk while she babysat.'

Matthew chatted to the others for a few minutes then went back to his friends.

'I don't know why you two don't get back together,' Jo said after he left. 'You get on so well.'

Abby sipped at her yummy non-alcoholic lemonade. 'I don't love him,' she said and then she turned to Becky. 'So tell us about work. Did you get the job?'

Becky gave a wide smile and told them about her promotion. And then they all started baiting Jo.

'What does Pete look like?' Becky asked.

'He's average height, about five nine, five ten . . .'

'Short then,' Becky said.

'He is not short,' Jo said in a voice that told Abby she cared. Maybe, just maybe this Pete did exist after all.

'Is he thin? Muscly? Fit? What colour hair does he have?' Fiona asked.

'He's quite fit but not overly big. Definitely not skinny though,' Jo said with a dreamy look on her face. 'He has dark hair, blue eyes.'

'Good in bed?' Becky teased.

'Oh yes,' Jo smiled happily.

'So when can we meet him?'

The smile disappeared. 'Soon. He works funny hours.'

Abby watched her fiddling with her glass. 'I thought he was manager of an IT firm.'

The fiddling stopped. And then it started again – more frantically. 'He is. It's a new company and he's working a lot of hours to get it running.'

Abby was just thinking that something still didn't seem right and that she'd have to do some more investigating when a familiar, spine-stiffening voice said in her ear, 'Good evening, ladies. Can I get anyone a drink?'

'Nick! Just in time,' Becky said, holding up her empty glass. 'Vodka and Red Bull please.'

'Same here please.' Fiona.

'Hi, Nick. I'll have sparkling water please.' Jo.

'Abby?' Nick said and Abby looked up into smiling eyes and a friendly smile.

And she was suddenly angry instead of bewildered. What right did he have to play around with her feelings anyway? 'Nothing,' she said shortly and looked away.

He disappeared and Abby forced herself to relax. She'd bumped into him in the pub before. No big deal. He'd be with his friends. He'd drop their drinks off, make some small talk and then he'd leave. Same as Matthew. Nothing to worry about. She took some deep breaths and crossed her legs. She'd had the most chronic period pain for the past week and since she hadn't been sleeping her back had been agony. It made sitting down very uncomfortable. For the first time that evening she wished she were tucked up at home in bed.

Nick came over with the drinks a little while later. 'Sorry it took so long; queues at the bar.' He distributed the drinks, putting a glass of lemonade in front of Abby, and sat down between her and Fiona. Abby listened while they chatted about Fiona's kids and then Tilly.

'How are you?' He asked Abby after he'd talked at length with all three of her friends.

'What are you driving?' she asked him.

'One of the pool cars from work. I asked how you were.'

'I'm fine. I've been fine for the past three weeks too,' she said, unable to help herself.

Nick grinned. 'Have you missed me?'

'No!'

'I've been busy at work.'

'Not too busy to see Jo.'

The grin widened.

'Have you met Pete yet?'

Nick sobered a little. 'No.' He glanced at Jo and then his eyes were on Abby again. 'I'm beginning to think you're right. I think maybe she is living alone. There were no signs of a man living there.'

'Apart from Sean you mean?'

'No sign of a man, full stop.

'Could be that she's living with a man she doesn't want us to meet,' Abby said, watching him carefully.

'Like someone we know, you mean?' Nick said slowly.

'Someone she met quite recently and hit it off with maybe?' Abby added and he looked thoughtful.

'You're thinking of Chris aren't you?'

Abby nodded again.

'Why would *you* think that? You weren't even there when they met?'

Abby took a sip of her drink. 'She mentioned him a couple of times afterwards and she's the worst person in the world at being subtle. It was pretty obvious she liked him. And I can't think of any other reason she'd keep a new boyfriend a secret from me.'

'Hm.' He thought about that for a beat. 'You could be right.' He shook his head. 'I don't think so though. I think she's going it alone.'

'What are you two talking about?' Fiona asked. Abby looked at Jo. She was deep in conversation with Becky so Abby leant across Nick and told her what they were talking about.

'I think it's more likely someone we won't approve of. She wouldn't be by herself voluntarily,' Fiona said.

'She's happy whatever,' Abby said, watching her friend. 'Maybe it doesn't really matter.'

'It matters to me,' Nick said, voice sour. 'I want to know who's raising my child.'

'Good point,' Fiona agreed. She stood up and disappeared in the direction of the toilets.

'How's the baby?' Nick asked, shooting Abby's stomach a quick look.

'Fine. I went for a check-up yesterday. Everything's normal. The midwife reckons he's going to be big.'

Nick smiled and downed some of his pint.

'Do you think Jo'll have a boy?'

'Nope. Girl.'

'Really? What makes you think that?'

He shrugged. 'I just know.'

'So it'll be called Jade?'

Nick grinned. 'What's wrong? Don't you like the name Jade?'

Abby grimaced. 'Not particularly.'

Nick finished his drink and got to his feet. 'I have to go. I'm meeting Martyn in the Arthur.' He kissed Jo and Becky and waved to Fiona who was talking to someone at the next table. 'Oh and on the subject of names. We are not calling our son Tom,' he said and walked out of the pub.

'Maybe you should call him,' Matthew suggested the next day. 'Make him talk to you.'

Abby finished loading the washing machine and measured out the washing liquid. 'And then what? I'll deny the baby's his and we'll be back to square one.'

'You can't deny it. It's too late for that.'

'What?' Abby stabbed the on button. The machine started filling with water and she turned to Matthew. 'You're not suggesting I admit it?'

'You already have. Think about it. If the baby wasn't his and he said the things he said you'd do anything to put him straight. By doing nothing you've admitted to it.'

'Shit.' Abby slumped through to the living room and dropped onto the sofa. 'I never thought of that.' She buried her head in her hands. 'What am I going to do?'

'Admit to it,' Matthew suggested.

'And then what? Nothing's changed. It'd still really upset Jo.'

'He's not with Jo anymore. And she can hardly blame you when she did exactly the same.'

'And he won't ever forgive me for lying to him.'

'He already has from the look of it. You need to talk to him, Abs. See what he says. Find out what he wants.'

'He can talk to me. Why should I talk to him?' Abby said.

Matthew sighed. 'Because you're an adult. Because you're carrying his child and you lied about it.' Abby didn't lift her head and she didn't speak. She heard Matthew stand up. 'I'm going. Think about it.' She listened to him step outside and call goodbye to Olly. And then everything was silent again. She struggled to her feet and shuffled to the window to make sure Olly was okay. He was lining stones up on one of the swings, mouth moving as he played his imaginary games.

'Knock, knock,' a voice said and Nick appeared in the doorway.

'Tilly!' Olly yelled, ecstatic to have something other than stones to play with.

'Hi. I just saw Matthew in the drive.'

'Yeah. He just brought Olly home.' Abby watched Tilly and Olly disappear into the playhouse. 'Why didn't you have Tilly last night?'

'I did. Mum babysat so I could meet Martyn. It was his birthday.' Nick sat down on the sofa and patted the seat next to him. 'We need to talk.'

Abby sighed and sat down just beyond his hand. 'I know.'

'Are you ready to admit the baby's mine?'

Abby nodded.

'And you lied because of Jo?'

Another nod.

'How do you know it's mine?'

'Matthew can't have children. He had testicular cancer just after Olly was born and the treatment left him infertile.'

'Is that definite?'

'Yes. We hadn't had sex since my last period anyway.'

'So he's definitely mine?'

'He's definitely yours.'

Abby watched him closely, trying to decide if he was pleased or not. He looked okay; just normal really.

'How come Matthew went along with it?'

'He's a good friend. And he thought you'd work it out.'

Nick acknowledged this with a nod. 'Would you really have let me go on believing you were carrying another man's child?

What about the birth? You'd have let me miss the birth of my child?'

Abby shrugged. 'Probably.'

Nick's mouth narrowed and Abby jumped in quickly, 'The reasons I lied in the first place still exist.'

'Jo has left me!'

'We don't know that. We don't know why she left. Maybe she suspected my baby was yours and she's moved out hoping we'll work things out.'

Nick snorted. 'Unlikely. And even if it were true, wouldn't we owe it to her to try?'

'I need to know for sure. I'm not hurting Jo,' Abby said stubbornly and Nick jumped to his feet.

'But it's okay to hurt me? And yourself? And Olly? And our son? All to save Jo?'

'I'm not hurting Olly.'

'Are you happy? Does he have a father figure in the house?'

'I am happy and he has Matthew.'

'Bollocks. He has a part time dad and an un-fulfilled mother. You don't even know that Jo would mind. Have you even tried talking to her about it?'

'No. Have you?' Abby stared up at him, wishing he'd sit back down.

'No. But I'm going to.'

Abby sprang to her feet. 'No! You can't do that. At least wait until the baby's born.'

'No. I want you living in my house before our baby is born. I want—'

'Oh fuck!' Abby looked down at her feet in dismay.

'What?'

'I think my waters just broke.' Abby stared at him, fighting back panic. 'It's too early. It's too soon. I've still got four weeks to go.'

'Have you had any pains?'

'No. Just period pain – no contractions.'

'We'd better get you to the hospital. Have you got a bag packed?'

'No. I've still got four weeks. I didn't even buy nappies yet.'

'Well if they keep you in I can get everything later. Come on, grab your stuff.' Nick led her to the porch, yelling at Olly and Tilly to come to the door. 'I'll drop the kids off at my mums for now.' He ran upstairs and got her a change of underwear and some jogging bottoms and she changed out of her wet clothes, too scared to be shy. He put her wet clothes in the sink and led her round to the driveway.

Abby followed him blindly, thinking please, please just let the baby be okay. She wobbled her tummy hoping the baby would move. Wanting reassurance that he was okay. But there was nothing.

The journey passed in a haze. She said goodbye to Olly, managing a bright voice so he wouldn't worry and ten minutes later they were at the hospital. Nick led her straight up to the maternity ward where they were taken to their own room.

'Someone will be in to examine you in a moment,' the nurse said and she left them alone.

Nick put an arm around her middle and led her over to the bed. 'Are you okay?'

'I can't feel the baby move,' she said, fighting not to cry.

'That's normal towards the end isn't it? Can you remember when you last felt him?'

Abby shook her head, 'I can't remember. This morning maybe.'

'Are you getting any pains?'

'Only in my lower back. And I still have period pain.' She turned to look up at him. 'I'm scared, Nick. What if something's wrong?'

Nick immediately yanked her into his arms, holding her tight, hand smoothing her hair and her back. 'You're both going to be fine.'

He held her for a few more minutes and then he pulled away. 'I'll go and see if someone's coming,' he said.

Abby watched him leave and then she sat on the edge of the bed. He was back in what seemed like seconds, a midwife close on his heels. And suddenly it was all action. She was laid on the bed and hooked up to a monitor. Beeping immediately filled the room and the midwife smiled. 'The baby's fine.'

She examined Abby then. It wasn't pleasant – was actually quite painful but Abby was so relieved that the baby was okay that she didn't care.

'You're five centimetres dilated,' the midwife said. 'Did you have a quick labour the first time round?'

Abby shook her head. 'Eighteen hours. How can I be dilated already? I haven't even had any contractions.'

'Have you had any other pains? Any cramps? Back pain?'

Abby told her about the period pain and her lower back and the midwife smiled. 'That's early labour my love. Now, can I get you any pain relief? Gas and air? Pethidine?'

'No thank you. I'm fine at the moment.'

The midwife left the room again.

'You need to call Matthew,' Abby told Nick. 'He'll have to collect Olly.'

'I'll go now. Will you be okay?'

Abby nodded and watched him leave. And then she relaxed back against the pillow. The baby was okay. Early. But okay. She looked at the clock. It was just after two. She wondered how long it would be before the baby came. She hoped it would be quick. And wouldn't it be wonderful if she didn't have any contractions. Was that even possible? She thought of the baby. Her son. Another baby boy and she didn't care if it hurt. She just wanted to hold her baby in her arms.

Nick got outside and unlocked his mobile; realising, as he pressed the contacts icon, that he didn't actually have Matthew's number.

He phoned Jo.

'Oh my God. Is she okay? Four weeks early isn't good is it? Poor thing must be beside herself. Hold on. I have his number here. I'll send it to you.' Nick ended the call, promising to call as soon as he had any news.

He waited for Jo's text to appear and pressed on the attached number.

Matthew answered after the first ring, 'Does she want me to come in?'

'No. I'm with her,' Nick said shortly. He told Matthew where to collect Olly from and again, promised to ring when there were any developments.

He hurried back inside. Abby was being examined again. 'Are you okay?' he asked, rushing to her side.

'The baby's distressed. The doctor's on his way but I think we're going to have to do a section,' the midwife said and Abby burst into tears.

The next few hours were a blur of activity. The doctor visited, closely followed by the anaesthetist. An Epidural was administered and then the nurse changed her into a hospital gown and took her jewellery away and suddenly Abby was being whisked off to the operating theatre. Nick disappeared briefly then was once again by her side, this time dressed in hospital clothes. A load of men in masks and funny hats introduced themselves, a screen was set up and then there was lots of stuff going on by her stomach. Abby watched Nick watch what was going on. He was pale, his hands gripping hers. There was a weird sensation, sort of like someone massaging her tummy and then there was a wail and her son was being held in the air.

'He's okay,' Abby said and started to cry again. Nick wiped the tears away and leant down to kiss her forehead.

The baby was taken to the side of the room to be examined and wrapped and then he was being handed to Nick who put him in Abby's arms. The baby was tiny, just over five pounds. He blinked at Abby with sleepy blue eyes. He was completely bald except for a tiny black tuft of hair on the right side of his head. 'He's so cute,' Abby whispered to Nick and then she smiled at her son, 'Hello, honey. I'm your mummy.'

The baby screwed his face up and started to cry. Abby automatically pulled the hospital gown from underneath her. She put the baby's mouth on her nipple and he moved his head around, still whimpering.

'His mouth is too small,' Nick said, 'squeeze it for him.'

Abby scissored her nipple and aimed it at his mouth again. This time he found it, latching on with mouth sucking hard.

'Well done,' the doctor said, 'premature babies don't always take to breast feeding.'

'Is he okay?' Abby asked.

'He's perfect. A little small but nothing to worry about. We're just going to stitch you up and then we'll move you to the ward.'

Nick and Abby watched their son feed while the doctors went to work with their needles. Abby thanked God she couldn't feel anything and tried not to think about what they were doing.

'What are we going to call him? Do you really not like Tom?'

Nick grinned. 'I really don't like Tom. How about Aaron?'

Abby screwed her nose up. 'What about Alex? Or Charlie?'

Nick cocked his head slightly. 'He looks like a Charlie. Charlie James.'

Abby pulled another face. 'Needs a middle name. How about Charlie Nicholas James.'

The smile stretched his face and Abby swore his eyes got a little moist. 'I love it.'

Charlie had fallen asleep, his tiny mouth still round her nipple. Abby watched him for a few minutes. And then she thought about Olly and how it had felt the first time she watched him sleep. 'What time is it?' she asked quietly.

Nick looked up at the clock. 'Five thirty.'

'Can you go and ring Matthew please? Check Olly's okay. Maybe Matthew could bring him in and stop by to get me some stuff.'

Nick talked to the midwife and disappeared. He was back within a few minutes and not long afterwards they moved Abby onto a ward. There were six beds, three of which were occupied. Abby was put by the door. The bed next to her was empty but there was a woman sleeping in the bed opposite.

'How do you feel?' Nick asked quietly. Charlie was sleeping in his little plastic crib – wearing a hospital nappy and wrapped in a blue blanket.

'Sleepy.'

'Are you sore?'

'Not yet. Everything's still numb. Is Matthew coming in?'

'Yeah, he'll be here in about half an hour.' Nick sat in the chair next to the bed. He glanced at Charlie and then turned the full force of his gaze on Abby. 'I want you to move in with me when you come out,' he said.

Abby shook her head. She took his hand and stroked his palm with her thumb. 'It's too soon. Jo hasn't had her baby yet and I need to speak to her first. And what about Olly? He's just got used to our new house. I can't move him again already.'

'I want to marry you, Abby,' Nick said. His voice was soft but he looked thoroughly pissed off. 'And if you're as loyal to me as you are to Jo, I'll be the happiest man in the world.'

Abby smiled and squeezed his hand. 'I love you. I really do. But I'm not going to upset Jo. Not yet. Once she's had the baby and she's settled, then I'll talk to her.'

Nick sat up straighter, 'Abby—'

'No,' Abby glared at him. 'Don't give me a hard time. I won't change my mind and it's not fair to hassle me. I just had major surgery. I just gave you a son.'

Nick gave a bark of laughter. 'Milk it for all you can,' he said.

Abby relaxed back against the pillows. 'I fully intend to. You can't yell at me in here.'

Nick gave in and went back to admiring his son. What else could he do?

Chapter Forty-Five

Matthew felt like crying. He'd seen Nick with Abby and the baby and he'd felt sick to the stomach. He hadn't stayed long. Olly was playing up. He was missing his mummy and he wasn't sure he liked his baby brother very much. Matthew took him back to his mum's and put him to bed. And then he went back to the hospital.

Thankfully, Abby was alone. She was feeding Charlie and looked so happy it made Matthew's heart ache. He kissed her cheek and handed her a box of chocolates. 'How are you feeling?' he asked.

'Itchy. The anaesthetic is wearing off and my legs are itching like crazy. Are you okay?'

Matthew looked at Charlie, avoiding looking at Abby. 'No. I wanted to talk to you alone.' He cleared his throat. 'I wanted to say sorry. For cheating on you. And for not being a better boyfriend.'

He felt Abby's hand on his arm and he swallowed. Hard. 'I was such an idiot.' He cleared his throat. 'I think that maybe it was because of the cancer. I was thinking about it. About how stupid I was. And I realised that I never even looked at another woman before that.'

'Because you couldn't have another baby?'

Matthew nodded. 'I would have liked a big family. Despite what you think, I really love Olly. I think maybe I distanced myself from him too. It's weird. You find out you can't have children and it takes something away from you. I felt like less of a man. Unworthy of having a family even.'

'Oh, Matthew.' Abby squeezed his arm and he looked at her for the first time. She was crying, big fat tears, which were running off her face and dripping onto Charlie.

'Don't cry. It's okay. I'm sorted now. I just wanted to explain. I know it's too late for us, but I love you and I wanted you to know why I was the way I was.'

'I love you too,' Abby said and pulled him down for a hug. Matthew returned the hug as well as he could without squashing Charlie.

'I'd better go and let you get some rest,' Matthew said, straightening up.

'Would you put Charlie in his crib for me,' Abby asked and Matthew took the baby, pausing to examine him.

'He looks like you,' he said.

'I know.'

'Let's hope he doesn't have your temperament,' Matthew grinned. 'I don't think Nick could cope.'

He put Charlie in his crib and gave Abby one last hug.

'Call me if you need anything. Otherwise I'll bring Olly in tomorrow after work. Mum's going to take him to nursery and look after him in the afternoon.'

Abby thanked him and he left. Glad to have got everything off his chest. Happy to have explained. And completely gutted that Abby wasn't in the hospital with *his* baby.

Nick stopped in to see Jo on the way home from the hospital. Her car was in the driveway and she answered the doorbell within minutes.

'What happened? Is Abby okay? Did she have the baby?'

Nick followed her through to the kitchen. 'Baby boy. Charlie. 5 pound 2 ounces. Abby had to have a caesarean but she'd doing fine. She's got a phone. I'll write the number down before I go.' He nodded to Jo's bump. 'How are you feeling?'

'Fine. I'm so happy for Abby but I wish I could have the baby early. It's really dragging now.'

Nick gave her a sympathetic smile.

'Do you want a coffee?' Jo asked, switching the kettle on.

'Yes please. Is Pete not here?'

Jo spooned coffee into two mugs. 'No. He's working.'

Nick cleared his throat. 'Does he really exist?'

'Sorry?' Jo looked up, eyes wide, expression genuinely surprised.

'Pete. You won't let anyone meet him. I just wondered if you were living alone and had made Pete up so we wouldn't worry about you.'

Jo carried on staring and Nick began to think he was wrong. But surely she'd have denied it by now. The kettle started to boil – steam shooting from the spout and the vent in the lid and then Jo seemed to slump.

'You're right. I'm sorry. I did make it up. I didn't want to live with you anymore but I thought you'd try and stop me if I just moved out.'

'So there's no Pete?'

Jo shook her head. 'No. There's no Pete. But I'm fine. I like living here. And when Sean comes back I'll probably rent somewhere. Mum and Dad have offered to help with money.'

Nick watched her and she slowly raised her eyes to meet his.

'And you're happy?' Nick asked.

Jo nodded. 'Very. All I want is a baby, Nick.'

'So you don't have feelings for me anymore?'

Jo's eyes widened in surprise. 'No.' She gave a little smile. 'Is that okay?'

'Of course it is.' Nick watched her pour the coffee and carried his over to the table. 'I have to ask you something. I hope it doesn't upset you, but I need to know.'

Jo took the seat opposite him and sat down. She gave him a wary look. 'What is it?'

Nick took a deep breath. 'It's about Abby.'

Jo didn't say anything; her eyes were steady over the rim of her mug.

'I'm in love with her.'

There was a long silence, broken only by the click of the dishwasher as it changed cycle.

'Is she in love with you?' Jo asked.

'I think so.'

Jo put her mug down and drew in a long breath. 'Have you slept together? When did this happen? Is that why you kicked me out?'

She looked so forlorn and Nick felt terrible. He moved to the chair next to her and took her hand. 'I don't know when I fell in love with her, but she's not the reason I ended it between us. Things hadn't been right for a long time.'

'I know,' Jo said and she looked down at their hands. And then she sniffed and Nick saw a tear roll down her cheek.

'I'm sorry, Jo,' he said and pulled her into his arms. She immediately burst into tears. Nick held her tight, stroking her back, feeling his baby wiggling between them.

'I'm sorry. I don't know why I'm crying,' Jo said between sobs. 'I don't want you anymore. It just feels weird.'

'I know,' Nick said, still rubbing her back. 'I do understand.'

'The baby's yours isn't it?'

'Yes, it is.'

'Can you get me a tissue please,' she said, pulling away slightly.

Nick got to his feet and looked around.

'They're in the living room.'

Nick went through and found a box of Kleenex. Jo was back to drinking her coffee and looking a little more composed when he got back. She thanked him and blew her nose. 'Does Matthew know?'

'Matthew knew right from the beginning apparently. I only just found out the baby was mine.'

'She lied to you too?' Jo looked aghast.

'She didn't want to upset you. We only slept together a few times, just the one night when she'd been drinking and she really fought against that. She refused to carry on because of you. You've come first for her the whole time.'

Jo was silent while she thought about that. 'Oh Jesus. What a mess. And now? What's happening now? Is she living with you?'

Nick shook his head. 'Nope. She's still refusing because she doesn't want to upset you.'

'But she's got your baby. And she loves you.' Jo shook her head in bewilderment. 'She's crazy. I can't believe what a good friend she is.'

She gave a big hiccup and Nick grinned.

'Sorry. God, I have such bad indigestion. Do you want me to talk to her?'

Nick shook his head. 'No. I want her to talk to you. She reckons she's going to tell you after you've had the baby.'

'But that's ridiculous. That could be two or three weeks away if I go overdue. Why don't you want me to talk to her?'

'I want her to initiate it. Call me dumb but I need to know it's what she really wants.'

Jo shook her head. 'You're so stubborn. You two deserve each other, you know that?'

'So you're okay with it?' Nick asked gently.

Jo smiled. It was a sad smile but it reached all the way to her eyes. 'Of course I am. I love you and Abby and I want you both to be happy.' She chuckled. 'I just don't want to be around when you fight.'

'No. Me either.' Nick stood up and put their mugs on the drainer. 'I'm going home to bed. Do you want Abby's number?'

'No. I'm going to go over first thing tomorrow. What ward is she on?'

Nick told her and she walked him to the door.

'Thank you for being honest with me,' she said.

Nick gave her a hug thinking that she was finally growing up. 'Thanks for being so understanding.' He kissed her. 'Call me if you need anything.'

'I will.'

Nick walked to his car and drove home thinking that he was going to have two children born within weeks of each other. How weird was that?

Chapter Forty-Six

Charlie slept through the night. Apparently that was normal for a newborn though Olly hadn't done it. Abby thought you were meant to wake premature babies for feeds every couple of hours, but nobody told her to so she let him sleep. He woke at six thirty, his little screams waking his mother instantly.

She rang the bell by her bed and a nurse came rushing through. 'Are you okay?'

'Charlie's crying. Should I try and get up?' Abby asked, feeling unaccountably lazy for calling a nurse to fetch her son.

'Not just yet. Maybe later on if you feel up to it.' The nurse changed Charlie's nappy and passed him to Abby to feed.

Abby spent a pleasant few hours feeding and admiring her son. Breakfast came and then Jo turned up. She handed Abby a wrapped parcel and gave her a hug. A really long hug.

'Are you okay?' Abby asked when Jo finally let go and sat down.

Jo nodded. 'Can I hold him?' She nodded at Charlie and Abby handed him over. She unwrapped her present. It was a little denim outfit.

'Thanks, Jo. I love it.'

Jo was gazing down at Charlie, finger caressing his face, his head, unclenching his tiny fists. 'He's gorgeous. What happened to naming him Tom?'

Abby shrugged. 'I changed my mind.'

'Will he be Whibley like Matthew and Olly?' Jo asked, looking up from Charlie, eyes meeting Abby's.

Abby gave her a long look. What a weird question. Unless . . . 'You know.' She threw her head back against the pillow and scrunched her eyes up. 'How?'

'Know what?' Jo asked innocently.

'You are the worst liar in the world, Joanne Gibson. You know about Nick. Did he tell you?'

Jo sighed. 'I wasn't meant to let on. He wants to see if you talk to me.'

'Really?' Abby perked up. 'Does he think I'm making excuses or something?'

'I don't know.'

'When did he tell you? Last night, right?'

Jo nodded.

Abby felt her throat close over. 'And? Are you okay? I feel so bad, Jo. But nothing's happened since we stopped the swap, I swear, and we never did anything until you split up.'

'I know. Nick told me everything. I'm fine. I was a bit upset at first. It felt a bit weird. But it makes so much sense. You're perfect for each other.'

'You think so?' Abby asked. She might love him but she certainly didn't think they were well suited.

'You're the only woman I know who'll stand up to him. And he'll look after you. And you both have kids and you're everything I'm not. Everything Nick didn't like about me – you're the opposite.'

'And you're really okay with it?'

Jo nodded. Her eyes looked a little damp but she was smiling and Abby felt so relieved she started to cry. And then Jo started to cry too and she had to put Charlie in his crib so they could hug.

'I'm so sorry I went behind your back,' Abby sobbed.

'Me too. I was worse. You and Matthew hadn't even split up,' Jo sobbed even louder. 'I'm so sorry, Abs. I was a terrible friend. I never realised how hard it was for you working and looking after Olly and being so tired. I just felt so jealous that you were a mum and Matthew always seemed so much fun. It's no excuse and I was such a brat. Please say you'll forgive me?'

'There's nothing to forgive; you're my best friend. Maybe if we'd been with the right men to start with, it wouldn't have happened.'

Jo pulled away and wiped her eyes with the back of her hand. 'Definitely.'

Abby reached for the tissue box and blew her nose, handing the box over to Jo. 'And what about Pete?' she asked tentatively. 'Is he the right man?'

Jo shook her head. 'I came clean with Nick last night. Pete doesn't exist. I just didn't want Nick to make me stay living with him. I wanted to go it alone.'

Abby smiled, feeling so proud of her friend. 'And you're happy?'

'Very. I just wish this baby would come,' she said and Abby laughed.

They spent another hour chatting, telling each other more about the swap. Talking about the birth, babies and the universe. And then Jo had to leave for her check up. 'You won't tell Nick I told you will you?' Jo asked before she left.

Abby shook her head. 'No.' She grinned. 'I have a plan. I need to think it through but it could be fun.'

Jo laughed. 'I can't wait,' she said and then she left.

Abby spent an hour phoning Becky, Fiona, Sally and her mother. They all promised to visit later on. She fed her son and even managed to stand up and change his nappy. And then she settled down to plan.

Nick appeared at three o'clock. He kissed her on the mouth and handed her a parcel. Too small to be clothes. He spent a minute or two admiring his sleeping son and then he sat down next to Abby.

'I told Jo. She's fine. Open the box.'

'You told Jo what?'

'About us. Open the box.'

Abby opened the box, mind racing. So much for her plan. Nick wasn't meant to admit to talking to Jo. He'd ruined everything. And then she opened the box and every thought flew from her head. It was a ring. An engagement ring.

Nick knelt beside the bed. 'Will you marry me?' he asked and Abby burst out laughing.

'What?' Understandably, Nick looked totally dumfounded.

'You're doing everything right. The ring; the kneeling down; the asking. But somehow you still make it an order. What is it with you?'

Nick grinned.

'Yes I'll marry you,' Abby said. She watched Nick remove the ring and slide it onto her finger. 'It'll be too big when I lose weight,' she warned him.

'We can get it made smaller,' he kissed her lightly on the lips. 'I love you.'

Abby smiled against his mouth. 'I love you too but I don't want to get married for at least a year. I refuse to get divorced.'

'I just asked you to marry me and you're already planning the divorce,' Nick complained, getting up to retrieve his son who had started whimpering.

He handed him to Abby who put him straight to her breast. 'I just want to be sure. We've lived together for two weeks. We've never even been on a proper date.'

'Fair enough,' Nick said. 'But you'll move in with me when you come out of here?'

Abby looked down at her ring. 'I don't know. What about Olly? Maybe I should go home for a while first. He's already got to adjust to Charlie. I don't want to overwhelm him.'

Abby moved Charlie to the other breast and he immediately resumed sucking.

'You should just ask him. See what he wants. Maybe he'll want to live with me.' He gave Abby a stern look. 'I don't want you coping alone. Charlie is my son and I want to be there.'

'I know. I'll talk to him.'

'Today?'

'Yes!'

'Good,' Nick gave the widest smile Abby had ever seen. 'I need to go back to work but I'll be back later on.

Chapter Forty-Seven

Abby couldn't believe she was thirty. Thirty years old. It sounded so old. Almost middle aged. And when she looked in the mirror she even looked older. More wrinkles. And she could have sworn her hair had a grey tinge to it.

Nick came into the bedroom while she was still standing in front of the mirror.

'Do you think I've shrunk?' Abby asked him.

Nick crossed the room and stood behind her. He rested his head on hers and smiled via the mirror. 'Nope. Not since I met you anyway. Are you almost ready? Fiona's downstairs.'

Abby nodded. 'I'm still fat.'

Nick did a body scan. 'You look fine to me,' he said and kissed her neck.

Abby shivered. 'Stop it – you're making my nipples hard.'

Nick looked at her chest in the mirror and grinned. 'I'd better go downstairs and wait with Fiona otherwise you'll never get out tonight.'

Abby watched him leave and grabbed her bag. She checked she had everything; face powder, lipstick, phone, money. And then she went downstairs.

Nick and Fiona were stood in the living room and Fiona was holding Charlie. She looked up and smiled when Abby walked in. 'He's got so big,' she said. 'What are you feeding him?'

Abby gave a rueful smile. 'He never stops feeding. I've had to express two bottles of milk just for this evening. And I bet he drinks the lot.'

'You're lucky you can express. I could never get more than an ounce or two.'

Abby nodded. 'It's God's birthday present to me. If I couldn't express milk I wouldn't be able to celebrate my thirtieth birthday.'

Nick and Fiona both turned to stare at her.

'I'm joking,' Abby said. 'Being thirty is nothing to celebrate.'

Fiona smiled and handed Charlie to Nick. 'Let's go and start the commiserating shall we?' She looked at her friend. 'You look really good by the way. Does it still hurt? Has the itching stopped?'

Abby grimaced. 'I'll never understand why women voluntary shave themselves. I feel fine now and thanks.' She smiled at Fiona and then she kissed Nick and Charlie. 'Ring me if you have any problems,' she said to Nick.

He looked at her as if she'd grown three arms and sprouted orange facial hair. Abby grinned. 'You never know,' she said and followed Fiona out to the car.

They picked up Becky and headed to the Oatsheaf for a pre-dinner drink.

'Where are we eating?' Abby asked, accepting a vodka and redbull from Becky. 'And where's Jo? Isn't she coming out tonight? Oh my God, she's not having the baby is she?'

'It's a surprise. And no she's not having the baby – or she wasn't an hour ago anyway. She's joining us later. She wasn't feeling very well earlier and she's running late.' Fiona told her.

'What was wrong?'

'Sick I think. She's okay now. Enough of Jo,' Becky said, putting down her glass and leaning across the table. 'We haven't seen you without Nick since you came out of the hospital. We want details.'

Abby grinned. 'Like what?'

'How's it going?' Fiona asked.

'Good.'

Becky rolled her eyes. 'Good? Come on, Abs. You can do better than that. How's the sex? Can you do it again yet? How're Jo and Matthew about it all? Are you and Nick getting on well?'

'And what about Olly? Is he okay?' Fiona put in.

'Olly is fine. He loves Nick. Jo and Matthew are also fine. Matthew was a bit upset at first but he met a new woman and he's been better since.'

More eye rolling from Becky. 'Matthew's always meeting new women.'

Abby smiled. 'I don't know. I think this might be different. I think Matthew's grown up a lot lately.'

'Since he told you he was unfaithful because he couldn't have more children,' Becky said, scepticism clear.

'I believe him,' Abby said. 'He was so upset when he found out he couldn't have more children. I just can't believe I didn't make the connection before.'

'You hadn't been together that long then. And Olly was just a baby. You had too much else to think about,' Fiona said.

Becky shook her head. 'Why didn't you tell us he had cancer?'

'He didn't want anyone to know,' Abby said with a shrug. 'We couldn't afford another baby so it wasn't an issue then.'

'Is Nick not pissed off that you lied to him?' Becky asked.

Abby nodded. 'Yeah, I think so. But he doesn't say anything. He kind of understands why I did it.'

'And you like living with him? It must be nice to live in a big house again.'

'His house *is* nice,' Abby said and then she gave a wicked smile. 'Though once I'm a bit more mobile I intend to make some changes.'

Fiona grinned. 'Such as?'

'More colour. And I've asked him to bring some of my furniture over. We're going to keep my house and rent it out. Nick wanted to sell it but I refused.'

'Why? Two mortgages is a lot of hassle and what if you can't rent it? It'll cost a fortune.'

'I've told him I'll cover it. What if we split up? I think it'd be stupid to sell it when me and Nick have only been together five minutes. Anyway, it's a good investment. We've got tenants lined up already and the letting agency doesn't think we'll ever have any problems renting it out.'

Becky nodded. 'Makes sense. It's in a brilliant location. By the station, M3 and town centre. Personally, I think you're doing the right thing. It means you don't have to rely on Nick and if things do go wrong you'll have somewhere to go.'

Abby nodded and Fiona snorted. 'You two are like a couple of teenagers. This is why there is so much divorce these days. Nobody works at their relationships anymore.'

Becky laughed. 'You sound like my Grandma.'

'She sounds like Nick,' Abby said with a smile. And then she sobered slightly. 'We had a huge argument when I told him I was keeping the house. He said he'd lock me up before he'd let me move out and if I thought I was running back to my house every time we argued I had another think coming. He only really agreed because of the investment aspect.'

Fiona rolled her eyes. 'You shouldn't have moved in with him let alone accepted his marriage proposal if you weren't sure it would last. It's not fair on Olly.'

'Who's ever sure a relationship will last?' Abby asked. 'And stop having a go at me – it's my birthday. Speaking of which, my glass is empty.'

Becky grinned. 'She's got a point.' She checked her watch. 'We should be moving on, it's almost eight.'

Fiona finished her drink and stood up with a sigh. 'You're right I'm sorry. Remind me to continue this conversation tomorrow.'

'I don't think so,' Abby said and they headed for Fiona's car. 'You're not driving all night are you?'

'Nope. We're meeting Jo at The Tweseldown and then we'll head off for dinner and I'll leave the car at the restaurant.'

'Why the Tweseldown? We never go there?'

Fiona shrugged. 'Ask Jo. That's where she said she'd meet us.'

They pulled into the pub car park a few minutes later and Abby followed her friends inside. The bar was empty.

'No Jo,' Abby observed looking around. She hadn't been in the Tweseldown for years.

'She might be through there,' Becky said, nodding towards another door and linking arms with Abby. Fiona pushed open the door and suddenly loads of people were yelling "Surprise" and "Happy Birthday". There were balloons and a Happy Birthday banner and loads of familiar faces.

Olly came running over and flung his arms round Abby's legs, 'Happy Birthday, Mummy. Daddy let me stay up for your party. Are you surprised? Can I have some birthday cake?' Abby crouched down, pulled him into her arms and looked round the room. There was her mother, Keith, her step-sisters. Tilly was dancing with the DJ's daughter - the DJ was Matthew's best friend. Matthew was stood by the birthday cake.

'Happy Birthday,' he called. 'I'm guarding the cake from Olly.'

Abby grinned and greeted a few old school friends. And then she spotted Nick. He was sat to the side of the room feeding Charlie. Abby went over and kissed his cheek. 'Whose idea was this?'

'Jo's believe it or not,' he said. 'Didn't you suspect anything?'

Abby shook her head and looked around. 'Where is Jo?'

Nick glanced around too. 'I don't know. She was here earlier.'

Becky came in with a tray of drinks and brought them over to Abby. 'Jo's at the bar.' She cleared her throat. 'And she's not alone.'

'She's not?' Abby put her glass down and headed for the door.

'Abby wait—' Becky called and then the door opened and Jo stepped into the room. She was carrying a glass of what looked like orange juice. She was wearing a black smock and white shirt. Her hair was in a French plait. And she was closely followed by Chris.

Abby stopped in her tracks. Chris? She met Jo's eye and her friend hurried over. She handed Abby a gift wrapped box and kissed her cheek. 'Happy Birthday,' she said.

'Thank you,' Abby returned her hug. 'And thank you for organising this. I'm impressed that you managed to keep it quiet – I didn't have a clue!'

Jo smiled. 'It wasn't easy.' She glanced at Chris as he kissed Abby and wished her a happy birthday. 'I hope you don't mind Chris being here.'

'Of course not. If I'd known I was having a party I'd have asked you to invite him,' Abby said, smiling happily at her ex.

'Congratulations by the way,' Chris said, looking at her much flatter stomach.

'Thank you.' She took Chris over to meet Charlie and then she got waylaid chatting to another old friend.

Drink after drink was pressed into her hand and by the time she managed to catch her breath she was feeling rather drunk. She took a moment to stand by herself and take stock.

Olly was asleep on Matthew's knee. He was chatting to his new girlfriend who Abby had been introduced to earlier. Tilly had been collected and taken home by Nick's mum a little while ago. Abby's mother and Keith had made their excuses and left about an hour after Abby arrived. There were a few people sitting around chatting but most people were dancing. Abby watched Becky and a man she didn't recognise dancing and then a slower song came on and they moved into each other's arms. Abby looked around for Nick thinking that a slow dance would be nice. Charlie was in his car seat next to Matthew. No sign of Nick though.

And then she saw Jo. She was dancing with Chris and there wasn't an inch of space between them. Abby swallowed a grin. She wondered if this was a new development. Somehow she doubted it. Either way, she was glad. Jo deserved to be happy and Chris was lovely.

She watched them for a few minutes longer and then went to look for Nick. She found him outside the back door, smoking a cigarette. 'Hi, sweetheart,' he said and slung an arm around her shoulders. 'Are you having fun?'

'Yeah. I wanted to dance with you.'

Nick took a last suck on his cigarette and stubbed it out in the ashtray fixed to the wall. He led her through to the hall and they joined the throng of swaying couples.

'Did you see Jo and Chris?' Abby asked.

Nick smiled. 'Yeah. It was actually my idea to invite him. Jo rang to check she hadn't forgotten anyone, she rang Fiona and Becky too, and I suggested it then.'

'For me or for Jo?'

Nick scowled. 'For Jo of course. Do you really think I'd invite your ex-lover otherwise? They hit it off that night you and Chris came to dinner. I didn't think she'd do it off her own back, she's too worried about upsetting you for that. I assured her you wouldn't mind.' He looked over her shoulder and gave a smug smile. 'Looks like I was right. They seem to be hitting it off.'

'I'm glad,' Abby said.

'I'm glad you're glad,' Nick said and held her a little tighter.

Abby snuggled her face into his neck and gave a sigh of contentment. 'Thank you for my birthday present,' she said. He'd given her a Ford Fiesta. It was fairly old but it was in good condition. And, most importantly, it was hers. 'It's the best present I've ever had.'

She felt Nick smile and she pulled back to kiss his mouth. He returned the kiss, parting her lips with his tongue and pulling her up against him. When he broke off, Abby clung to his shoulders, breath coming fast. 'Is it time to leave?' she asked.

'It's your party. You have to stay until the end,' he said. Abby opened her mouth to argue and he pressed his finger to her lips. 'Remember Jo arranged it for you. You should talk to her – reassure her you don't mind about Chris.'

Abby looked to her left and chuckled. 'It's lucky I don't mind with the way they're behaving.' They were still dancing – oblivious to their surroundings – alternately gazing into each other's eyes and then holding each other so close it was a wonder they didn't fall over.

Nick followed her look and smiled. 'Just reassure her,' he said again. 'Like she reassured you.'

Abby nodded. And then her eyes caught on his and she felt her legs give way. 'And then can we go home?'

Nick ran a fingertip over her lips. His lips followed his finger and Abby fell into the kiss. Her last coherent thought was that Nick's house was home now. She thought of Matthew and Jo and the swap. And she thought of swapping living with Nick to going back to her own house and she knew she'd offer to sell her house. She wouldn't be going back there. She and Nick were for keeps.

No more swapping.

The End.

If you would like to hear about future releases and promotions please sign up to my mailing list. I only ask for your name and e-mail address and you can unsubscribe at any time.
Sign up here: http://eepurl.com/dlS08P

If you've enjoyed reading The Spousal Shuffle, it would be amazing if you could leave a review on Amazon.co.uk so that others might buy it.

I would love to hear from you with any ideas/suggestion/views. I can be contacted in the following ways:
My website: http://paulambrooks.co.uk
Email: paulambrooks@hotmail.com
Facebook: https://www.facebook.com/Paula-Brooks-Author-198913940857987/
Twitter: https://twitter.com/paulambrooks4
Instagram: https://www.instagram.com/paulambrooks4/

About the Novel

I wrote this book while working nights in 2003. My new boss, on learning I had young children and no opportunity to sleep during the day, decided there was to be no more napping. I therefore had a lot of time on my hands and started this novel. I dragged it up to date for publishing purposes, to 2018 when there is sadly no more Woolworths and we can no longer smoke inside pubs.

A friend told me that my main character is frustrating in her loyalty to her best friend and said best friend is too thoughtless and selfish. Unfortunately, these are traits that exist in many people, and as I pointed out, novels would be very boring and unrealistic if all the characters were perfect.

Acknowledgements

I would like to thank my children for giving me the courage/urgency to publish this book. Without them I wouldn't be so deeply in debt that I was forced to ignore all my fears and insecurities. My ex-husband also needs some credit as if he hadn't been so boring, I would never have started writing in the first place.

And finally, a huge thank-you and lots of love to my friends for all their support, proofreading and encouragement. Special thanks to my BFF, Rebecca Handyside, for designing my cover, proofreading multiple times and boosting my confidence a million times.